The First Time I Saw Her

The Gossamer and Pitch Trilogy: Book One

Jae Mazer

A HellBound Books® LLC Publication

www.hellboundbooks.com

Also by Jae Mazer

Novels
- Landing in Eden
- Delivery
- Pal Tailor
- Gahl's Door
- Chrysalis and Clan
- Notch (written as J.M. Adler)
- Crone: A Witch's Tale
- Beautiful Beasts: A Collection of Visceral Horror
- Ripples of Silence (co-authored with Gerry Mazer)
- Tales from the Den (co-authored with Jessica Raney)
- The Sisters Three
- Tales from Ramnon
- Mister Picket Blackmaw
- Sometimes We Don't Escape
- Salt of my Blood
- Mother Mare

Inclusion in Magazines and Anthologies:
- *The Wish* in Sicklit Magazine
- *Flight of the Crow* in Eclectically Heroic by Inklings Publishing
- *The Waif and the Witch* in Hair-Raising Tales of Villainous Confessions by Madgirl Publishing
- *Hurt* in Hair-Raising Tales of Villainous Confessions by Madgirl Publishing
- *The Ballad of Big Sammy Purdue* In Monster Party
- *Death Served* in Books of Horror Volume I
- *Of Your Own Creation* in Books of Horror Volume 2

- *Mozart in the Flames* in Books of Horror Volume 3, Part One
- *Blubber Murray* in Twisted Legends by From the Ashes Press
- *That's a Peculiar Stain on the Carpet ...* In Roadkill Texas Volume 8
- *I Didn't Hate This Goodbye* in Dead Heat: An Anthology of Summer Horror by From the Ashes Press
- *Behold, Death Arrives, A Duet of Ash and Fang* in These Lingering Shadows by Last Waltz Publishing.
- *Aisle Four* in Trapped: A Dark Dozen Anthology from Uncomfortably Dark Publishing
- *The Rise and Fall of the Corn Kings of Appalachia* in Harvested: An Anthology of Reaping What You Sow by From the Ashes Press
- *That's a Mighty Fine Head of Hair You've Got There* in Head Blown Too by Merrill David and Texas Authorcon
- *To Never Know* In Lucky Number 13 by Limitless Ink Press
- *Please* In Deviants and Decadence by Stitched Smile publishing LLC

Audioplays/Dramatizations:
Down with the Ship: Episode on July 27th, 2021 of Hearing the Haunted: A Sirenicide Production
Straight on Through: Episode on January 25th, 2021 in Hearing the Haunted: A Sirenicide Production

The First Time I Saw Her

Chapter One

The first time I saw her, she had no head. Blood oozed from her neck and dribbled down her pinafore, soaking in and spreading like rot. In her hands, she held a bowl; it was a plain, old cereal bowl, just like the ones I had at home, when I had a home. But the bowl the headless girl held didn't contain off-brand fruit loops or flakes of corn. No stale marshmallows or sticky, icky sugar. The bowl contained a red liquid that stank of copper.

"Is that blood?" I asked, and I pointed at her bowl.

She couldn't confirm that. Not without a mouth to speak or a head to nod. She held out the bowl, as if to suggest I should find out the answer on my own. So I did. I dipped a finger in, plunging it knuckle deep until the tip bottomed out. The liquid was thick. I pulled my finger out, stuck it in my mouth. Gritty. Warm. Metallic. She held the bowl to my lips. I slurped in a mouthful, swishing thick crimson from cheek to cheek, coating my teeth with it.

Definitely blood.

"Anna, come here, please."

Mom's voice was kind but firm, a tangled chorus of exhaustion and fear. *How could it be,* I wondered, *that she is both deathly tired and desperately afraid*? Fear takes energy. Fear keeps you wide awake, keeps you running from whatever monsters are chasing you, nipping at your heels. But yes, my mom was both, in equal measure.

How long had we been driving?

I went to Mom's side and pressed against her so she could rest the pads of her fingers on my shoulder. She pressed her fingertips into my flesh, almost to the point of pain, but I knew it steadied her. Perhaps, without me there, she would have toppled over. And without her there for me to hold on to, I feared the wind would blow me away into some monster's belly, so I grasped her coat until my fingers ached.

My new friend stood watching. I knew she was watching, even though she had no head with which to house eyes. Her shoulders were square with mine, the toes of her black patent shoes pointing at my faded Converse. I'd always wanted fancy shoes like that.

A woman who stood beside my mom spoke. "Anna? My name is Allison."

I peeled my eyes away from the girl and her bowl of blood. It would be rude not to acknowledge the person that Mom and I had driven so far to meet.

"Hi," I said.

"Would you like to sit and have a doughnut?" Allison asked me, her voice high, catering to a child. Which I was, but not so young as to require coddling. Besides, I was basically an adult already. It felt like I'd endured ten lifetimes in my short twelve years.

"I would like that," I said. Because I did like doughnuts.

Allison led the way to a booth in the corner of the

diner. The vinyl seat was icky, with raggedy tears, gross stains, and it squeaked as I scootched my bum across it to sit next to the window. I liked sitting next to windows so I could watch the outside. I preferred trees and birds and flowers, but this diner didn't have anything like that outside its smudged, dusty glass. I had to look out at a half-empty parking lot and the old, potholed highway beyond. It was a secondary highway, so no traffic zooming by. I couldn't even count cars—I liked to pick out all the red ones.

"I'm so proud of you," Allison said to Mom.

Mom responded by sitting next to me, her teeth pressed into her lower lip hard enough to draw blood. She always bit on her lip when she didn't want to start crying. Or rather, have me see her cry. And once she started crying, she had a hard time stopping. So she said nothing to Allison, and Allison said nothing back. They just sat there, Mom looking at the table and Allison looking at the top of Mom's head. I didn't want to say anything either, so I just stared out the window, cataloging all the pebbles and broken glass littered about the parking lot. Just as I had discovered a shiny green piece of glass sparkling in the sun, a black patent shoe stepped on it. I couldn't hear it, but I imagined the sound of that broken shard crunching beneath New Friend's weight.

Mom and Allison started talking, but I didn't pay attention to what was said. I was more interested in New Friend, who stood outside the window right beside me. I wondered what her hair would be like if she had a head. Would it be long and straight, the colour of burnt chocolate? Or would it be red and curly, bouncing off her shoulders each time she took a step? Maybe she had a pixie cut the colour of pale, malnourished daffodils. It didn't matter. She was interesting no matter what might or might not have been atop her head.

New Friend balanced her bowl of blood against her hip and dipped the other hand wrist deep. When she drew her hand out, it was coated in thick blood. The window squeaked as New Friend pushed and pulled her finger across the glass, stopping a few times to wet her writing instrument with new blood. When she was done, she took a step back, as if to admire her art. But there wasn't much to admire, to be honest. It was a trio of hearts, two big ones on the outside and a little one in the middle. They were all squished together, blood drooling down like they were actually hearts being squeezed by phantom hands.

"What are you looking at, Anna?" Allison asked.

The noise of her voice startled me. I had clearly forgotten Allison and Mom were there. Except that Mom wasn't there anymore. The booth beside me was empty.

"Where's my mom?"

"She needed a minute," Allison said.

"For what?"

"It's been a hard day. Long."

I nodded. Day, week, year. Years. It had all been so long and terribly hard.

"I just want to go home," I said to my lap.

"I know," Allison said.

"How?" I snapped. "How do you know?"

There's no way she knew. I wanted to go home. I didn't understand why I had to be whisked away from all my things. My collections. My gardens would die, I wouldn't know the new place, and everything would be wrong. Change made my skin crawl and my bones shift. At least my loneliness would remain the same. I had no friends at home, and I would have none at the new place. I hadn't had friends in a very long time.

Allison was uncomfortable. I could tell by the way she shifted in her seat and sipped at her tea. I wondered if she had kids. She certainly didn't have kids like me.

"So, what is your favourite subject in school?"

I shrugged. Did it matter anymore? School was very

far away now. And what did school matter? What did the future matter when it was a blank piece of looseleaf, but my pencil had been stolen from me?

Allison was pretty. She looked like a dancer, all long and slender, soft and hard at the same time. Her fine, wispy hair was tied back into a ponytail, flyaways dancing in the air moved by cheap plastic ceiling fans.

"I like reading," I said. Because I did. And I said it because Allison wanted me to say something. I could tell.

"That's wonderful!" she said. "What kinds of things do you like to read?"

"All sorts of stuff."

"Like what?"

"Harry Potter."

"Oh," she said. She looked quite displeased by this. "Anything else?"

"Roald Dahl."

"Ooh, he's a good one. What's your favourite?"

"*The Witches.*"

"So you like witches, huh?"

I nodded. Because I did like witches.

"I'm named after a witch," I said.

"Is that so?"

"Uh huh." I loved telling this story. "Mom named me after the daughter of Malin Matsdotter, a famous Swedish witch from the 1600s."

Allison didn't look pleased. She looked suspicious. Disgusted.

"Was Anna Matsdotter a witch too, like her mom?"

I wondered the same. I had always wondered the same, and the thought of it now fluttered sad moths in my belly.

I shrugged. "Well, the books don't say so, but I like to think she was. All witches were super strong women that men and bad women were afraid of. That's why the men and bad women killed them, because they didn't want good women having power. But good women always had power, so the men were already afraid."

"Vicious cycle," Allison said. "So why was this particular family famous? Why are you named after Anna?"

"Anna was brave," I said, puffing my chest out. "Her dad was a bad man. He was mean to Anna, and then Anna caught him having sex with a cow, and she told on him, even though she knew she would get beaten up. And after she told on him, she *was* beaten up, but her dad was executed. For the cow sex."

"Ah."

"But … she was strong. And good. She did the right thing."

And her dad died.

I regretted telling so much of that story. Allison did not look as impressed as the kids at school had. Though anything about sex impressed the kids at school.

"And your mom named you after this Anna?"

"Are you telling stories again?" Mom said as she slid back into the booth. Her face was red and her eyes puffy. She had little white flecks on the tops of her cheeks. She must have tried to use toilet paper as a Kleenex. Diner toilet paper always crumbled like that.

Allison smiled at Mom. "Anna was just telling me she was named after the daughter of a famous witch."

Mom looked at me.

I shrunk into my seat.

Mom smiled. "She likes to read."

Mom put her arm across my shoulders, pulled me in for a hug. She felt so cold, so thin; I could feel her ribs through her jumper.

"Imagination is a great thing," Allison said. "We should all have the imagination of a child."

Mom forced a laugh. It was high and squeaky,

nothing like her normal alto tones. I suspected she was doing it for Allison's benefit. Mom was always worried about everyone else—if everyone else was comfortable, if everyone else was getting what they needed.

I wondered what Mom needed and if she ever got it.

I ate my doughnut while Mom and Allison talked about things. Movies, what Mom used to do for a living, if either of us had any medical conditions or health concerns. My doughnut was stale, but I liked it anyhow. It would have to be a pretty awful doughnut for me not to like it, and besides, I hadn't eaten that whole entire day. Cardboard would have been delicious.

After I polished off the last bite and—much to Allison's chagrin—wiped powdered sugar from my lips with the sleeve of my jumper, Allison gathered her purse and coat and stood from the booth.

"Shall we?" she asked, jangling her keys at Mom.

"Yes, I …" Mom trailed off. Her eyes searched the parking lot, and I looked too.

New Friend wasn't there anymore. I wondered where she went. I didn't know her, so I couldn't possibly miss her, but I missed the wonder of her. And the possibility that I might have a friend I could keep.

"Yes?" Allison said, prompting Mom to finish her statement or ask her question.

Mom hesitated. Stared out the window, then looked at Allison's keys. "What about my keys?" Mom asked. "My car, I mean."

Allison nodded. "Yes. Well, I know it's hard, but it might be best to leave it."

"Leave it?" Mom said, incredulous.

Allison nodded. Mom stared first at Allison, then down at the keys in Allison's hands, then back out the window to the parking lot beyond. I wondered what Mom was thinking. Was she wondering how Allison could have said such a preposterous thing? Who leaves a car? Not that our car was anything special, but it was almost all we had. Besides that old Chevette, we had the clothes in our suitcases, and I had one box of books because Mom said we only had room in the boot for one. Mom had her jewelry box and her special trunk, and some grocery bags filled with snacks.

"Leave it?" Mom said. Seemed like she said it more to herself, though. Like she was evaluating the idea.

"I can have someone come and retrieve it," Allison assured her. "You parked around back, yes? Where no one can see?"

Mom nodded.

"It will be fine," Allison said.

What would be fine? I wondered. *The car? Us?*

Didn't matter. Mom was up and moving. She reached into the booth and tugged the arm of my jumper, prompting me out. Mom followed Allison, and I followed Mom, and our little parade marched out to the parking lot. Mom and I went to the Chevette, which was parked between an old red and white Ford that was up on blocks and a two-meter-high pile of firewood covered in moss and mold. Mom opened the boot, and we gathered our belongings as Allison pulled up in a bland white SUV of some sort. They all looked the same to me, those nondescript soccer mom cars. Which was good. I supposed we were trying not to get noticed.

Allison helped Mom and I load our stuff into the hatch, then she got back into the driver's seat as Mom slid in shotgun. I took my place in the back with a book tucked under my arm that I had secretly snatched from my box. I would have sat in the middle of the backseat, but the seat behind Allison was occupied. New Friend sat there, seatbelt strapped across her blood-soaked pinafore, bowl of blood held tight in her lap. As we pulled out of the parking lot and onto the highway, the blood sloshed out of that bowl, splashing onto Allison's seats and even, as we hit an impressively deep pothole, onto the light grey roof of the tidy SUV. Allison might be mad about something like that. She looked like someone who liked monogramming all her clothing and making sure her house always looked precisely staged. But I also knew that despite the fact that the blood was everywhere and despite the fact that the SUV now carried the stench of a sweltering slaughterhouse, Allison would never know. No one would ever know about the blood, or about New Friend. No one but me.

Chapter Two

It wasn't a terribly far drive to our new home. We followed the highway—first pavement, then gravel—to a giant campground-looking place bearing a wooden sign with smiling moose, squirrels gnawing nuts, and cardinals singing in the trees.
EDEN'S EDGE
the sign declared, was tucked off the highway about four songs deep down a narrow gravel road. A winding, haphazard lane snaked around sites, much like the campgrounds and trailer parks I knew, but instead of prefab mobile homes, Eden's Edge was littered with a half-dozen cozy bungalows perched atop concrete slabs. And it wasn't open and naked like a trailer park. There was a great deal of space between each home, with lots of trees and bushes to designate the yards. Just like a campground.

"We only have about a dozen residents right now," Allison explained. "The large home on the right is actually a foster home. One mom, Martha, is minding six kiddos."

"Official foster home?" Mom asked.

Allison didn't answer.

This was a place for hiding, I thought. But it felt more like a place to hide from. Unlike a trailer park, it wasn't cluttered and lived in. There were no toys or derelict vehicles strewn about, no chubby, shirtless men cooking chicken fingers on portable barbecues atop the bonnets of their cars. Yards were tidy and precise, with lawns that looked sculpted by barber's sheers, meticulously tended flowerbeds, and windows devoid of the dust and fade the outdoors brings to glass unloved. As Allison drove, navigating with care as if herds of children might be running about, I searched for a bike, a ball, any evidence of potential friends. But there was nothing. Only clean lawns, spotless porches, and empty swings.

"Here we are," Allison said as she pulled the SUV onto one of the lots with a lovely little green bungalow. And not sea foam green like an ugly bridesmaid's dress. A deep emerald green.

The butterflies in my tummy fluttered their wings as my eyes came to rest on the car window beside New Friend. For the duration of the trip, she had drawn dozens of her little hearts over the inside of Allison's back window. In some places, New Friend's finger had been a bit too coated in blood, and the drawings dribbled down, staining the fabric on the car door. Some even dripped on the seat, but that was nothing compared to the mess that had splashed out of that bowl every time we hit a bump or took a turn.

I found it curious that the bowl wasn't empty, what with every drop that had been spilled. It was quite the opposite, in fact. It was still full to the brim, maybe fuller than when we'd first met at the diner.

"C'mon, Anna," Mom said. "We're here."

Both Mom and Allison were staring at me. Mom looked loving and worried and tired. Allison looked something else. She was staring at me funny, like she was suspicious. Which she should have been, given the extra passenger messing up her ride.

"Long couple of days for you, huh, sweetheart?" Allison said. "Let's get you inside, get you settled."

I said nothing, just stared into Allison's eyes until she shifted in her seat in discomfort and looked to Mom for rescue. Mom said nothing either. As I slid out of the car, I watched Allison, even though Allison made a show of not watching me, even though I knew she was. Secretly. In her peripheral.

There was a wet bite to the evening air. Like mint that made my mouth taste cold, the dampness of the breeze and scent of the pines gave my skin that little extra prickle of chill. Maybe because it made me think of Christmas, of chopping down trees in the back forty with Dad and hauling them home strapped to the roof of his old Buick. That impact of his axe against bark was thunking in my mind like a heartbeat as Mom took my hand and led me to the porch of the dark emerald green bungalow.

"You can sit here," she said, pointing to the porch steps. "I'll get our stuff from the car."

I looked around. There were a few houses, but they were hidden in their own nests of trees. The windows were dark, even though twilight had only just begun to dim the day. The only houses with lights on were the two bigger ones, set back further than the rest. The foster house and one other. Allison's, I supposed.

"Can I explore?" I asked. "Just a little."

Mom nodded and ruffled my hair. "Stay smart," she said, and moved towards the car.

That was our thing. Stay smart. Not be careful because to be careful, you had to be smart. Being smart was knowing your surroundings, what they meant, what you needed to do, and what you were capable of. And knowing what wasn't in your surroundings that you might need. You had to be smart to be careful.

"No, no, let's not do that," Allison said, and she hurried towards me, then grabbed my shoulder. "Best if you just stay here for now, until you know the place a bit better."

Mom was on her like a viper.

"Do not touch my daughter."

Allison recoiled like she'd been slapped. "I just—"

"She's fine," Mom said. "Or is this place not safe?"

Allison was flustered. I could see it in the blush of her cheeks and hear it in the stammer in her voice. "Well, of course it's safe, but—"

"Then there should be no problem with her exploring a bit. This place isn't that big, so she won't get lost. And she's smart. She will be just fine."

Allison's mouth pinched into a hard pink line. She nodded, even though it seemed like her head did not want to; the motion was tight and forced, like someone had hands around her neck. She was irritated with me. When she looked down at me, I could see the impatience in her eyes.

But I knew she had nothing to worry about. I was smart, like Mom said. And besides, I wanted to see where New Friend was going.

The little headless girl had slid out of the car, blood splashing onto the ground with every movement, and was strolling away down the lane. I followed her, keeping an eye on the glistening trail of blood puddles rather than the girl herself. She didn't walk fast, so it was easy to keep up—just a leisurely promenade. We turned, curved, walked, turned again. We passed a few little bungalows, a spectrum of colours, all dark windows and silence. Beyond the houses, the woods encircling Eden's Edge bristled and hissed with the sounds of life—wind through the trees, the cackle of animals, the occasional snap of a branch or crunch of weight on forest debris.

New Friend stopped quite suddenly, and her shoes turned until she faced a little bungalow on a corner lot. It was crooked, with the roof sitting atop the structure like a crumpled hat. The wood walls were bowed this way and that, and each board was painted a different colour. I imagined it would be quite the sight in the sunlight. And the base of the house wasn't a concrete slab like all the other houses, at least the ones I noticed. The foundation of this little place was shiny, black, and crumpled in like a mattress compressed beneath a great weight.

New Friend set the bowl of blood on the ground, then wrapped her arms around me. I hugged her back, grimacing at the wet meat of her exposed neck against the collar of my jumper. When our embrace was finished, she retrieved her blood bowl and walked up to the house. I followed, mostly because I was intrigued by the curious little structure, and partially because I'd become attached to the odd little girl. I should have been terrified, but she was warmth and safety. She hopped up the three steps to her porch and set the bowl on a post at the top of the bannister. With a crackle like burning wood, the bowl fused to the pole, marrying into a uniform pillar that looked like it had been there and together all along. On the opposite side of the stairs was another pillar with another bowl attached. Similar to stoups, but I felt like neither bowl was very holy.

I dared to walk up the stairs, even though it felt rude. I had not been officially invited, but how could New Friend invite me? She had no mouth to ask me up or to suggest I come inside for a hot cocoa or snack. She did have hands, though, and those were free now that she no longer carried the bowl. If she didn't want me there, she'd surely let me know I had to go with a point or a wave.

When I reached the top of the three steps, I grabbed the bowl she'd been carrying and pulled. It was attached, just like I thought. I squinted my eyes and bent at the waist to inspect the fusion a little closer. The whole thing was molded concrete, with no splits or join lines or creases or anything.

But she had been carrying it, I was sure. And it was still filled with blood. I looked over at the other bowl, the one that had presumably remained there while its partner was traveling. The liquid in this bowl was clear and sparkling in the twilight. I touched my lips to the surface and drew a mouthful, swished, then swallowed. It wasn't water. It was refreshing and light but also salty and tepid.

Tears.

I turned to ask a question, but New Friend was gone.

No.

Please don't go.

I don't want to be alone.

I don't want to be here.

I was so concerned about the bowls, both old and new, that I hadn't noticed her disappear into the house. The doorknob was large and beautiful, chiseled like a diamond and glistening just the same. There were swirls of sparkles and precious metals veining through whatever clear gem the doorknob was made of. I was hesitant to touch it, worried that my fingerprints would mar its beauty. I did, though, because I wanted to go inside and see what New Friend was up to. But the beautiful gem would not turn. The door was locked. New Friend did not want me to visit yet.

The thought of retracing my steps, finding Allison and my new home, was a punch to my guts. New home was not my home. My lip quivered, my chest tightened, and bile crawled up my throat.

I wanted to go home, to my place, my space, with my things and my mom and my dad and everything as it was. But it was all gone. My routine was smoke dispersed by the wave of a hand. My life ripped from me.

Because of me.

I stood on the porch, on my tippy toes, and peered down the lane. Barely visible through the walls of trees, illuminated by now-full moonlight, was an emerald green chimney with a brick rim. My new house. I descended the porch steps, aiming myself towards that house, *my* house, planning to cut through the woods to get there in a straight line so I wouldn't get turned around on the curvy, swervy lanes. As I reached the pavers beyond the bottom step, I decided to have a peek back at the shiny black foundation of New Friend's house. It shouldn't have been a shock, but I gasped regardless.

Compacted black patent shoes had been formed into a haphazard foundation. Shoes just like the ones New Friend had been wearing. There had to have been thousands of pairs making up the entire slab. I took a step, dropped to my knees, and then to my belly so I could get my face right up to the slab of shoes and examine them further. What I found wasn't only shoes but shoes complete with their matching feet. Gnarled bones pierced the toes of some of the shoes, and globs of bloated blue flesh swelled out of some of the wider gaps. I poked one particular bubble with my finger, and pus oozed out in a viscous glob that stank of hot meat and wet hair.

I stood and found the line of sight to the green and brick chimney again, then I walked, my feet following that imaginary line through the trees. I was curious about the feet supporting New Friend's house, but I was also tired, and it would take me a while to fall asleep in a new bed in a new place. I would have to ask New Friend about the shoes and feet another day.

Chapter Three

Mom cracked the egg like a skull. Her hands trembled as the clear white and thick yolk oozed into the pan like sick snot. A second egg fell victim to her wrath as she prepared our breakfast in our new pan, in our new house, in our new life, far away from the old one that had been stolen from us. Was this life going to be shiny new? Would it smell good, like fresh paint or a new car? Or would it stink like thrift store clothes, tattered and ready to fall apart before we even tried them on?

"Would you like some toast?" Mom asked.

I nodded, but Mom didn't see. Her eyes were glued to the pan, which might as well have been on a stove in some far away borough for all the attention she paid to anything outside its heat.

"Yeah," I said. "I'll get it."

I opened the cupboards, searching for a toaster, but found only a sparse collection of CorningWare and mismatched pots and lids, none of which looked to fit each other. It was no mind. I didn't much like toast anyway. Soft bread would do just fine to mop up my eggs.

The bread box on the counter was very pretty. It looked like pine, with intricate mandalas painted everywhere, spattering its surface in a rainbow of swirls. I opened it up and found a loaf of what looked to be homemade bread—a fat, puffy top, unsliced. I grabbed the bread and laid it on the cutting board, then retrieved a knife from the block.

Mom turned her head when she heard the metal of the knife slide from its slot.

I sliced four pieces of bread, then placed the loaf back in the bread box. Mom finished up the cooking, and we convened at the table, where she had set out plates decorated with eggs and bacon. It was delicious. We didn't often have full, hot breakfasts like this; cereal, frozen waffles, or Wonder Bread were all time would afford us back in the days of employment and school and commutes. But now we had all the time in the world, and that endless expanse before me was somehow claustrophobic.

"I love you," Mom said.

"I love you too."

"I'm sorry," Mom said. "For everything."

I cocked my head. Mom was beautiful. Her golden hair swooped across her forehead at the line of her brow, accentuating the warm cocoa of her eyes. Her face was soft and familiar, with lines etched there by smiles at the beach and by furrows of concern from reading emotional chapters in her favourite novels.

"Sorry for what?" I asked.

I watched Mom's face. The slight clench of her jaw as she tried to form words that wouldn't trickle down from her brain. The gloss of her eyes. And pain. There was a lot of pain on that face, but it wasn't the same as before The Incident. Mom had two different faces. Her before-face and her after-face.

Before The Incident, the pain was there, quiet and

hidden. It struggled to break free, stretching her expressions taut like a rope when Dad was in a mood. It was subtle, the way the pain strained her face every time Dad swore, or stomped his feet, or sighed. It was there in loud moments when Dad was around and worse in quiet moments when he wasn't. I figured her brain thought about it more when he wasn't around.

He never hit her, or me, but he was awful just the same. I did not like my dad.

After The Incident, the pain changed. It was somehow softer. An acceptance. I couldn't decide whether it was worse or better than before, but I could pinpoint the very moment the before-face had changed into the after-face. When Mom had first walked into the abandoned lot behind the grain elevators at the edge of town, she had the before-face. When she saw me, it was still the before-face. Even when she saw him there, standing in front of me, she still wore the before-face. But it only took a few seconds for it to change. It was almost instantaneous. One moment, the before-face, full of fear and silence and ambivalence. The next, that face was gone, replaced by the after-face. The after-face was full of uncertainty, but it held an odd confidence I hadn't seen before. Well, maybe I had seen a flicker of it once or twice—when we took a ferry out to the island for a weekend by ourselves. Mom looked out over the ocean, and the after-face made an appearance for the briefest moment before the salty wind swept it away.

In that lot behind the grain elevators, with the paste of grain dust thick on our tongues, Mom's after-face was covered in blood from Dad's arterial spray. Mom's lips looked so pretty that day. She often wore clear gloss to make her lips shine like they'd been freshly licked. On fancier days, she'd swipe them with a bit of sparkle so she looked like she had kissed the stars. But the lips on her after-face were gleaming with damp crimson. Her golden hair was soaked with it, turning the tendrils of sunlight into mud. Mom stood there that day, only a few days ago, wearing her after-face, her gardening spade clutched in her hand. It dripped dark ruby droplets onto her bare feet. I remember the sound, how thick and wet it was. The hands holding that spade were not the same hands that had just been cooking eggs in our new home. The spade hands were completely still, completely sure.

What happened?

I remember being in our house, then I wasn't. I blinked, and when I opened my eyes, I was staring at my bare feet, at my toes that were curled into the dirt.

"No child should have to live such things," Mom said as she pushed egg onto her uncooked toast. "And for that, I'm sorry. But it's over now."

I nodded. "Yeah. Over."

"We are strong women, Anna, and we will be just fine."

I believe she said that to both me and herself. More to the latter.

But why were we here? What had happened that caused Dad's blood to flow like a waterfall, which set us running to a place where we had nothing? I couldn't remember. I only remember the flowing blood, the rush to get out, get away fast.

And we ran here. To this place that was all sorts of wrong.

Just like me.

"Do you trust Allison?" I asked.

Mom shook her head. "Not really, no. But all I can trust is us. She might be good people, she might be bad. But we are strong, and we are smart, and this is an option. And we needed an option."

"We haven't got money."

"I know."

"Is that why you didn't leave?"

Mom paused. Thought. Nodded, though it was small. "In part, yes."

"And what were the other parts?"

"Are you resentful?" Mom asked.

My turn to think. Then, "No. I'm not. Just wondering. Because I'm curious to know why someone would choose unhappiness."

Mom took a bite of her egg, chewed, swallowed, dabbed her lips with the napkin. There was no blood there, not anymore, but they still seemed so red to me. That blood would always be there now.

"I did choose unhappiness, Anna. Because other choices have unhappiness too. Poverty, legal battles, the possibility of losing you." There was no food in Mom's mouth, but she swallowed. Hard. "So I chose the lesser degree of unhappiness, I suppose."

"It wasn't horrible," I said.

"No. It wasn't."

"But it wasn't good either. It was pretty bad."

"Yes. It was."

"And bad is not okay."

Mom's lips pulled, twitched, curved into a smile. "That's right, Anna. Bad is not okay. We can do better. And the only thing that stops us from doing better is fear. It grabs us by the ankles, pulls us back, wraps its long, cold fingers around our throats until we can't breathe, not until we let it have control. But *we* have control. We always did. We have always had the fingers and could always choke fear until it has no more breaths to draw."

I liked that. I would choke fear when I met it again. And I knew Mom would too.

"So, what happens now?" I asked.

"We live. We go about our day, settle in, figure shit out."

I gasped. Mom laughed.

"Oh please," she said as she reached over and ruffled my hair. "You've heard worse."

Yeah. And seen worse too.

"Do they have school here?" I asked. I liked my composition books. Green for science, blue for social studies, red for writing, and yellow for math.

"Yes," Mom said. "There's one here, Allison said. She will give us a tour tomorrow."

Ugh.

"How do we get around?" I asked.

"Walk, I suppose. For now. Everything should be close if what Allison said is true."

"Will we get our car back?"

Mom shook her head. "I'm hoping we will get a new car soon, but I just don't know."

"Why did we come here, Mom? To this place?"

Mom was quiet. She took the dishes to the sink. Rinsed them long and slow before sitting back down.

"We are far away from everything," she said to the floor, as if convincing herself. "Off the beaten track. If the police should come out here, which I can't imagine they would, we have support. Allison …"

Mom trailed off. I didn't push. We'd been through enough, and most of it was my fault.

But underneath it all, like the stench of greasy smoke, was a lie. Mom was lying. I didn't know what about or why, but there was something concealed. Something ugly and dangerous.

One thing was for sure, we had driven several hours, at least. To get us, the police would have to come an awful long way and know exactly where they were going and why they were going there. But they would have no reason for coming. Not now, maybe not ever.

A rush of heat in my memory sizzled my skin. The

flare of Dad's flesh aflame in the woods. He smelled like bacon on Christmas morning, except not quite. His burning smell was more sour.

"Anna," Mom said as she took my face in her hands. "We are strong. We are smart. And we will be just fine, whatever that looks like."

I nodded, the pressure of her hands on my face transferring calm to me in a gentle current.

"I love you," she said.

"I love you too."

Breakfast concluded with no more talking. After I washed the dishes, I headed to my room. My suitcase was on the floor at the end of my bed. We had arrived late, and I had been asleep in no time without bothering to unpack. I took my clothes out of my suitcase one by one, carefully folding rumpled shirts and jumpers and slacks before assigning them their own drawers in my new dresser. Everything was quite wrinkled; though we hadn't left in a panic and had taken time to pack thoroughly and properly, our suitcases were fuller than I would have imagined possible. Cramming what would be my entire wardrobe into one bag meant leaving behind some of my favourite things. But at least I still had my unicorn t-shirt with the rainbow sequins and my leggings with the gold snowflakes.

After all my clothes were put away, I took the remaining trinkets out of the side pockets of my suitcase. The Wetbrush for my hair; my hair was long and thick and got easily matted in the bath. I had my fat journal where I did my sketches and wrote my stories, and my favourite pen with the glitter ink. A menagerie of plastic animals—horses, chickens, dogs, a pretty Jersey cow I named Lulu.

The last possession I had taken from my old-and-stolen-from-me home was a jar. It was a mason jar we had in the cold storage room. It had been meant for preserves, but that wasn't its destiny. At home, due to the lateness of the hour and the urgency of our departure, I was not able to go out and obtain formaldehyde, glutaraldehyde, methanol, humectants, and wetting agents required for proper preservation. We did have gin, though, and lots of it. Dad always drank gin, so I supposed he'd have been happy with my choice. While Mom was putting our luggage in the car and retrieving bedding from the attic, I filled the jar with Dad's gin, then plopped his heart—perfectly intact, save some ripping and jagged tears on the arteries—into its temporary embalming container. Blood swirled like lava, muddying the gin as the heart came to rest on the bottom.

Now, sitting on my new bed in my new house, with Dad's heart staring at me from the confines of its jar, that night seemed a million eternities away. I stared at the bloody muscle, and it stared back at me, distended and still. No eyes, but it looked at me. Stared right into me.

There was a far-away knock, then Mom appeared in my doorway.

"Allison's here," she said. There was no urgency in her voice.

"We should go then," I said.

In my peripheral, Mom nodded. Then she walked in and sat on the bed.

"Allison can wait," Mom said. "Take your time."

"Where should I keep this?" I asked as I tilted the jar so Mom could see the heart through the now-murky liquid.

Dad's heart rolled, drunk in its gin, until the tangle of veins floated above it like hair.

"Wherever you like, sweetheart."

"I'd like it on my windowsill, I think. The sun shining through the jar will be quite pretty."

Mom took the jar and polished it with her sweater before placing it on the windowsill. Outside, a beaming red cardinal sat on a nearby tree branch, and when it caught sight of the heart, it sang a lovely ballad.

"I agree," Mom said. "It won't keep long like this, but I'm sure I can find a way to get some epoxy. Keep it from decaying to mush."

"Maybe we could put a light underneath to make the whole jar glow."

"Yes," Mom said. "That's a lovely idea."

I went to Mom, and she wrapped her arm around me as we admired the sunlit jar on the windowsill. The alcohol had done its job so far, but the tiniest bit of decay was already eating at Dad's meat. I hoped we'd get that epoxy soon enough to save most of the ugliness from gorging itself completely, but either way, it would be lovely.

Allison knocked again, this time more obnoxiously, so Mom and I left Dad's heart behind to go on our grand tour.

Chapter Four

Eden's Edge was unremarkable. Bland and muted. The forest designating the lots was lush and perfect, but the yards were too clean, the people too quiet. There was no mess, and I preferred a mess. As we wandered the lane, I searched for something my eyes could consume and my brain could digest. Broken toys, thriving weeds, mushroom rings. Something. Anything. But there was nothing, only boring bungalows with minimal decor, tidy lawns devoid of toys and glee and life. I would have even enjoyed some signs of misery—vandalism, abandoned gardens, unused rocking chairs. But everything was in its place, unused and staged.

"Is this place real?" I asked.

Allison nearly tripped as she looked down her nose at me. Her glasses had boring brass frames, and her beige suit had pleats. She was cardboard.

"Pardon?" she said.

"Is it real?" I asked again, in case something was wrong with her hearing. "I don't see any life."

"People?" she asked, her head cocked to the side like

a golden retriever.

"No. Life," I repeated. There was definitely something wrong with her ears. Or maybe her whole head.

"I don't quite understand," she said.

Ah. So it's her head.

Mom rested her hand on my shoulder. "Signs of life, Anna means. It's quite neat and tidy here."

"Well, yes," Allison said. "We like to keep it presentable. Mess can get out of hand, and besides, cleanliness is next to godliness, don't you agree?"

Mother's fingers tightened around my shoulder. Not to the point of pain but to the point of passion.

"I don't agree, no," Mom said.

Allison stopped walking and spun on the balls of her feet to face my mom. They stared at each other. Mom's chin never dropped, and her eyes never strayed from Allison's. I admired my mom's strength. It was the only thing keeping me from giving myself over to fear and letting it consume me.

There was no further discussion about God, or cleanliness, or agreement. Allison gave a curt nod and spun back to her strides, carrying on down the final leg of our tour. We'd seen all the rows of bungalows, which looked nearly the same. Allison yammered on the entire time about who lived where and who did what, but without seeing faces and hearing voices, I was never going to remember a single thing she said. I hoped that I might eventually get to meet these elusive folks who were oh so quiet and oh so neat. But for now, we moved on to the bigger structures.

"This is the second largest house here," Allison said. "The Foster Home, as I told you last night."

"What's the biggest?" I asked.

Allison smirked down at me. "Mine, of course. It was the first I had built out here when I bought the land."

And lavish too. It was tucked way back from the

others, up the hill a bit, sheltered by trees. I imagined it had white carpet and peach wallpaper, and boring pictures and Live Laugh Love signs.

"Is there a market close?" Mom asked.

"No," Allison said. "Which was intended. You know. To keep it quiet and safe out here."

"Food?" Mom asked.

"We do deliveries. Once a week. But if you find you need something, we can make arrangements."

I could tell by the look on Mom's face that she did not like that arrangement.

"Is there stuff to do?" I asked.

I liked my garden back home. And playing in the creek. I used to collect the chips from the beaver-whittled trees and arrange them like fairy paths through my rows of roses, peas, and dandelions.

"School," Allison said. "And we have social groups that meet up."

"But on my own," I said.

"Well, we do have the library."

I perked up. "Library?"

"Why, yes!" Allison said. "That's right! You like to read."

"Where is the library?"

Allison pointed a finger tipped with a magenta nail towards the other side of Eden's Edge, at a peak poking through the trees.

"But that's just another house," I said.

"Yes," she said, her tone suggesting it should be obvious. "Same footprint as the rest. But I left it empty to put in some leisure activities. Books, a turntable, some art and craft supplies."

I supposed that made sense. There were not many people here—a dozen at most, I concluded from Allison's chatter. There would be no need for much.

We came around the corner and came face-to-face with an oppressive, irregular shaped building. It wasn't on either side of the lane but right smack in the middle of the end of the road. The Beast. It loomed like a predator, tall and hungry and violent.

"What's that?" I asked as I pointed at The Beast.

The smile of a proud parent bloomed on Allison's face. "Our church. Serves as a community center and town hall as well."

"It's all integrated?" Mom asked. I could tell by the sound of her molars grinding together that this idea did not please her.

Allison's head tilted again. I fought every urge in my every nerve ending to not roll my eyes.

"May I go to the library?" I asked.

"It isn't open," Allison said.

"But it's daytime."

"Yes, but it's a Wednesday. There's school and work."

"Where is the school?" Mom asked, but before Allison spoke, realization spread across Mom's face like pain, drawing her features taut. They both looked at The Beast, and Mom sighed.

"It won't hurt for Anna to go explore while we discuss things further," Mom said.

"She is welcome to join the children in class," Allison said, holding an open palm towards The Beast. "It's only 9 a.m. They'll be just starting math."

"No." Mom's voice was firm. "Anna will have some time to settle in. It's been a traumatic few days, and she is a child." Then to me, "Go ahead, love. We'll meet back at home later."

Allison's brow furrowed into a petulant, well-groomed caterpillar. "But—"

Again to me, Mom said, "I love you." Then she gave

me a slow, solid kiss on my forehead and spun me away from Allison and The Beast.

Thanks, Mom, I thought at her as she faced both woman and Beast, both of which seemed quite unpleasant.

I wanted to go to the library, but I was afraid. I shuffled my feet and kicked rocks, killing time until Allison and Mom were swallowed by The Beast so I could run to my new house and hide. I had no desire to get in trouble, and I was quite certain Allison wasn't going to change her mind about me going to the library. But I didn't feel safe out and about in this place that tasted like decay on my tongue and in my throat.

Air shifted behind me, ruffling my hair. The fine hairs on my body stood at attention, and I froze in fear. I didn't want to turn to see what predator approached. What monster put its hand upon mine, slipping its finger through mine and squeezing with the tender love of a sister?

My fear dissipated as I smelled her. It was New Friend standing with me, holding my hand. She still had no head, but she also had no bowl of blood in her hands, which I was grateful for. I smiled at New Friend, and I can't say how, but I felt her smile back.

"Hello," I said.

She raised a hand and waved. At first, I thought she was wearing black nail polish, and I was jealous. Mom didn't let me wear nail polish yet. But New Friend wasn't wearing nail polish either. Her nails were bruised and rotting, the tips of her fingers shriveled and necrotic. The nails on her pointer fingers were completely gone, the bare skin covered in a layer of thick yellow pus. It looked like they had been gnawed off.

"I'm sorry that happened to your hands," I said. "Oh, and your head, I guess."

New Friend shrugged.

She knew exactly what I wanted. She absorbed all

my fear and uncertainty and led me to the library house. We snuck around to the back of the bungalow that housed books instead of people, and I turned the knob on the back door. No resistance. It wasn't locked. Probably not a good sign. Nothing valuable or important was kept behind an unlocked door. But then again, few people saw the value in books. I understood their value in my soul. Cerebral gems waiting to be mined.

It didn't matter that Eden's Edge was sterile and boring, and that the people were neat and tidy and quiet. Books were books, and no matter the words on the pages, they would not disappoint. When I stepped into Library House, I was greeted by the aroma of parchment and book dust; it was an intoxicating medley that reminded me of adventures and quiet spaces, heroines and villains, creatures and places that formed the folklore of my childhood.

We walked down the hallway, which led to various rooms throughout the house. There was a kitchen, which had a fridge and sink, but the cupboard doors had all been removed to display rows of books stocked within. The living room had a few armchairs and a cozy rug, and each wall had floor-to-ceiling bookshelves with zero space left for a television or paintings or anything other than reading material. Aside from the bathroom, which was a normal bathroom with all the expected equipment and amenities, every room was the same. Each of the three bedrooms had books, ceiling to floor, and some sparse seating.

"How do you check out a book?" I asked the void. There was no computer or checkout counter.

New Friend glided like silk to a bookcase, pulled out a novel with plants and dogs on the cover, and handed it to me.

"We just take it?" I asked.

There was a slight movement of her shoulders, then a pause, then she gave me a thumbs up.

I supposed she had tried to nod, but that wouldn't work, now would it?

I put the book back. I had read that one before. It was about two Irish Setters who grew up together and were best friends, and when one died, a plant grew, and the other laid down beside him and died, and a plant grew there too. Too sad for my liking. Death and dogs and plants.

"Any history books?" I asked. "I like true stories."

A slight movement of her upper body, then a thumbs down. Couldn't shake her head either.

"No history books? What about nonfiction?"

Another thumbs down. Then New Friend lifted her finger and pointed out the window. At The Beast.

I didn't understand. Maybe I was thick like Allison.

"The nonfiction books are there?" I asked.

Thumbs up.

Before I had a chance to ask any follow-up questions, there was the rattle and click of a door opening. My heart swelled and percussed against my ribs. I didn't want to get Mom in any trouble with Allison, but here Allison was, come to bust me for breaking and entering.

But it wasn't Allison. The voices were many, and they were young. Guilty whispers, naughty giggles, the patter of small, sneaking feet.

I stepped into the hallway, exposing myself like a timid specter.

They all screamed. Two girls and a boy. They looked to be about my age, and they all had heads.

"Holy shit," one girl said. Her hair was red and bouncy, and her face was a palette of ginger stars on a pink morning sky. "Are you the new girl?"

"You know about me?" I asked.

"Yes," the other girl chimed, but in a whisper. This girl was taller, with poker straight hair that shone so black it was a lake at midnight. "Allison told us at service yesterday that we had new residents. A mom and daughter."

"What are you doing in here?" the boy asked. He was grubby and dirty, with super short hair and gross grey sweatpants. That made me so happy. There were real people here after all.

"Looking at books," I answered. "Mom says I can take some time to settle in before I go to school."

"I bet Allison didn't like that," Ginger Stars said To Midnight Lake.

"What about you?" I asked. "I'm guessing you aren't supposed to be here either."

Looks were exchanged, then all three snickered.

"I'm Liza," Midnight Lake said. "And this is Laz and Mary."

Ice formed in my stomach, a burg that was cold and sharp and deep. A funny tingling beneath my fingernails flared like heat as panic threatened to take hold. All at once, I noticed the air from the cheap, single-paned windows moving about the room, drawing gooseflesh on my arms. New Friend, seemingly sensing my sudden discomfort, stood next to me and laced her fingers through mine. Her rotten fingertips were cold and slimy with the spongy texture of liver. But that didn't bother me. It distracted me from my swelling anxiety.

"Are you okay?" Laz asked.

"Yeah, you got real pale," Mary said.

Like I always did when panic stalked me, I babbled. "Witches. Did you all know you have witch names?"

Glances were exchanged, but there were no giggles this time. New Friend squeezed my hand. I wondered if she meant for me to stop. But I didn't.

"Lazare Lizotte," I said to Laz, "Was an Acadian nicknamed 'Le Canadien' because he was Quebecois. He was accused of casting spells and turning into a dog."

Another squeeze from New Friend, this time harder,

her bones piercing through the tips of her fingers and stabbing into the flesh of my palm. But still, I could not stop.

"And Mary Dunbar from Belfast. She puked up nails and threw bibles at people."

New Friend dropped my hand, stood in front of me, and wrapped her arms around me. When she compressed me in a hug, my chin dipped into the gore of her neck. I could feel the sharp stab of her spine in my throat, the strings of her tendons against my neck, and the pulse of her pumping blood on my face.

"Liza Barnes was also Irish," I continued, "But she moved to Canada and was known as Mother Barnes, or The Witch of Plum Hollow. She was the seventh daughter of a seventh daughter, and she told fortunes, and she helped solve mysteries and crimes and found treasures. One of her clients was the first Prime Minister of Canada, and—"

New Friend squeezed me so hard that she compressed out all my breath and stuck my words to my ribs.

"Are you okay?" Mary asked.

I wasn't, clearly, but what else could they say?

Once I stopped attempting to speak, New Friend loosened her grasp. I sucked in a deep breath, thankful for the oxygen, then took another slower breath to compose myself.

"Sorry," I said, examining my shoes, too embarrassed to see their eyes. "I get flustered around … I've been through a lot."

"I have panic attacks too," Liza said. "Just like that."

I looked up at her. She was beautiful. Her hair was black glass, and so were her eyes. Her skin was warm and olive and smooth as can be.

"We've all been through a lot," Laz said, and Mary poked him in the ribs.

"What Laz means to say," Mary said, "is that you aren't alone. If you're here, something about your life sucked. Real bad. Allison takes in all sorts of folks like us. But we don't need to know what your malfunction is, and we won't judge if you do decide to tell, okay?"

They assumed abuse. Probably sexual. Everyone always assumed abuse, and sexual was the most lurid. But that was not the case. Not at all. I did not like my dad, but it was never like that.

"Look," Liza said, slowly taking a step forward. "One moment at a time. That's what my dad told me when we got here. And that's what I do. One breath at a time, one moment at a time, until time flows easier."

"You're smart for kids your age," I said.

They giggled. It was nervous but not awful.

"You seem pretty mature yourself," Liza said. "Knowing all that stuff about witches."

"You, um, have that ass burgers?" Laz asked.

Mary gasped and punched him in the arm. "You idiot! It's *Aspergers*, and don't be rude!"

"I don't have that," I said, "but I can see why you'd think that. I'm weird …"

These kids wouldn't like me either. They were gonna make fun of me. Hate me. Avoid and ignore me.

"You like witches so much because maybe you are one," Laz joked.

They all laughed.

I didn't.

New Friend took me by the shoulders. Squeezed me so hard I lifted off the ground ever so slightly, millimeters, just enough so these new kids wouldn't see. Wouldn't know. I could smell and taste the gas from her belly, the food rotting in her intestines, the ash on the soles of her black patent shoes. Music played in my ears, a symphony of screaming, of fire crackling, of flesh sizzling, and hair singeing. They all laughed at me, and I burned there on the spot as New Friend tried to protect me from the shame.

"No," I said, trying not to choke on the smoke. "I just like history."

"But it's not history," Laz said. "History is real and witches aren't. Just like ghosts aren't real."

"They are so!" Mary said. "What about Old Man Merle out by the cemetery?"

"Your momma just says that to keep you outta those woods," Laz said.

"Not true!" Mary screeched. "I seen pictures of Merle! He's real!"

"He *was*. Now he's dead," Laz said. "And there ain't no such things as ghosts."

"You don't know," Mary said. "Because you have a penis and men are idiots!"

Liza stepped in. "Hey! Cut it out. Don't be rude."

Mary looked properly scolded and stepped back.

"Listen," Liza said to me. "It's obviously not been an easy road for you. For any of us. But you're here, and we're here, and you must be kinda cool cuz you busted into the library on your first day. Crime and books. Winning combo."

These kids weren't so bad. Yet. Despite the taste of soot on my tongue, despite not knowing what fresh horror awaited me, I felt like I might do okay here. For now, at least.

"And look. Mary likes witchy stuff. She doesn't go anywhere without her lucky crystal."

Mary beamed, reached into her pocket, and pulled out a sparkling rock.

"It's bloodstone," Mary said. "Protects me from negative energies."

And with that, she held the crystal out at Laz and stuck her tongue out.

"It's pretty," I said. And I meant it. It was dazzling, in fact. Mom liked crystals too. Anything that came from the earth.

"What's the cemetery you mentioned?" I asked.

They all gave me a look.

Again, acting like a weirdo, Anna.

I clarified. "I mean, you can tell a lot about the history of a place from its dead."

"Old Man Merle could tell you a lot about it, for sure," Mary mumbled.

Laz rolled his eyes.

"You had the tour from Allison, yes?" Liza asked.

I couldn't contain it. I rolled my eyes, which ignited belly laughs in the whole crew.

"Looks like you know Allison well," Liza said, wiping tears of laughter from her eyes. "Let us give you the real tour. We'll have to sneak cuz Allison will send us straight back to school. Or … don't worry. We know how to keep out of sight."

I wasn't sure. Part of me wanted to link arms with New Friend and head back to the house I was staying at, crawl into bed, and watch Dad's heart floating in his gin. Imagine it was still beating.

"Come with us," Liza said. She touched my arm. It felt safe. She looked a bit older than me, but her eyes were kind, and her movements soft and calm. "We'll hang in the woods for a bit, then we'll get you home safe."

"Will your mom be mad?" Laz asked.

I shook my head. Mom wouldn't be mad at me. She rarely was. She only got mad if I was rude or mean or inconsiderate. If I was smart and kind, Mom was happy.

"I'm in," I said.

The kids were a flurry of whispers and giggles again as they crept out the back door. I stopped in the threshold, frozen in hesitation until New Friend took me by the hand and led me out into the woods.

Chapter Five

Mary was in the lead, but not because she was the leader. Mary was the youngest, maybe nine or ten, and full to the brim with energy and sass. But she seemed impulsive and not very careful. She bounded off into the woods, a deer prancing through the flora. Laz followed close behind, snatching up rocks and ricocheting them off trees as he went. I came next, with New Friend attached to my hand. She and I moved as one, our shoulders pressed together so we could fit side-by-side down the narrow path through the birch and pines.

Liza was the leader. She walked silently, her black eyes flickering at every movement, her head tilting towards every sound. She appeared calm, even, and aware. That's why she quietly fell to the back of the pack, I imagined—to watch over us. A dark guardian angel haunting our footsteps.

"Here!" Mary squealed, and Laz answered with hoots and hollers as the two of them charged.

I quickened my steps, and New Friend matched my pace. Pretty soon, our path, which had been dimmed by tree cover, birthed us into a clearing flooded with warmth and light. And, sure enough, speckled with tombstones.

"Oh." I had nothing more to say about it. It was a cemetery, all right. Nothing fancy—no tombs, no intricate headstones, no fresh or rotting flowers set atop graves. But there was a couple dozen folks buried there, maybe more.

"See?" Laz said to Mary. "No ghosts."

With a hand on her hip and a roll of her eyes, Mary said, "Duh, you idiot. It's daytime. They're allergic to the sun."

"They ain't vampires," Laz said. "That's not how it works."

"If it ain't real, then how does it work at all then?" Mary said, head tilted so her curls draped on her shoulder.

"Stop." Liza stepped around me and strolled into the center of the cemetery. "Show some respect."

"The dead don't care," Laz said.

Mary opened her mouth, an argument on her tongue, but Liza held up a hand. "I meant respect each other."

The argument died before it aired, and everyone shuffled into the cemetery. Mary took a stick to draw hearts and stars and smiles in the dirt and gravel at the foot of each grave, and Laz dug around in the dirt collecting various sizes of rocks to throw. New Friend unlatched from my hand and strolled around, resting her hand on the top of each headstone. Her chest moved, heaving ever so slightly, and I wondered if she was speaking.

Liza laid down in a patch of grass in the middle of the cemetery, turned her face to the sun, and closed her eyes. She didn't seem as interested in the cemetery as the other two did.

"Who died here?" I asked.

"Nobody, silly," Mary said. "They're just buried here."

Liza groaned.

"Sorry," Mary said, then continued doodling in the

dirt.

"Just people from the area, I suppose," Liza said.

"You don't like it," I said.

She looked at me. Her eyes were beautiful.

"My mom passed before we came here. Cancer."

"Oh." I said.

I wish cancer'd been the one to take my dad. Cancer didn't have a face. Or a heart. A faceless monster wasn't as scary.

Laz kicked some dirt at Mary, and Mary shrieked before launching at him and chasing him in figure eights around the graves. I noticed her fist was closed around her crystal. New Friend was like my crystal. I felt safe and strong when she was around.

New Friend laid down in front of a headstone like Sleeping Beauty on her funeral slab, and blood oozed out of her neck into the soil beneath. I pushed some rocks around with my toe. I wanted to sit by Liza and visit like normal girls would, but she intimidated me. She was beautiful, and confident, and mysterious.

My mother's voice sang in my head like a song.

Only thing to do when you're afraid is to do the thing anyway. Fear is not as strong as you, my love, but it is deceitful and will convince you that you are not enough.

So I sat. I didn't even ask if it was okay and tried not to worry if it was awkward. I wasn't too close to Liza, and I wasn't facing her. I sat crisscross applesauce and turned my face to the sun just like her.

"How long have you been here?" I asked.

"Too long."

"You don't like it?"

"There's nothing much to like."

"Sure there is."

Her face turned from the sun towards me. "You've been here all of half a day. How do you know what's here to like?"

"I can see." Plump, juicy leaves shuddered in the breath of a gentle breeze. I saw the trees, some dead and rotting, some solid and healthy. All the wood, dead or alive, was teeming with life—insects, incisor marks from deer and rabbits, hidey holes that rodents used as homes and playgrounds. I saw the emerald shimmer of the grass and the roan dirt of the forest floor.

"I can hear." Birdsong trilled in my ears, twittering and warbling in time with the rustling of the leaves. In the distance, there was water, but it was far, bubbling and gurgling and streaming over boulders, lapping against shores of mud and roots.

"I can smell." Forest. Pine. Critters. Flowers. Wood fires burning in the distance.

"I can taste." No salt water—the ocean must have been far—but I could taste the mustiness in the air from mold and dust. And there was the lack of taste as well. No smoke, no petrol, no stench of concrete jungle.

"I can feel …" breeze caressing my skin, the tickle of grave grass poking through my tights, the soft petals of a wild rose as I pinched it. I rolled the petals until they smeared between the pressure of my fingertips, and I thought of flesh—of me pulling and tearing, pinching a vein until it burst like a balloon. The wet of the annihilated wild rose became crimson gore rather than smeared fuchsia on the milky hue of my skin.

"Huh," Liza said. "Nature nut, eh?"

I was no longer nervous. Nature had calmed me, like it did. I gazed at Liza, right into her dark eyes. *How beautiful*, I thought, *should stars glitter there in the black.*

"Yeah," I said. "I am. Nature is far more interesting than people. And more gentle too."

"Gentle?" Liza laughed. "Tell that to the people living in Tornado Alley. Or on a hurricane-battered coast. Or the victims of avalanches."

"Nature is neither gentle nor rough," I said. "It just *is*. It's not doing those things *to* anyone. It's just being itself. No malicious intent."

Liza's mouth opened, then closed, then opened again. She was going to ask me a question that made her uncomfortable, which meant she'd been thinking about it for a while, perhaps since she'd heard a new girl was coming.

"Are you okay, Anna?" she asked.

"I feel fine," I said.

"Yes, but … are you … did someone hurt you? I mean, you came to live *here*."

I broke eye contact. I should not be uncomfortable about it, Mom said, but I was. And Mom said when I started to feel uncomfortable, I should just own it. See the truth in my emotion and I would grow more comfortable in my own skin. Acceptance.

"I bet you think my dad beat me," I said. "Or diddled me."

Liza shrugged. "Or your mom's boyfriend did."

I shook my head. "Nobody hurt me."

I did not want to talk about it anymore.

"Why are you here?" I asked.

Liza shrugged. "Dad had a … problem. When Mom died … he didn't work."

"Oh."

"Drugs and shit," Liza said.

"Oh."

I should have said something more. But I liked Liza, and I was balancing on a knife's edge. Be too weird, say something wrong, and I'd be alone again. But the words and emotions swelled in my body, straining against my skin, desperate to get out. I wanted to vomit those words all over Liza. Tell her I cared, tell her that I understood how she was feeling and I that felt bad things too.

But Liza said nothing. I bet she didn't want to talk about it because it hurt. There was no more conversation to be had, and that was okay. Our brains had enough to ponder. I took in my surroundings, happy to be in the woods, where time stood still. Mary and Laz were making a ruckus in the trees, snapping and striking each other with wooden light sabers. New Friend was still lying on the grave, but she was wriggling ever so slightly. It caught my eye, and I looked away, but something didn't sit right. So I sat up and looked again. Closer.

New Friend was struggling against unseen bindings. Red marks appeared on her wrists as she rotated them back and forth, her fingers clawing the dirt for purchase. Her feet flexed and her ankle bones knocked together as she tried to free her legs from something that grasped her that I could not see. Was she screaming? Maybe. Her stomach was heaving, her shoulders lifting off the ground as her core twisted and turned. An imaginary weight was upon her, pinning her down.

I rolled to my hands and knees and crawled over to her as the sounds of Mary and Laz's play faded to a muffled droning. Liza was saying something, but her voice, too, was far away and encased in maple syrup.

Once I reached New Friend, I examined her further. The blood in her exposed neck had clotted and turned to thick, black pitch. Her flesh was as thin and translucent as onion skin, and purple veins moved like millipedes living in between her top layer of dermis and her fat and blood, manic and panicked and wriggling every which way. So many worms, so many veins, her insides scrambling to find an exit from their meat casing.

I wanted to help. Panic rose in my own chest, and I wanted to cry out and ask Liza to help me, to help New Friend, to do something because Liza was so calm and cool and beautiful, and she was older, and she could help. But I didn't say a single word. I leashed my panic, snapping it to heel. Only I could help because only I needed help. No one else could see.

I placed my hand on New Friend's arm. The tips of my fingers froze instantly, my nails and pads turning black and stiff. It hurt, but I did not pull away. I bit my lip until I tasted blood, and I sucked on it, using the copper tang to distract me from the pain in my hands. Most importantly, though, was that New Friend had calmed. The millipedes beneath her skin were gone, as were the striations on her wrists and ankles. Her chest was not heaving, and the blood trickling from her neck was wet and thin and crimson. She was back to her normal, but all was not well. Something was off. The sound was still muted, and the forest had stilled. No playing kids, no breeze, no smells or tastes or colours. But a sight in my peripheral cause me to leap to my feet.

There was a man standing at the edge of the cemetery, watching me. He had to be about eight feet tall, but he was hunched over into an arc, leaving him a good foot shorter. One leg was much longer than the other, and that would have caused him to stand at quite a slant if it weren't for his single Logan; that boot was a bright yellow beacon in the otherwise muted tones of the forest. His body went this way and that like a gnarled root, and his face was long and wide, puffy and bloated. His tongue was thick and distended and covered in tiny mushrooms, and his teeth had rotted away to blackened posts. He had empty sockets where eyes must have once been, but now they were just caverns dripping with a slimy layer of rot and pus that hung there like globby stalagmites. Ribbons of tender flesh fluttered from his eye sockets as he blinked; I figured those were probably, at one time, his eyelids. He had no hair and barely any flesh on his bones. I could tell because other than that blaring yellow Logan, he was wearing not a single stitch of clothing. The length of his manhood had shriveled up into his body, but his testes had swelled and drooped and were now swinging full and heavy between his thighs. They were dark purple and distended, their veins as mobile and frantic as the millipedes had been under New Friend's flesh.

"Old Man Merle," I said. And indeed, the specter before me huffed out a wheezy, wet breath of acknowledgement. A gasp drowning in sludge.

"What about him?" Liza asked.

"Is he here?" Mary shrieked, and she and Laz came bounding back into the cemetery.

Liza rose to her feet and greeted the two other kids by my side. Old Man Merle swayed, his drool swaying with him. He wasn't coming any closer, and for some reason, faced with this behemoth of a rotting monster, I felt no fear.

I waited. Someone else would have to say something first.

"Did you see something?" Mary asked as she tugged on my shirt. "Some*one*?"

"You scared?" Laz asked.

I was. But not of Old Man Merle.

There was something else there. Something behind Old Man Merle, over his shoulder, hiding in the trees. As I looked past him, he turned and looked over his shoulder. He saw what I saw, and it scared him too. He took off through the woods, shit flowing from his bottom as he disappeared into the trees.

Scared shitless.

Me too.

"What's that?" I asked.

My hand levitated and my finger came up and pointed without me ever realizing I was lifting my arm. It was my finger and always had been, but it looked foreign and too big. All eyes followed the line of that finger into the trees.

"That?" Mary said.

Mary crept into the woods without hesitation or concern for safety, but this time, we were all close behind. The thing I'd pointed at was only a stone's throw deep into the brush, but it was overgrown with tangles of weeds and limbs and deadfall.

"That's nothing," Liza said. "Just a back entrance to the cemetery, I suppose."

Laz sighed, probably disappointed it wasn't something more interesting, like a corpse. But …

"A corpse gate," I said.

They all stopped.

"What?" Liza said.

"A lych-gate," I said, thinking that might clarify. It had not, judging by the confusion on their faces. "Eden's Edge. The Beas—I mean, the church. Is this a religious cemetery?"

The three kids gave each other strange looks I couldn't decipher.

"Religious?" Liza said. "Well, yes. Probably."

There was more to that, but I was most interested in the structure before me.

"A corpse gate, or lych-gate, is simply the entrance to a cemetery," I explained.

It was an entrance. Or a former one. But it was on the opposite side of Eden's Edge, meaning there must be a community further out. Which made sense. We were not an island. But the woods were thick. No evidence of roads or paths or any kind of clearing.

The structure itself leaned to one side, very much like Old Man Merle, but it was in much better condition than him. It was simple—four heavy wooden posts and a roof, like most lych-gates, but this one had certainly stood the test of time. With no fence attached on either side, it had devolved into more of a monument than a gate. An abandoned covered bridge between the cemetery and the forest.

"They used them to gate-keep cemeteries from body snatchers," I explained.

Among other things.

Mary pulled down her sleeve and started wiping the wood. Where debris blocked the way, she pulled down branches and vines to reveal the beauty beneath.

And it was beautiful. Horrible, depraved beauty. Images had been whittled into the wood—faces contorted in ecstasy and pain, pleasure and torture. Human forms intertwined with wings and claws and hooves and jaws, knotted amongst trees and stars, with bones and flowers sewing everything together.

My hair whooshed towards the lych-gate, sucked by an impossible vacuum. And heat seared my flesh—I could smell the cook of my own meat and the boil of my own blood.

I couldn't breathe.

"It's pretty, I guess," Liza said.

"Awfully dirty and moldy," Mary grumbled as she tore away branches and polished the carvings.

I was choking.

"Hey," Laz said. He was the perceptive one of the bunch. "Are you okay?"

Boils swelled on my skin, bursting and seeping into my clothes, weighing me down as I tried to back away. My hair fell out in clumps, and where it didn't, my scalp itched so badly I ripped the hair out of my head. My teeth chattered together, splintering and stabbing into my gums until my mouth was bloody and I could not speak. I turned to leave, to run, to submit to my fear, but New Friend was there, and I slammed into her. She did not falter or budge even a millimeter. Instead, she embraced me again, held me until my teeth grew back, and my boils healed over, and new hair sprouted from my head and rested upon my shoulders.

"You're acting real weird," Laz said.

"It's just …" I was still facing the lych-gate. I hadn't taken a single step away. "I need to go home. I'm thirsty and tired."

They weren't convinced. Mary was too busy revealing the lych-gate in its entirety, but Laz gave me the side eye, and Liza had strategically placed herself between me and the other two.

"I can find my own way back," I said. "Thanks for hanging out with me."

I didn't give them a chance to respond. I walked away, trying to feign calm and casual. I stepped around New Friend, headed in the direction of Eden's Edge, when I noticed her shoulders were squared towards the lych-gate. Her body trembled and sound crescendoed deep in her belly—a rumble like thunder laced with rage. And even though she only had a throat and no mouth through which to emit a voice, she was making sound, nonetheless.

She was growling. And it wasn't until I had sprinted through the trees, away from the lych-gate, away from the graves and the kids and Old Man Merle and burst out the other side into the yard behind Library House that I realized the noise—the rage, the growling—was still with me even though New Friend wasn't.

Placing my hand on my own belly, I realized that it was I who had been growling.

Chapter Six

Mom wasn't thrilled about me going to school in Eden's Edge.

"It's quite religious," she said as she held my hand tight and locked our front door. "I know you aren't used to that."

"I know all about that already," I said. And I did. I had read about all sorts of religions from all sorts of places in all sorts of books.

"Yes, but knowing and living it are two different things. You know about religion—practices, ideologies, conflict. But what they'll teach isn't history, and they will try to feed you heaping spoonfuls of belief. They'll try to convince, not teach."

Mom did not like religion. Mom hated nothing because hate is such a strong word, but her feelings towards religion came close to hate. She said spirituality was beautiful but religion was violent, judgmental, hypocritical, tainted. An excuse for behaviour and power and pride.

"It's okay, Mom. I'll nod my head and smile."

"Do not feel you have to agree or offer an opinion."

"I will do my schoolwork."

"Facts and science."

"Yes."

"Creativity and exploration."

We both smiled. Mom's smile was the sun, absorbed into my flesh and warming my bones.

Mom started down the lane, still grasping my hand, but I tugged back.

"Anna?" she said. "You have to go."

She was on edge. I wished I could calm her nerves. At our home, our old home, I had a tea garden in the back, and I would make her some chamomile lavender tea, just like she liked.

"I'm okay, Mom. I was just wondering if we could go the long way to school."

"Sure," she said without hesitation.

I had never given Mom a reason to question me. Even when I messed up, I learned. I was smart and safe, just like she'd taught me.

I wanted to collect New Friend. She was a kid, just like me, and the only person here I felt truly comfortable being around. I assumed she would go to school just like me. And I was right. As we approached the property with the crooked little house on a foundation of black patent shoes, the door creaked open, squawking like a raven. I stopped, and Mom's steps stopped with me. New Friend's pale blue leg stepped over the threshold of her door, then the other leg appeared, and she slipped through before pulling the door shut. She paused while the door clanked, locking behind her.

Someone was on the other side.

Her mom?

New Friend was wearing her shiny black shoes again. A moment of worry fluttered in my chest as I pictured her feet severed from her ankles, propping up the house from which she had just emerged. But for now, her feet were attached to her ankles, which were attached to her legs, which stretched up beneath her blue pinafore dress.

As she passed between the two bowls, she stopped and considered. Turned her body from blood to tears and back again, as if looking at each bowl in turn. Then she chose the blood bowl, laid her hands on it, and lifted it from its post. As she descended the stairs, blood sloshed over the front of her outfit, rolling down her pale legs in thick drops, leaving streams spidering down her skin. I imagined that's what it would look like if she got her period and had no panties on. I didn't know for sure, though, as mine hadn't come yet. But blood is blood, no matter how it spills. Mom did say that it was a bit thicker than water, dribbling out of vaginas and making splotches on clothing, bedding, and tacky patches on the insides of thighs.

Mom didn't hide things from me. She told it like it was, or how it could be. Sometimes I was scared—many times, in fact—but Mom was always there. When she told me about periods, she was honest. They'll hurt, she said, like someone squeezing your belly parts in their fists. And you'll have to keep a straight face while people are talking to you and a blood clot slithers around a tampon or out onto a pad. Or when you don't know it's coming and you have to tug your jumper down to mask the spreading crimson on your pants or the stream of blood dribbling down your inner thigh, racing to expose itself below the hem of your skirt.

Periods aren't scary. That's what Mom said. Some things were, though. But Mom was there. She tucked me in at night, held me when I cried when the nasty old nurse with the salt and pepper hair gave me my vaccines, fed me peanut butter and marshmallow sandwiches when I felt sad. And she was there, standing sentry at my door, when Dad came home drunk from the bar. Mom was strong and Dad was not. That's why he acted the way he did.

New Friend joined me at the side opposite where

Mom stood. I felt Mom watching me, but I would not meet her eyes.

"Anna?" she asked.

I did not know what she was asking. I did not have an answer to a question that wasn't asked. So, I walked, and New Friend walked with me, and after a few steps, Mom joined us. We did not speak on the way to The Beast, but it wasn't uncomfortable. I was thinking, and I'm sure Mom was thinking, and New Friend couldn't speak because she had no head. It was a peaceful stroll; Mom's shoulders were relaxed, and her steps moved in time with some music in her head. New Friend skipped every few steps and kicked bigger rocks down the path. I drank in the birdsong, the smell and taste of the damp plants waking with the morning and enjoyed the tingle of the sun as it burned away the fog.

Things were not so jovial when we reached The Beast. It was ugly, it was cold, and it was hard as stone and dull as a spoon. It was shaped like a Protestant church, with a tall steeple and bell atop, but it had no curves. Humans had curves, and humans had hearts and souls and warmth. This building was square and had none of that. It was hateful. I could feel its apathy, its loathing, the indifference it offered its occupants. It was gross.

"I don't like it, Mom."

"Neither do I."

Mom never sugar-coated anything for me. I appreciated it; I was always prepared. Still, I felt unease gurgling at the top of my bowels, a squelching protest for what I might find behind those double oak doors. Would the kids point and laugh? Would the schoolwork be too hard, and would the teachers think I'm dumb and put me back a grade where I would be too tall and stick out like a pokeweed in a field of sweetgrass? Or would my period start, staining my outfit and telling all the boys and all the girls that I was gross and different and something to be avoided?

Mom put her arm around my shoulder, and we bumped off each other while we walked until we fell in step.

"It's okay, Anna. It's a new school, and new things are scary. Unknown things are scary and uncomfortable, but growth is never comfortable. Doesn't make it bad."

"I think this place is bad."

Mom sighed from deep in her belly. "Might be, Anna. Might be. And that's okay. You know why?"

I shook my head, and Mom stopped walking. She placed her hands on my shoulders, got down on one knee, and looked up into my face. Even below me, she was the sun.

"It's okay because you aren't bad. You are good, and you are strong, and no bad person or place or thing will make you otherwise."

I nodded. I didn't believe that in my feelings, but Mom said even if you didn't believe things with your emotions, you should pretend you do, and eventually, it will become truth.

We continued walking. In a very short time, too short for my liking, we were at the front steps of The Beast, staring up at the white paint slathered over plain wooden doors.

My lip quivered, and I bit it hard until I could taste copper.

"It's okay, Anna."

"It's not."

"But it will be."

I clutched on to Mom's jacket, clenching it in my fist until my hand hurt. "I don't want to go."

"I know. But sometimes we have to do things we don't like. It is safe in there, and you need to go to school. Learning is important."

"I can learn at home. From books."

"You sure can. But you can't learn independence. You can't learn to navigate people from behind the pages of a book."

I had no idea what that meant, and I didn't care. I didn't want to go.

"You are going," Mom said.

I hesitated, seeing an opportunity in the sheen of tears over Mom's eyes. She didn't want me to go either.

"Of course I worry, Anna. Of course I'll miss you. But you need school, you need structure, you need other people, and everything will be fine."

She looked down at me and tilted her chin. A prompt.

"Everything will be fine," I repeated like a Catholic callback.

"You are smart."

"I am smart."

"You are strong."

"I am strong."

Mom pulled me to her body. The rhythm of our breath matched in tempo and depth, and I could feel her heart beating, pushing against my own.

"I love you, Anna. Right from my roots to my soles."

I smiled, and tears leaked out from where my eyes crinkled.

"I love you too, Mom. From my soles to my roots."

As if to punctuate our exchange, the door to The Beast swung open with no shortage of dramatics, and a hefty woman in an olive apron clomped out to the top step.

"Oh, look here!" the plentiful woman said, her solid shelf of monoboob heaving with each step she took. "And who is this little goat?"

I opened my mouth, but my voice retreated, hiding in my stomach. The woman seemed so large, and behind her, the open door of The Beast looked like a mouth, wide and hungry and sharp.

"This is Anna," Mom said as she rose to her full height, her chin held high.

Mom was sad and scared too, but she was acting

brave. For me. And because she was. Or was trying to believe she was to make it true.

The large woman waddled down the stairs and bent in half in front of me, so we were eye to eye. But she didn't come too close. At my level, but out of my space. I liked this woman.

"Well, it's a pleasure to meet you, Miss Anna. I'm Mary Jo. But the kids here call me Miss Mojo."

That was a funny name. I giggled and curtsied. I did weird things when I was uncomfortable. Miss Mojo curtsied too, and a laugh erupted from her jiggly belly.

"Well, aren't you quite the show!" Miss Mojo said.

And despite all her weight, which was a lot, and her height, which had to have been two meters or more, she took a knee in front of me so she could look up at me, just like Mom had.

"Now, girl, I understand you are scared. And so you should be! You don't know me, and you know nobody inside, and this building is really ugly, and this isn't quite a town …"—Miss Mojo leaned in and her voice diminished to a wisp of a tone—"and Miss Allison for sure has some sort of broomstick up that tight ole booty, but don't pay attention to any of that mess. This school is *mine*, and I *promise* you that you will be just fine inside as long as I'm there. And I'm never not there."

My ribs relaxed, allowing my heart to beat free of constriction. I looked up at Mom, and her cheeks were rose-petal pink, her eyes shiny with joy tears. Miss Mojo was good, and everything was okay. For now.

Miss Mojo took a moment, maybe two or three, to get upright again, then she took my hand, and we headed into the mouth of The Beast as Mom watched, her hands wringing behind her back so I could not see.

It's okay. I'm smart, I'm strong, and this will all be okay.

Chapter Seven

"Class is important," Miss Mojo said.

I scrunched up my forehead super hard so she would know I wasn't happy. We were sitting on the long benches in the belly of The Beast. Pews, I supposed.

"I'm already smart," I argued.

I did not want to leave Miss Mojo. She was good, and I liked her.

"A smartass, that's for sure."

I gasped. She laughed. Her laughter was full and breathy, right from her belly, which warmed my blood.

"I'm quite certain you've heard worse language," she said. "Probably the F-word, and the S-word, and that C-word."

I wanted to lift my hand to cover the giggles leaking from my mouth, but one hand was in Miss Mojo's, and the other was held tight by New Friend, who was sitting beside me in the pew. Miss Mojo noticed me tug my hands—first the one she was touching, then the one she wasn't. I tried to relax my hand, to make it seem like it wasn't threaded through fingers that weren't there.

"What's the C-word?" I asked, trying to distract her from the nothing that sat beside me.

"You know what it is," Miss Mojo said out of the side of her mouth. "Like you said, you're smart."

I did know. Dad had called Mom the C-word on more than one occasion. Mom said men did that as an insult, but it was actually a secret compliment. It meant that a woman made them angry, made them lose control, and men spat that word because they were all out of smart things to say.

Thoughts of the C-word and its meaning in a larger context were a nice distraction from the belly of The Beast. The interior of the building was ugly too, just like it was on the outside. It acted like it was pretty—crisp white walls, silk flowers in vases on every surface, billboards with laminated pictures of apples and rainbows and bluebirds perched atop math equations and Comic Sans lines of the alphabet. But there was no heart. No soul. It was barren and ugly and lacking any sort of genuine personality.

"Is this building new?" I asked.

"Not terribly," Miss Mojo said. "Thirteen years or so, I think. Miss Allison bought the property way back when. Had some houses built in the campsites and put up the chapel around then too."

The Beast wasn't big. It was like an ocean behemoth. Its hallways were tentacles, the rooms like suckers, and the main room—the chapel—was its belly. The altar was its beak. That's where all the noise comes out. And that's where it eats people alive.

I swung my feet beneath the pew, and New Friend mirrored my movements. The sunlight filtering through the stained-glass windows shone like kaleidoscopes on her shiny patent shoes. Not on mine, though. Nothing on my feet but dirt and threadbare fabric worn from playing in the dirt and dragging my toes instead of braking my bike properly. I wished I could have brought my bike here. I wondered if I would ever have a bike again.

"Now, Miss Anna, you're going to go to class. You are gonna study the books and pay attention to what's written on the board."

I didn't like it. Not one bit, but I couldn't say why.

One of the suckers down one of the tentacles opened, and a frail man with glasses on the end of his nose stepped out, looking frazzled and lost.

Miss Mojo heaved herself to her feet. New Friend and I jumped up as well, and New Friend stood in front of me, protecting.

"Mr. Charles," Miss Mojo bellowed. "Over here, boy."

He wasn't a boy. He was a full-grown man with thin hair and a roadmap of wrinkles on his skin. But he sure jumped like a little boy when Miss Mojo hollered for him.

"Ah, yes then," he said as he shambled towards us.

Miss Mojo made no move to go to him; he had to come all the way into the belly of The Beast to retrieve me. When he reached us, it was uncomfortable. For him. He looked at his shoes—not my eyes, not my face, not me at all.

"This is, um … welcome!" he said.

"Anna," Miss Mojo reminded him. She didn't sound impressed.

"Pleased to meet you," I said.

Neither of us reached our hand out for an introductory shake. Maybe he was like me and didn't like touches.

"You good?" Miss Mojo asked.

I thought she was asking him, and maybe she was, but she was looking at me.

I wasn't, but I nodded. Because it didn't matter if I was good or not. I had to go to school, to this school because it was right here in front of me. My old school, where I wanted to be, was very far away.

"Okay then," Miss Mojo said. "I'm gonna go talk to your momma for a spell. You go on. Both of you."

Miss Mojo left me with Mr. Charles. She walked out of the mouth of The Beast and back into the sunlight. I was jealous, and I think New Friend was too. Her shoulders turned to the door, to the sunshine, to freedom.

"Come then," Mr. Charles said as he motioned a hand down a tentacle. "Class has started, but that's no mind. We'll go in, introduce you, and you can settle right in."

Right in. Sure. Parade me like livestock in front of a bunch of predators and I'll be totally comfortable. The new kid. Great.

Mr. Charles's feet clip-clopped down the old wooden floors, and it made me think of horses. He acted like an old work horse, the way he was all hunched over and grey.

He disappeared into a classroom down the hall. I hesitated. I couldn't see around the door. Couldn't see what might be waiting for me in that room I had never seen, in this place that I didn't know.

"Coming, Anna?"

My mom spoke in my brain. *You are strong. Be strong.*

I squared my shoulders, jutted out my chin, puffed my chest out, and entered the classroom.

"Everyone, I'd like you to meet our new student. Anna?"

What was I supposed to do? He said my name like a question. I looked at him; he still wasn't looking at me. The classroom contained half a dozen normal-looking kids, all eyes on me. There were empty desks peppered here and there, so I eyed one towards the back and made my move.

"No no, dear," Mr. Charles said. "Stand up by the board and tell us a bit about yourself."

My worst nightmare didn't involve pain, fires, death,

or teeth. It was this: people looking at me, judging me, evaluating me.

You are strong, my mom said in my head.

I took my place in the center of the chalkboard and looked over the heads of my new classmates rather than into their eyes. The eyes are too intimate. New Friend's arm curled around my waist as she propped me up. My rock.

I spoke, but the voice came from nowhere and everywhere all at once. It boomed, it rumbled in my belly, swelled out of my throat like a frog wriggling free.

"I am Anna," the voice said. "I am a witch, like my mother before me, and her mother before her."

No reaction from the crowd. I continued.

"I came here because my father was murdered and we didn't want the police to know because they wouldn't understand and we'd go to jail, so we had to hide."

A kid in the back row picked her nose, and a dude in the front scribbled circles on his paper, bored.

"I see things that are there but aren't meant to be seen. But I'm not schizophrenic. I'm a witch."

Mr. Charles uncrossed his arms and rolled his hand in a circle, motioning for me to continue.

I sighed. It wasn't easy to sum up.

"My father wanted to kill me because I was a witch. And because Mom was a witch and didn't tell him, then she birthed him a baby witch and that's not what he wanted, so he wanted to kill her too. He was scared of me, and of Mom. I did things that made total sense, but he didn't understand. I ate flesh and burned furry things. I raised animals and walked naked through the woods and drew pictures on my body with broken glass, and it was beautiful, but he thought all of it was awful. Dad was scared of me, and of Mom, and he was so mad at Mom for not letting him take me away and fix me …"

My fingers traced the jagged silver lines on my arm,

scars of the cuts I'd made repeatedly like poetry on my flesh.

Everyone was looking at me now, even the boy drawing circles, even Mr. Charles. New Friend was squeezing me so tight that my breath was held prisoner below the vise of her arms, but that voice from within me kept on coming.

"And we came here to this place, but I don't like it. It's not my home with my garden and my smells and all the things I know. And we left our home so quick, and—"

"It's okay," Mr. Charles said as he stood and came over to me.

I looked at him. At the class. Back at him.

"You can tell us about yourself later, when you're more settled in." He bent and whispered in my ear. "Sorry to put you on the spot like that."

He patted my back. I didn't hate his touch because it was well-meaning.

I headed for the desk I had initially set my sights on and slid into the seat. New Friend sat on her knees beside the desk, her arms tight around my calf.

There had been no words at all. Not said out loud, anyway. I had wanted there to be words, a cleansing confession, but none had any meat behind them. They had only been smoke in my mind as I stood there like a buffoon, silent, mouth agape at the front of that classroom.

That was all right. These people were not ready for my truths. Probably never would be. I know I wasn't.

Chapter Eight

Classes at The Beast were similar to classes back home—sterile, obligatory, boring as all get-go. Mister Charles was nice enough, but I could tell he was bored just like the rest of us. Back home, kids would be whispering and passing notes until the noise of their restlessness boiled over and the teacher had to bark at them to quiet down and pay attention. And then the cycle would start again—the crinkle of notes passed, whispers hissing, rising in volume like a swelling wave.

The kids at The Beast did not whisper. Notes did not crinkle; feet did not tap the floor in a restless staccato. Everyone was eyes forwards, hands folded in front of them, full soles—toe to heel—pressed firmly into the wood beneath their feet. It was creepy.

"Miss Anna?"

Mister Charles was looking at me. They were all looking at me.

"Just Anna is fine," I said. I was no *Miss*.

"Do you have any thoughts on the assignment?"

What assignment?

"No, I'm good," I lied.

"You understand?"

Nope.

But I nodded anyways. I figured maybe one of the other kids could tell me. Or I just wouldn't do it.

Mr. Charles was on to me. His eyes bored into me, but they were soft. He wasn't going to challenge me or put me on the spot anymore, at least not today.

The church bell rang, and I almost fell off my seat. It wasn't the electronic ding of the bell back home. It was an actual church bell, all big and rough and brass, and it shook my molars in my skull. The others seemed unfazed. They were used to it.

"Okay, kids," Mr. Charles said, "on to arithmetic."

The kids stood in unison and gathered their things.

I had no things to gather. I didn't know if I needed school supplies or if there was even anywhere to shop for them. Mr. Charles had given me a piece of paper and a pencil to take notes during his class, but I didn't. His class was language arts, and I certainly didn't need any help in that area. But I didn't want to draw attention, so I had spent the first period doodling and writing poetry, looking busy busy busy. Very much like I intended to spend the last half of the day.

I missed my own pencils that wore my teeth marks like scars, and my old notebooks, fat and bulging with my words and drawings.

I want to go home.

I have no home.

"It's across the hall," the girl next to me whispered. "We switch with the other class."

The other class was only four people, and three of them, I knew. Liza, Laz, and Mary.

"Hey!" Mary said as she bounced past me.

"Having an awesome first day?" Liza said as she

glided by.

I wondered why I couldn't be in that class. Because there were so few of us, we were a mix of ages and grades, all clumped together. The schoolwork was individualized; they gave us worksheets, tests, and projects based on our grade level. I had heard about school like this back in the old times in the north. Single room schoolhouse, everyone at every level crammed in the same room. Being in this school, in The Beast, in Eden's Edge, made me feel like I had been thrust back in time.

My three familiars were gone into the classroom I'd left behind. I was left alone, moving across the hall with my cohort of strangers. I stepped on one girl's heels on purpose, and she glared at me. But I hadn't meant to hurt her. I felt so alone. I wanted to feel her. I wanted someone to notice me.

The afternoon was spent on arithmetic, which I didn't prefer because I wasn't good at it. The time went fast, though, because I had to pay attention and take notes; I didn't have to doodle or write poetry to pass the time in this class. Thankfully, I wasn't that far behind. My math class at home was doing about the same things when I was forced to run away in the middle of the night.

After a while, the bell sang out again, and the children marched in an orderly fashion down the hall to a set of stairs leading to a basement. I didn't want to follow. Basements never contained anything I cared to bother with. Instead, I hung back from the crowd and snuck into a dark classroom. Once the last patter of footsteps had disappeared down below, I closed the door to the room and flicked on the light.

It was a library. Perhaps. There were lots of books, but not floor to ceiling like the library house. There were some tables, some green lamps, and cup holders containing pencils. There were no computers. In fact, I hadn't seen a computer since arriving in Eden's Edge. Not that I should have—I hadn't been in very many places, and it was only my second full day—but surely I should have seen one in the library house, or somewhere in The Beast, which was supposedly both a school and the heart of the whole community. I tucked that information away for later. I was in this room to see the books.

My steps were soft as my fingers found spines, dragging over plastic dust covers and embossed lettering, riffling the tops of pages. There were books on animals, on the continents and bodies of water, on weather. And lots of self-help books and religious texts. Not religious. Christian. And only Christian.

"Oh, my word, Little Goat, you're gettin into it from the first, are you?"

Miss Mojo swayed into the room, and I jumped back from the bookshelf like I'd been manhandling forbidden fruit. But she didn't seem mad. In fact, she closed the door behind her and turned on the light.

"Is this the library?" I asked.

"Library House is where all the good reading is. The fun stuff, anyways."

"I like history. That's fun."

"Well. You won't find too much of that here, I'm afraid."

The books contained in this room amounted to a meager, pathetic collection. The bookshelves were so starved for words I could almost hear their wooden bellies clench and grumble.

"But social studies …" I said. "What about research?"

"Folks here learn about internal politics and structure. And religious teachings, of course."

I sighed and crossed my arms.

Miss Mojo grinned. "I know, I know. You're a child of knowledge and fire. Like me, and I suspect, just like your momma."

I didn't know what that meant and didn't care to ask. I had other things that needed knowing.

"Is this a cult?" I asked. "Eden's Edge?"

A braying laugh escaped Miss Mojo's mouth before she brought her meaty hand up to stifle it. The laughter continued, muffled, for a full minute before she regained her composure.

"Well then," she said, coming close to me so her breath could land on my cheek. "You are a cheeky one, aren't you?"

She hadn't answered my question.

"In its way, yes," she said. I wondered again if she had read my mind.

I was a bit startled.

"It is?" I asked.

"Uh huh."

"A cult?"

"It's got its particulars and its rules."

I took a minute to process that. I wasn't used to anyone being so forthcoming with me.

"Is Allison bad?"

"Does a butthole stink?"

I thought about that too. "It does, but only because of the shit that passes through."

That enticed another of those big, beautiful Miss Mojo laughs that made me feel warm and safe.

"Well, in simpler terms, yes. She's a bad apple."

"Why?" I asked. "How?"

I had so many questions.

Footsteps tapped up the stairs beyond the door and around the corner.

"No time for questions, and certainly no time for answers, Little Goat."

The door opened, and Mr. Charles entered the room,

preceded by his rodent-like nose. I half expected him to twitch it and sniff the air, looking for cheese.

"What's all this then?" he asked. "Anna, you are missing lunch period. The cafeteria is downstairs."

I opened my mouth, but words came from Miss Mojo's mouth instead.

"You mind yours, Mr. Charles. I was just having a quick yarn with Little Goat, making sure she was doing okay on her first day. Been quite a turmoil for her the past little while, as I'm sure you can imagine."

"Yes, yes, quite so," Mr. Charles mumbled. "But Allison—"

"Can mind her own as well," Miss Mojo said.

There was a tap tap tap at the window. A buzz. My eyes found the sound and accompanying movement. It was a cluster of blue bottle flies bouncing off the glass. I looked back at Miss Mojo and saw the gleam of a blue body and a few furry legs as a fly crawled into her left nostril.

"But yes, Anna, you should eat. Keep up your strength. You have a few hours of learning yet to do before you can scamper on home. Would you like me to take you downstairs?"

Yes. Very badly.

"No, I'm fine."

Miss Mojo nodded towards the door.

"Go on then. If you have any troubles, just call for me."

"Like, yell?" I asked. "I don't have a cell phone."

She laughed. Then didn't answer the question.

Miss Mojo walked to the door of the classroom with me and shut off the light, even though Mr. Charles was still inside. I headed to the end of the hall, to the stairs, and looked back at Miss Mojo. She was standing in the center of the hall, filling the space. The corners of her mouth were curled up into a smile. My head felt quite funny. The doors on either side of the hall blurred, and the floor beneath Miss Mojo blurred, and her eyes seemed to light up, bright lights, gold and sparkling and spinning. They were glass jars filled with fireflies frantic to escape. And her fingers were millipedes, fat and drooling, and hornets poured from her ears with clumps of meat trailing from their stingers. I blinked hard, again and again, but I couldn't clear the fuzz from my vision or the bugs from Miss Mojo, and my tummy did a weird clench.

I nodded, curtsied, and stumbled all at once, then got my footing and grasped the handrail leading to the basement. I descended one step at a time, but I didn't feel well. It was hot, I was hot, everything was hot. My palm sizzled against the rail, and the soles of my shoes got so soft and tacky that the rubber stuck to the stairs. Sweat dribbled down my face, pasting my hair to my cheeks in snaking tendrils. Each step was a mountain, my legs concrete, the heat boiling my very blood. I called out for Miss Mojo, but I had no voice, and besides, not even my legs would listen to me. They kept going even though I screamed at my muscles to stop and obey and behave, but on I marched, step by sticky step.

I finally reached the bottom, where I was greeted by a set of double doors. I peeled my hand from the railing, leaving my flesh behind, and touched one of the door handles. It was scorching hot. Pure fire, in fact, glowing white and flickering with the heat of flame. And on the other side of the door were sounds. Awful sounds. Screaming, squelching, the splintering of bones and the shattering of teeth. A girl cried out—in ecstasy or pain, I wasn't sure. Glass was breaking, wood snapping, dogs yelping, lambs mewling.

The door swung open, and I stepped inside.

The children were all there, standing, hands folded in front of their tummies, facing the door, facing me. Rows of them, precise, evenly spaced. In the middle of the room was a long table full of serving platters, upon which was New Friend. She was all broken up. Her fingers were on one platter, arranged over a bed of raven-black hair

her hair?

that had been shorn and laid out in a basket. Her feet and fingerless hands were on a pretty serving plate with blue flowers. Her ribs, spine, and femur were hung from the ceiling like wind chimes rattling together, swinging in the breeze from the air vents. Her organs, still pumping and churning and working, were on the largest platter in the center of the table. Feces, urine, and bile pooled around the meat of her like gravy, glistening under the bulbs overhead, most of which were cracked, yellowed, and sparking.

The children no longer had their hands in front of their tummies. They were eating New Friend. Her meat dangled in strips from their gluttonous lips, her juices squelching between their teeth and dribbling down their chins. Their clothes, which were all white gowns, were stained with the blood and leavings of New Friend. They gulped and belched and gagged as they ate, and I gagged too, vomit stinging the backs of my eyes and my throat.

I was screaming, I think. Air passed through my lips; I sprayed hot, wet spittle and tears into the air in a dense mist. My hair didn't blow in my wind because it was stuck to my face with sweat and tears. I ran to the table, to the platters, desperately trying to hold New Friend's hand, to tell her I was there, and everything was going to be okay, but I didn't know what to do. Did I have to reconstruct the hand to hold it? Tack the fingers together with the gravy of blood and bile? And where were her palms? Her arms? Which bones were which? She was a puzzle to which I had no box for reference. I did not know how to assemble her, so I, too, fell apart.

I screamed and all the children screamed with me, bloody noise spewing into the air in a crimson spray until the room darkened with red rain that coated everything, thick and horrible, including my eyeballs, coating them thicker and darker with blood until everything went black.

Chapter Nine

"I don't understand." My mom's voice was firm but calm. She didn't seem worried.

"She passed out," Miss Mojo said. "I think maybe the day overwhelmed her. The new place, the other kids. You know." Her voice wasn't worried either.

"Had she eaten anything off?" Allison's voice was a chorus of worry, but not kind worry. Worry that centered on herself.

"I'm sure the food is just fine," Miss Mojo said, impatience deceiving itself in her tone. "And she hadn't been gone from me but a moment. She wouldn't have had time to get a seat, let alone eat the cafeteria food."

"What was going on in the basement?" Mom asked.

Outside, a song ignited. A solo voice, singing in the trees. It was the red cardinal again, and she sang me fully awake.

"Mom?"

The three heads turned to me. I had just opened my eyes to this discussion and was surprised to find myself on my new couch, in my new home.

Mom quickly joined me at my side. When she sat, her warmth was a comfort. I rested my head on her lap, and she stroked my hair. She smelled like musk and lavender.

"How are you feeling?" Mom asked.

"What happened?" Allison asked. She sat at my feet, and I pulled my knees into my chest. I didn't like her there, not one bit. Allison shifted closer, and I scrunched tighter, pressing into Mom. Drawn in by good and repelled by evil.

Mom held her hand up to Allison and repeated her initial question to me. "How are you feeling?"

"Okay," I said. "Weird."

"You had a spell," Miss Mojo said.

"Is she prone to *spells*?" Allison asked. Her arms were folded across her chest, and her stare was firmly affixed on Mom. Accusatory.

"Does anything hurt?" Mom asked.

I shook my head.

"Is your tummy upset?"

"No."

"Dizzy?"

"Nope."

I felt just fine. Physically.

"I'd like to speak to my mom," I said. "Alone."

I looked at Allison. It was much easier to look at the blue shimmering line of her cheap, flaking eyeliner than right into her hateful eyes, so I watched that line lift and crinkle as she scowled at me.

"It's important I know what happened," Allison said. "If she has a preexisting condition I should be aware of—"

"Thank you for your time," Mom said. When she stood, my head rolled back onto the couch. "And for bringing her home, Miss Mojo. I will let you know in the morning whether she's well enough to attend school."

"You will let *me* know," Allison corrected.

I sat up and moved to the edge of the couch, far away

from Allison, in the warmth where Mom had just been seated. Mom stepped in front of Allison, who was still seated; Allison did not look impressed with Mom standing above her staring down at her. Allison glanced at Miss Mojo, maybe looking for support, but Miss Mojo had already moved to the door. It was closed, and beyond the wood, on the other side, something scratched. Clawed. Rhythmic scraping against the flaking paint. Miss Mojo heard it too. I know because her head tilted, her eyes widened, and she made eye contact with me before opening the door a slit.

"Look here," Allison started as she stood to match Mom's height.

New Friend slipped through the door as Allison spoke, and she curtsied to Miss Mojo. It was oh-so-subtle, the slightest dip in her stature, but Miss Mojo curtsied back. I was sure of it. New Friend rolled in like fog, settling on the couch beside me. The cushion did not move, my weight did not shift, but I felt her body, her arm around me, and the hard stone of the bowl cradled in her other arm. Blood splashed out. It was cold on my crotch, not warm like if I'd peed my pants. I felt the tingle of embarrassment between my legs, but everyone was too busy sparring to notice what wasn't actually there.

"Eden's Edge is mine," Allison said. "*My* responsibility, and if there is something I should know about, something that might endanger the other residents, you must tell me."

"And I would," Mom said, "Were it a danger. But it isn't, nor is it any of your business, or theirs."

Allison's eyes narrowed to slits, and her teeth ground together before she spoke again.

"Everything here is my business," Allison said.

Mom smiled. It was wide and warm and threatening.

"No." That was all she said. And that was enough.

Allison sputtered, shifted her weight, but then the

door opened wide, permitting a gust of wind inside that swept my hair 'round like a cyclone. Again, I wondered what New Friend's hair would look like disrupted by that billow of a breeze.

Allison said no more, but her actions screamed her frustration. The stamp of her feet as she moped to the door, the huff of a sigh to rival the wind blowing in from outside. And had Miss Mojo not firmly affixed her hand around the doorknob, taking responsibility for closing the door, I was quite certain Allison would have slammed it hard enough to rock the house. Before she stepped out, Miss Mojo tilted her head at me and offered a wink. I don't know why, but I winked in return before she pulled the door closed.

"Cunt."

My mom rarely used language like that so openly. Whispered curse words, yes. All the time. And louder when she thought I couldn't hear. But she belted this out with intent and meaning, and part of me hoped Allison heard.

"I don't like her," I said.

"I can't imagine anyone does," Mom muttered as she crossed the room and locked the door.

A thought that had been a shadow in my brain since we'd sat in that diner only a few days before appeared on my tongue.

"Why are we here?" I asked.

Mom tugged at her jumper, then smoothed the front of her pants.

"It was an option. Like I said."

"Yes, I know," I said. And I did, but we'd only touched on this. I wanted to know more. "But how did we find her? What is this place?"

"I met Allison at the Women's Center. After yoga."

Mom loved yoga there. Bonding with her tribe of women. But the Women's Center was for abused women. Mom wasn't abused. Not quite. Not enough to necessitate a center.

"What was she doing there?" I asked.

"Not yoga," Mom said with a smirk. "Advertising. Recruiting, I suppose."

I said nothing. Mom needed to elaborate, which I told her with my stare and crossed arms.

"She chatted me up," Mom said. "And asked me if I needed help. Told me she had a place that was contained and safe, and that she could make all the arrangements. I declined, until that night … when you and I had to go and go quick."

I couldn't remember, and it bothered me. Really bothered me.

"What happened?" I asked Mom, like I'd asked so many times before.

"It doesn't matter," she said, like she had so many times before.

But it did matter. We were here, and my home was back there, and Dad was dead.

"Was he really gonna kill me?"

Mom didn't answer. She'd said it once as blood dripped from her hands

he would end you, Anna

as she convinced me that we had to leave, to run. But my memories were thick fog, dense, choking me, but the blood dripping from her fingers so brilliant and glistening …

"Your father wasn't good for us," Mom said. "He was a dangerous man, Anna. You'll come to see."

Will I?

He ate dinner with us every night, taught me to ride a bike, came to all my school plays, and worked to put food on the table. We had a house where I could grow my very own garden, a huge garden, with mint and sage and lemongrass.

I wondered what kind of work Mom could do here to

support us. Or maybe she could leave to make money and come back in the evenings. But we were far away from anything and everything, buried in the middle of the woods.

"Will you have a job?" I asked.

She shrugged.

I had no grandparents, not on Mom's side anyways. Grandma had passed in her fifties with a nasty combination of heart failure and mental illness, and Grandpa had held on until his sixties, passing with the same. Carbon copies of broken bodies and minds. Mom had no siblings, so we were all that was left. I don't count whatever Dad had on his side. I'd never met a single one of Dad's line.

"I think this is a cult," I said.

Mom considered this, biting her lip. "Doubtful. But Allison seems extreme in her beliefs."

"Cults are dangerous."

She nodded. "Cults are manipulative and smart and organized. But Allison is only one woman. We just have to be smarter. And prepared. We'll wait and see what comes at us next."

"Can we leave?"

"Of course."

"Did you sign anything? A contract?"

"Nope."

But she looked worried. We weren't legally bound here then, but the law threatened us from the outside, panting at us from every direction by now, I was sure.

"I'm tired," I said. And I was. I was still rattled by my encounter in the basement of The Beast, even if it wasn't real.

But …

"Mom, am I a witch too?"

That question startled her. She gathered herself with a deep breath, cracked her knuckles, then looked me in the eye.

"Why do you ask that now?"

"Things are strange with me."

"Everyone carries strangeness with them."

"But not like mine," I said.

"You either tuck your strangeness away, let it rot who you are on the inside, or allow it to breathe and flourish on the outside, leaving your insides to peace and discovery."

"Yes, but … am I an *actual* witch? Like you?"

Mom smiled. "You've always loved stories of witches," she said as she twirled a tress of my hair between her fingers, the individual strands nestling into the grooves on her knuckles, etched there by work and time. "Perhaps you simply want to be a witch."

I find the best way to get people to talk is to say nothing. That tactic didn't usually work with Mom because I was so much like her that she knew what was up. But this was an uncomfortable topic, not one that could linger stagnant in the air without causing her to fill the silence to break the tension.

"Do you know the story of Isobel Gowdie?" Mom finally asked.

"Scottish witch," I said with enthusiasm.

Mom grinned. "But do you *know*?"

I shook my head.

"She's an interesting one. She was accused of witchcraft in Scotland in the 1660s, as were countless other women. The witch hunt was a nasty process, as it was in many regions around the world. They used coercion and torture to garner confessions from these poor girls and women."

"They were forced to say they were witches," I said.

Mom nodded. "Even if they were witches, we would never know. And the methods for testing for witches was ridiculous. Aside from that, prosecuting witches was typically a tactic used to strip women of power and strengthen the patriarchy and the church."

"But you're a witch."

Mom nodded.

Like trail mix, bits and pieces of memories tumbled in my mind: Mom tending to wounds with words and poultices. Mom sitting naked under the moon. Mom speaking to animals and listening as if they spoke in return.

"Like my mother," she said.

Dad hated that. He was nervous about me being alone with Mom. He always hovered, tried to spend time with me away from Mom and all her things.

"So I have witch blood in me."

Mom nodded. But it was slow.

"So … I'm a witch."

Mom bit her lip.

"Well, I'm not sure, Anna. You will discover that for yourself as you grow older, but I suspect …"

"Why?"

"You're … I see something different in you. And not all witches bear witches."

So I was ordinary. That discovery was worse.

"Fix your face," Mom said, wiping a tear I hadn't felt roll down my cheek. "Why the sadness?"

"What's wrong with me then?" I asked, thinking of the things I felt, all the things I could see, all the things I knew. If I wasn't a witch, I was flawed.

"Nothing is wrong with you," Mom said. "And I never said you weren't a witch. I just pose the question—what is a witch?"

"A witch is … a witch."

"Hard to answer, yes?" Mom said. "Isobel was tortured. That much is true. And once her confessions started to flow, they became grand, exuberant claims. Talk of bedding the devil at night, of performing rituals, of transfiguration, and the description of a coven and attending the Sabbath. But the thing was … this was the first the world had heard of these things. And Isobel's confessions were all documented. Thoroughly. They influenced other confessors and subsequent witch trials, and the written confessions have been unearthed and translated time and time again throughout the years."

"A false history," I said.

Like the bible. Like a Stephen King novel if found in five-hundred years by a reader wondering if it was fact or fiction. Dark fantasy.

"Her accounts were detailed," Mom continued, "That's for sure. And the imagery and rituals she spoke of are the basis for many a vision of modern-day witchcraft. She was tortured physically—beaten, sleep deprived, burned, held under water. All those things can make the brain go wonky. Tall tales are not a surprise. She told them what they wanted to hear so they'd stop their torture and put her to death."

"Did they?"

"No one knows what happened to Isobel after her trial. She vanished. A dandelion seed in a storm."

"Was she a real witch?"

"Only Isobel knows that," Mom said, "But it begs the question. What is a witch? A *real* witch? Are modern witches forged from the suggestions of Isobel's forced confession? Or are there actual witches? Beings who are things we cannot imagine or define. Perhaps Isobel spouted no truths, but maybe there are different truths."

So there was a possibility I was … something.

"Stands to reason," Mom said, "That women with … *differences* would keep quite quiet about them, yes? Based on the consequences demonstrated through history."

This was all true, but none of it helpful. I didn't know what I was, but I was something. I wondered if even Mom knew.

"Did something happen at school?" Mom asked. "Something that would spark this discussion?"

New Friend was still sitting beside me, but now she was holding my hand. She was looking at me. I could feel it. But I couldn't see her expression, so didn't know her intention.

"No," I said. "Not really."

"Not really," Mom parroted. "Okay then."

I was scared to tell her, scared of how she would react. Would she be shocked and upset, like the first time she saw me holding flame to my own flesh? Or eating insects in the yard? I would think after twelve years on the planet, she should be getting used to me by now. I needed to talk to her. Tell her the whole of me.

But I was stuck in the dark, in an unfamiliar place, where nothing made sense. Especially not me.

Chapter Ten

I slept most of the day and half of the next. I wasn't sick, not exactly, but I was exhausted. It was probably my mind. It was running, constantly chasing thoughts I couldn't quite catch. *Am I not a witch? Then why is Dad dead? Why are we here?*

There are other options for women like Mom and kids like me. People escaping their dads. I figured we were only here because I was different, and different was hard to explain and even harder to accommodate. Mom picked this spot in the middle of nowhere, highly hidden and very controlled by that shrill, stale soda cracker of a woman, because she wanted to keep me away from normal eyes.

My legs could not stop moving. I rapped the tops of my feet on my footboard in a manic rhythm, trying to distract myself from worry.

What's wrong with me?

I'd read about mental illness. Perhaps it was that, but it didn't feel like it. I didn't look like those people in the movies with their delusions and their extra animated flights of fancy and destructive behaviour. I was not prone to mania or bouts of tears enough to flood a valley. In fact, I didn't feel much at all, most times. Mom kept me safe. That's all I needed to know. My fears, my doubts, my everything was bundled in the membrane around her heart.

And that's why we're here. Because it's safe.

But is it?

I had to get out of bed. The tops of my feet were bruising from banging them off the footboard for … how long? Hours, I supposed. I gave Dad's heart a wink and a bow, then went down the hall in search of Mom. To my surprise, the house was quiet and the doors were locked.

"Hello?"

Nothing. Maybe Mom was resting in her bedroom. Or out perusing the neighbourhood, if you could call it that. I'd had quite enough of exploring, so I decided to hang out in our backyard. I rifled through the stack of books I had brought and hauled out my worn and extra-loved copy of *The Malleus Maleficarum*. Maybe I wasn't a witch, but I clung to that maybe. Because maybes come with another side. Maybe I *was* a witch. And that was enough for me. Mom did always say I could be whatever I wanted.

The backyard was neatly manicured. I didn't like that. I liked trees and bushes, flowers and weeds. This bare and short-sheared yard made me feel exposed and vulnerable, its cleanliness a violation leaving me stripped bare. Thankfully, the forest wasn't far behind the back fence line, so whenever I felt the suffocating anxiety swell, I could look off into the trees and imagine I was dancing in their midst.

In the meantime, I had no tree to lean against and read. I could lay in the grass; it was so clean and tidy even wee life couldn't take shelter there, so I wouldn't have to worry about ant bites or mosquitos or lurking serpents. I went to the back fence and nestled into the corner. It felt like a little box if I faced the corner, the two sides confining me to my own safety. But the fence was bright and white and far too clean. I sniffed it. Fresh paint. Allison the Bland must have painted it right before we came. She seemed the type to stage everything so it wouldn't look lived in, like living was a bad thing. I liked smelling the things that had been cooked, seeing the stains of life, and hearing the memories embedded on the surfaces. There was none of that here.

I read for only a few minutes before the noise of silence was ringing in my ears. There was little wind, and no people around, and no wildlife. Just me, my thoughts, and the white noise of solitude. Fearing madness was approaching, I scooped up my book and climbed over the fence. The cardinal was perched atop the fence, and it shrieked a wicked warning as I strayed from the property. I was unfamiliar with the woods, but I would be much happier lost in there than found in a tidy yard, alone and murdered by the quiet.

The crunch of deadfall beneath my feet sloughed my anxiety away. The trees grew tighter together the deeper I submerged myself, and the branches nipped at my flesh. I lifted my arm and licked a trickle of blood away, and the warm, wet grit on my tongue made me think of New Friend.

She was not with me.

Where is she?

What does she do?

I wondered about her in that house. Was New Friend all alone? I wasn't—I had Mom—but I still felt lonely. And suddenly, I missed New Friend. The forest was too confined and too large all at once. It had darkened considerably as I walked due to the heavy canopy of branches, needles, and leaves overhead. I turned on my toes and headed back the way I had come, trying to focus on the music of the woods. But my body had other plans. My heart beat against my ribs, my trachea contracted, allowing only squeaks of air to leak in and out, and cold sweat formed beneath my eyes and my nose and along my hairline, sticking my hair to my face like spider webs

beads of semen

and I giggled at the naughty voice in my head as I swiped the moisture from my face. Seeking sounds wasn't helping, so I used my nose as distraction. Pressing my lips together, I pulled a deep breath through my nose, inhaling the aromas of pine, of wood, of damp mud. There was a faint hint of manure, and maybe a touch of decay—a rodent or two rotting in the loam, perhaps a rabbit.

The smell got stronger. Sour, hot, salty. My mouth watered, filling to my throat, so I released my lips and let the drool pour over the front of my jumper as I coughed and sputtered. I couldn't catch my breath. Panic still had its meaty hands around my trachea, so I desperately sucked in air, which only made it worse and angered my cough to a whooping hack. I dropped to my knees and plunged my fingers in to the forest floor. It felt both glorious and awful. The mud was cool and soothing, but the sticks tore my skin. I kneaded and squeezed the earth, willing the tactile sensory experience to calm my nerves and ease my breathing. And it did. My breathing came to rest on a gentle rhythm, and the darkness spinning around my vision lightened to a warm glow.

But the aroma of decay was still there. Not just there but stronger. A stench I could taste on my tongue. I looked around, shuffled some leaves, crawled on my hands and knees, wincing at the piercing of stick and rock until the reek was so strong my eyes watered. Whatever it was, it was close.

Chitter.

My eyes darted to the sound just as a flash of roan emerged from a pile of leaves. It was a squirrel—quite young, judging by the size—and the cloud-hued fluff of fur on its chest was soaked in glistening crimson.

"What did you find there, little sir?"

He was nervous—he trembled, but he didn't run. I scootched closer to him, to the stench hidden under bushes and leaves, and he stayed still, watching me with eyes so dark and so black that I could see my reflection in them.

I plunged my hand into the pile of leaves, and when I pulled it out, it was wet and warm with a coating of blood and rot. I brushed the leaves away, revealing the corpse beneath.

"Poor thing."

It was a bull moose with his rack lodged in a tangle of trunks. I felt along his spine, but his hide was too thick to tell if he had broken his neck or he simply starved to death, entrapped by nature.

The squirrel had burrowed a hole in the moose's distended gut. I thought at first the squirrel had been eating him, but then I saw a little cavern filled with nuts and berries and other forest goodies tucked in among the muscle, gristle, and layers of fat.

"It's a great hiding spot, Gus, but your stash will rot with his body."

The squirrel looked at me with those big black eyes, its nose twitching every which way, trying to sniff out what I was saying.

"I'm sorry, but you look like a Gus. Do you mind if I call you that?"

He didn't answer. I figured he didn't care.

"Well, Gus. What do you say we move these nuts and berries? I can make you a little storage box closer to my yard, then maybe you and I can visit once in a while."

I reached for the moose's belly, and Gus lunged through the air and sank his teeth into my arm. I screeched, jumped to my feet, and shook my arm, sending Gus flying through the air and smashing into a thick poplar trunk.

"Oh, no no," I said as tears welled in my eyes. I ran

to the tree and gathered Gus's limp body in my hands. My tears spilled over his glossy fur as I rocked him and hummed, trying to will him back to life.

But I had no magic, no powers. Not that I knew of. No spells, no tinctures, nothing. Just me and Gus, rocking in the forest, my weirdness impotent to help.

I screamed, and my voice echoed through the trees, back into my ears, and stabbed into my brain. I wailed, and rage flew out, rage that had been sitting on the top of my stomach like acid, festering and frothing and building until it finally overflowed in an explosion of tears and noise. Something was wrong with me. And Dad was dead, I had no home, no friends, and I was no one and nothing. I had nothing.

Gus's powder soft fur brushed my lower lip as I sobbed, tickling it. I bit my lip, scratching the itch, then nibbled the fringe of Gus's tail. He was motionless but warm, and his eyes were open wide, still black, still wet and staring. I saw myself in those eyes—the strings of my hoodie, the shudder of my shoulders as I sobbed, but I had no head. Only a stump of a neck oozing gelatinous blood. I closed my eyes and pressed my lips into Gus's body, into the wet moose blood that marred his little chest. I licked him, then I bit, tearing away fur until I found flesh, then ripping at that too. Soon, the ribbons of Gus's entrails were hanging down as his heart popped between my molars and his fur was packed between my teeth. I gulped Gus down, sucking every bit of meat from his bones.

I saved his eyes for last. They burst when I popped them from their sockets. I was happy to see my false reflection disappear into my stomach as I swallowed the meager gel of his eyes. Then I touched my face. Pulled my hair until it hurt and a clump came out in my fist.

It wasn't real. The reflection. It lied.

I had a head. I knew that for sure. It was probably the

only thing in my life I was absolutely certain of.

But Gus was gone. I tucked his bones into the pouch of my jumper, then fished his nuts and berries from the moose carcass and put them in the pockets of my pants. I admired the moose for a moment—his massive rack, thick hide, and long legs—before heading towards home. I shuffled my feet, thinking only of the rack, of Gus's soft fur, and my headless reflection in those black eyes, when a splash of pink caught my eye.

A single wild rose was growing among the dark foliage of the woods. I knelt next to it, got my face real low beside it, and breathed in its perfume.

I decided how to make my corner of the world a bit better. I buried my hands in the dirt once more.

Chapter Eleven

Mom arrived home later in the day. She poked her head out the back door and lingered, checking on me, on what I was up to. She did not interrupt, nor did I offer an explanation. I went in and out of the woods many times, stretching my hoodie out in front of me and using it as a basket to carry flowers, roots, and sprigs of life.

Stars like flicked paint speckled the indigo sky when Mom finally came out and spoke.

"You've been working hard," she said with a smile on her lips and in her voice.

I had. With an old rake I found in the shed, I'd torn up most of the grass in the backyard. Then, starting at the back, arranging and planning on the fly, I planted. Every flower I could find in the woods, seeds that had fallen on the forest floor, bushes that I uprooted. The yard was no longer a yard but the beginnings of what would become a spectacular garden.

"I would like some more flowers," I said. "And maybe some herbs? Plants too. Green, fluffy ones."

Mom was smiling, nodding, and there were tears in

her eyes. Mom loved gardening. She always had her flowerbeds, and her nails were always caked with dirt. My new garden made me happy, but it gave her great joy as well. It wasn't the same as my garden back home, but I would grow it, and maybe it could become something as good. Or better.

Mom's eyes dropped to the front of my hoodie, and her smile wilted. I looked to see what killed her joy. I'd forgotten about Gus. Now it was my eyes' turn to get damp.

"It was a squirrel," I said, my voice quivering. "Gus."

Mom's mouth was a tight line. Her eyes were dry as bone.

"I see me in you," she said as she looked over the garden. Then she looked back at me—not into my eyes but at the front of my hoodie. "But you are your father too."

I didn't know what she meant, but I didn't like it.

"I am not a bad person," I said.

"Neither was your father. He was who he was."

I focused my attention back on the dirt, tilling it with my fingers rough and hard, trying to direct my anger there.

"But you married him," I said. "And had me, and then he had to die and we had to come here because he was a bad person. You said so."

I couldn't look at Mom, so I didn't know what her face was saying, and she had no words for a few moments. I filled the silence with the sounds of squishing, kneading mud.

"Your father and I were a good match," she said. "Balanced. I loved him, and he me."

"But he hurt you."

"He never laid a hand on me."

"Your mind. Your heart."

"Love is deep, and passion is intensity that sometimes causes pain."

I stood.

"If that's all, then why is he dead?"

"So you would be safe," Mom said.

Something flashed in her eyes. A darkness, powerful and large. She was suddenly taller, wider, without having grown so much as a millimeter.

My stomach gurgled, and air popped and shifted in my abdomen. I wondered if Gus had given me food poisoning.

"I will answer all your questions," Mom said, "in time."

She stepped towards me and began extending her arms for a hug, but then stopped when she looked at the carnage over my hoodie and slid her hands into her pockets instead.

"And some answers are better discovered on your own."

Mom went back inside. Something was changing. Mom was pulling away from me. And she was hiding stuff from me. I supposed she'd been hiding stuff all along. But now we were in Eden's Edge, and I had no idea who I was and what was happening, and I didn't like this place.

I charged after Mom, determined to scream and shout and get at least one answer, but a fist slammed into my guts and twisted, bringing me to my knees. I gasped and clenched my belly, and another wave of pain cramped me, shooting from my belly to my groin and down the insides of my thighs. I stuck my hands in my leggings and felt my stomach, my legs, my vagina. I was really wet, but it wasn't like I had peed my pants. It was hot and thick. I pulled my hand out, and even in the last murky throes of twilight, I could see the blood coating my fingers.

"Oh."

Was it my period? I figured maybe so. But it hurt really badly. So bad it took my breath away. I stayed on my hands and knees, arching my back, then bending it back, trying to relieve the pressure and cramping, but nothing worked. I curled onto my side in the dirt and brought my knees to my chest, squeezing my organs together.

It was too much. I was sweating, nauseous, freezing cold. I clawed and crawled my way towards the house. I needed Mom. She would help, she would tell me what was going on and what I needed to do.

I called out

Mom!

but the words wouldn't come. I was breathless, unable to squeak out noise. A gush exploded from between my legs, and my wet clothes weighed me down, pinning me in the dirt. I writhed like a dying animal, my hands pressed between my legs, trying to calm the flow of blood. The patio door creaked open, and my stomach relaxed.

Mom is here to help.

To tell me.

To fix everything.

But it wasn't Mom. It was New Friend and her goddamn bowl of blood or tears. She came to me, set the bowl down, and embraced me. It felt both awful and splendid, unnatural and comforting. She rolled me on my back, then wriggled me out of my leggings and panties. I was ashamed, with my private bits exposed to the chill of the night air. New Friend placed her palms on the inside of my thighs and spread my legs, splaying me out, exposing me further. I wanted to resist, but I couldn't. There was nothing I could do. My arms would not move, and I couldn't feel my legs. All I could feel was the searing pain like a knife in my belly, cramps and pressure between my legs, and throbbing from my bellybutton to my tailbone.

New Friend placed one hand on my abdomen, below my bellybutton, and inserted the other inside me, one finger at a time until I could feel her whole hand moving, grabbing, pulling. I opened my mouth to scream, and she shoved her other fist in my mouth. I bit into her hand, and blood poured down my throat.

With one final gush and crush of pain, New Friend pulled her hand out of my vagina, and everything in my body relaxed. No more pain, no more cramping. New Friend sat back, cradling a bloody mass in her arms. Rocking. If she'd had a head, I bet she would have been singing or cooing.

I reached my arms out, and New Friend set the bloody mass on my chest. I wrapped my arms around it, holding it close, and looked into its big, black eyes.

"Gus," I cried.

He was covered in blood and creamy yellowish goo. I wiped the mess from his face and scooped it from his mouth with my pinky finger.

"There, there," I said as I cuddled him close, stroking his slick fur.

New Friend closed my legs. I was too wet and dirty to wriggle back into my tights, so I just held Gus tight to me with one hand and New Friend tended to me. Using her hand to scoop tears from her bowl, she washed away the fluids between my legs and off my thighs. After she was done, she gently pried Gus from my grasp and put him in her bowl, where we both tenderly bathed him until his fur was clean.

After all that was done, I took Gus in my arms again, and the three of us snuck into the house and into the bathroom, where I locked the door while New Friend drew a warm bath. Once the water was almost to the brim, I dipped my toes in, then lowered myself in, taking care to keep Gus's head above the water. We soaked, and New Friend washed us, carefully scrubbing away any remaining blood and dirt and slime coating both Gus and I. After the water turned cold and my fingers wrinkled to prunes, we got out and toweled off. I gave Gus a little puff with Mom's hairdryer, which he seemed to love, then he scampered around the bathroom, sniffing and exploring while I dried my own hair.

I was in no pain—maybe a little cramping, but blood still trickled out of me and ran down my legs in little crooked lines. They looked like brooks through a forest, red and streaming, going this way and that down my pale legs and pooling into little ponds on the floor.

The doorknob wriggled.

"Honey, are you okay?"

New Friend reached for the knob.

"No!" I shouted. Not at Mom but at New Friend.

Don't open the door!

How will I explain this?

New Friend opened the door, and Mom came inside.

"Oh," Mom said. But she smiled. Knowingly. "It's okay. I wondered if this would happen soon."

I did a quick scan of the bathroom. New Friend was gone, but Gus was there, sitting on the back of the toilet tank, chittering away and grooming himself.

"I …" I didn't know what to say. Thankfully, Mom didn't require an explanation.

"Got yourself a new friend, do you?" she said as she tilted her head to Gus.

I nodded, and Mom reached out, giving Gus a scratch behind the ears.

"Several new friends," she said, pointing at my leaking vagina.

There was a box of tampons under the sink. How they got there, I wasn't sure. I was going to ask, but then I realized that Mom probably had a period too.

"I don't have pads," she said, "which would be easier for your first period, but tampons are way more comfortable. They don't bunch up in your clothes and are less likely to leak. Here. Let me show you how this works."

Mom explained thoroughly what to do, and after wasting a few tampons on failed attempts, I managed to get one comfortably inside. Mom gave me a towel to wipe myself and the floor clean as she fetched a cozy pair of pajamas from my room. Once I was all dressed and the room cleaned up, Mom made some hot chocolate and popcorn, and we settled onto the couch to watch a movie. We didn't speak, but I cried. I don't know why my emotions were so violent and sorrowful, but they were. And there was no stopping them. Mom didn't seem worried. She just stroked my hair as I petted Gus's fur, and New Friend sat cross-legged on the floor in front of us, her body jiggling with laughter at the movie.

Chapter Twelve

I stayed home the following day, but the day after that, Mom said I could go to school. I was still bleeding like a stuck pig, but Mom packed a bunch of tampons in a pouch for me, tucked it in my backpack, and sent me on my way. My belly was okay, thanks to the ibuprofen I'd taken, but I felt tired and heavy.

I walked the long way to school so I could meet up with New Friend at her house. We walked together, hand in hand, while Gus trotted along faithfully beside us, occasionally taking detours to scurry up trees or shove acorns in his already distended cheeks. Once we arrived at The Beast, I shooed him on his way. I figured no one would want a critter roaming the halls. And besides, Gus wouldn't much like being inside, I figured. Like me, he'd choose trees and dirt over linoleum and fluorescent lighting any day. I felt like Gus preferred running free. I could feel the breeze in my own hair as it rustled through his fur, could smell the pine as it lingered in his nose. My jaw ached as he stretched his wide, cramming in as many nuts as he could.

It was my first day back at school since the incident

downstairs in the cafeteria. I wondered what it had looked like from the outside. Had I been screaming? Crying? What were the other kids actually doing while I imagined them devouring New Friend in a buffet of carnage?

Most of the kids stared as I walked in, and no one said a word. I was the weirdo. As always. I took my seat, and the staring continued, right until class began and Mr. Charles directed everyone's attention to the front of the room. Then it was my turn to stare at them—at the backs of heads, wondering what it was like to be inside their normal, carefree minds.

The morning moved too fast. It careened at breakneck speed towards lunch, when I would have to go back to that basement. I didn't know what I'd find there and had no desire for discovery. Thankfully, I didn't have to go down there yet.

"Hey, witch," Liza said.

Liza, with Mary and Laz behind her, approached me in the hall as the other children stared, rubbernecking their way to the stairs to descend to the basement for lunch.

I pulled the strings on my hoodie tight to hide most of my face.

"Hey," I mumbled.

"You okay?" Liza asked. "That was quite the spectacle the other day."

I looked into Liza's eyes. They were kind and curious.

"Was it?" I asked.

Mary and Laz shot each other looks I couldn't decipher. Liza's eyes stayed locked on mine.

"You were pretty upset."

I nodded. I sure was, but they didn't know why. I glanced over at New Friend, who was beside me, whole and intact, save her missing head.

"Hey, why don't we eat lunch outside?" Liza offered.

"I can grab us some food from downstairs and bring it out back."

"Yes please," I said, far too eagerly. I wasn't afraid of basements. I didn't want them to think I was a little baby. But I didn't want to go down there.

Liza smiled and disappeared down the stairs. Mary took me by the hand, the one that wasn't clenched around New Friend's, and led me out the back door of The Beast. I hadn't been out back before. It had a small playground, a smattering of picnic tables, and a maypole. There was a fence around the entire back, creating a barrier between The Beast and the woods. *Shame*, I thought, *for beasts should be one with the forest.*

"Don't be embarrassed," Mary said, and she rested her head on my shoulder as we walked.

"I'm a weirdo." I didn't mean to say it out loud. "And now they all know."

"Don't mind those other little shits," Laz said as he hopped up on a picnic table behind the building. "They're just boring."

Mary scowled at him, then sat next to me at the table.

"They are uptight," Mary said. "So don't mind them. You're pretty cool, even though you cry at lunch."

"I wish we were in the same class," I said.

"Good thing we're not, I guess," Laz said. "They have to spread out the cool kids so we don't take over the joint."

Me?

I'm a cool kid?

Mary laughed, and Laz flashed her a smile and a wink. They were playful, but underneath it all, there was something more there. I could tell by the smirk of her mouth and the flush of pink on his cheeks.

"Why are they so uptight?" I asked. "The other kids."

"They aren't used to things being out of place," Mary

clarified, though it still wasn't clear.

"Everything is pretty strict here," I said. An observation and a question.

They both nodded.

"We get in BIG trouble if we misbehave," Mary said. "Allison spends lots of time making this place perfect and safe. She doesn't have time to go fixin' things that we muck up."

Big trouble. I wondered what that meant. Mary and Laz had no obvious signs of abuse, though a strap would typically be applied to the bare backside.

"What do the parents do?" I asked.

Mary shrugged. "Aren't many parents here. Liza's dad, when he's not out working. My mom and Mrs. Henderson. They help keep the place clean, tidy, make meals, get supplies."

"All the time?" I asked. "I mean, I never see anyone."

"There aren't many here. Mostly kids. Homeless kids, fosters. Allison is a registered foster. But the kids that do have parents, those parents head off and work, eventually. So … mostly just kids."

Something was wrong with Laz's face. It was slight, barely noticeable, but there was a strong emotion there, drawing his expression taut. Sorrow? Rage?

"Where are your parents?" I asked Laz.

He shrugged. Mary answered for him. "He came with his dad, but his dad left to find a job. Been gone for months."

Liza came out the door with a plastic tray full of sandwiches and bags of chips. After she deposited that on the table, she fished four juice pouches from the pocket of her hoodie.

"I can get more if you're real hungry," she said. "It's all I could carry at once."

"It's fine," I said. And it was. I wasn't really all that hungry. When I looked at the sandwiches, cold turkey and processed cheese smooshed between a little white bun, all I could think of was that those pale folds of meat were flesh off New Friend, and the mustard, the bile from her stomach.

It was quiet while we ate. Laz was upset, and Mary was watching Laz, probably worried she'd upset him. And Liza was watching me.

"Will I stay here for long?" I asked.

Everyone stopped chewing.

"What do you mean?" Liza asked.

I didn't know what I meant. But I knew I didn't want to stay here.

"I started a garden," I said.

They quietly chewed their food, watching me. I regretted saying anything, but Liza spoke up.

"Cool. Vegetables?"

"Uh, no. Plants, flowers, stuff like that."

"Awesome," she said. "I'd like to see it sometime."

My cheeks got hot. Was she just indulging me, or did she really want to see my garden?

"And I have a pet squirrel," I blurted.

"Cool!" Laz said, breaking out of his funk.

"A squirrel?" Mary said, brow cocked. "We aren't allowed to have pets."

Liza rolled her eyes. "How's anyone gonna know?"

"You keep it in the house?" Laz asked.

I didn't know yet. Maybe.

"I just met him," I said. "His name is Gus."

"Weird name," Laz said.

"That's just what it is," I said.

"Where did you get him, if you just got him?" Mary asked.

I couldn't explain that. Wouldn't. I needed to change the subject.

"Can we go back to the cemetery some time?" I asked. "That was fun."

Liza laughed. "For a witch, sure."

It wasn't a mean thing to say. She meant it in a good way. Like a witch in the way I wished I was.

"I like history," I said. "And there are no history books here."

"Miss Allison don't like facts," Laz said, and Mary smacked him on the arm.

"Shhh," Mary said, her eyes darting to The Beast and around the yard. "You're gonna get us in trouble again."

"Well I like cemeteries too," Liza said. "I love a good ghost story."

"Wanna hear a ghost story?" Laz asked.

Liza sighed and started clearing our trash.

"I love ghost stories," I said.

"I hate them!" Mary said, and she poked her fingers in her ears and ran off to the swings at the edge of the yard.

"Scaredy cat!" Laz shouted after her. "Anyways. Old Man Merle."

"The ghoul by the cemetery?" I asked.

"Yep," Laz said. "He's real, you know."

I knew that. I'd seen him. But I wasn't ready to tell Laz about that. People didn't respond well when I told them what I could see, even if they said they believed it was real in the first place.

"Merle was a fisherman that fished for salmon off the coast of the Haida Gwaii. He made a party and a living of it. He had chums up and down the coast of British Columbia that would join him out on his boat, *The Surfin' Dogwood*, at every possible chance. Rumour has it they carried equal parts bait and Canadian Club, and they had to piss out the excess so as not to swim the boat."

"Laz!" Liza scolded as she wiped down the table with a paper towel.

"It's true!"

"How do you know?" she said.

"Anyways," Laz said, turning back to me, "One weekend, just as the fall colours painted the coast, Old Man Merle headed out for one of his favourite events: The Coho Fishing Derby. He loved the massive gatherings and parties, but even more, he loved the bright silver coho salmon that came in from deep in the Pacific. They were tasty AND beautiful, he said."

"Again," Liza said. "You can't know that."

"It's legend!" Laz whined.

"Pretty specific," Liza mumbled.

"A-n-y-w-a-y-s," Laz said, drawing out and articulating his impatience. "Merle had the catch of a lifetime. He didn't return to shore until his boat was heavy with the silver of fish and he was light on the gold of liquor. Once his boat was moored, he decided to have a few celebratory shots at the Coho Derby Dance, maybe squeeze a few boobies before unloading his catch."

I giggled, but Liza clucked her tongue.

Laz continued, ignoring Liza's displeasure. "Well, lemme tell you, Anna, Merle never got to squeeze no boobies. He went and danced with some ladies, drank some, and when he went out back to drain the snake, if you know what I mean, he heard a rustling in the woods. When he went to investigate, he found quite the commotion. There was a young girl there gettin manhandled by Bobby Pickton."

I knew that name. "The pig farmer?"

"The very one," Laz said. "That one they say raped and murdered all them girls up the west coast, then fed them to his hogs."

"Enough," Liza said.

"It's okay," I said. "I'm familiar."

"Rumour has it that Merle's last encounter was with that sack of shit. He pulled him off and out of that poor girl, and as she ran away, naked and screaming, she looked back and saw Merle and Bobby throwing hands in those woods.

The police came out and found Merle's shirt and a boot, but not much else. They questioned old Bobby, but there was nothin to say he was there that night, and the girl couldn't identify him."

"And Merle?"

"Never found him. His boat stayed docked, and no one checked on it until the stench from the rotting fish overtook Moresby Island."

"Huh." I thought about him. About the grey, translucent ghoul lurking in the cemetery.

"He must be lonely," I said.

Like me.

"What?" Laz said. "Who?"

Shut up, I scolded myself.

"Why would he be here?" I asked. "We're nowhere near the ocean."

Laz shrugged. "No one knows. We are inland here, far as I can tell. An hour from the ocean, at least. Not sure why he'd be here, but he is."

"Bollocks," Liza said. "That's all bollocks."

"It's true!" Laz shouted. "I heard it from Tommy!"

"Tommy don't know his head from his chocolate balloon knot," Mary shouted from ten meters away.

"Thought you were scared of ghosts stories?" Laz said.

"You's talking about Merle, not his ghost," Mary said, then she stuck out her tongue.

A bell rang inside The Beast, and the three kids were suddenly edgy and serious as they hustled inside. Liza hung back a bit and walked with me.

"We can eat out here every day if you like," she said. "If you don't want to go downstairs and eat with the others."

Then she did something I both liked and disliked. She hugged me. Full-on, shoulder to shoulder, chest to chest. And she held me for several uncomfortable seconds before letting go and walking inside like nothing had happened. I wanted to laugh, to cry, to hug her back, but I did what I was supposed to and followed her into The Beast, calm and orderly, and carried on with my classes. Almost like a normal kid.

Chapter Thirteen

As I filled a large mason jar full with hot water at my kitchen sink, I hoped for two things. First, I hoped Mom wouldn't get home before I left. I was surprised that she wasn't home to greet me after school, but she'd left a note saying she'd be out shopping with Miss Mojo and might be a tad late. I didn't want her to get home because she might ask questions about where I was going.

The second thing I hoped was that I could find my way to the cemetery. Laz and Mary had led the way the last time, and I'd been paying more attention to Liza and them than to where we were going. But I figured that if I started off from behind Library House, I could follow the general direction and get there just fine.

After the mason jar was ready, I stuffed it in a backpack with an old book of mine and headed out the door. The sun was low, probably kissing the horizon, judging by the pink-orange tones of the sky; I couldn't tell for sure where the sun was through the wall of trees surrounding the community, but I knew that soon the colours would be enveloped by the purples and navies of night, and I would need to be alert for whatever thrived in the darkness.

Gus ran alongside me as I trekked to Library House, then as I walked straight back into the woods. I walked about twenty meters, stumbling in the spreading dark, before clicking on my flashlight; I didn't want anyone to come and tell me not to be wandering around on my own or, even worse, try to come with me to see what I was doing. No one would understand, and people not understanding tended to get me in trouble.

It didn't take long before I spied the white gleam of the moon resting atop the gravestones. The forest's maw opened up and spit me into the clearing. A chill licked my bones, the open air reminding me of how exposed I was now that I no longer had the shadows and cover of the trees. I hunched in on myself, shoulders rolled forward, trying to be as small as possible. I wished there was a wall at my back so I could see what was coming at me, but there were no walls or large structures. Only stubby, cracked headstones and the mystery of the woods on the perimeter. I scoured the marble and stone, finally deciding upon a crooked headstone that was marginally taller than the rest, covered in weeds and moss. I sat on the ground, pressed my back into it, and slid down, hiding as best I could and watching all angles.

The night was fully upon me and the cemetery, save the hints of moon silver resting here and there. But that light birthed shadows and movement that were wreaking havoc on my nerves and my resolve. I was about ready to give up this crazy idea and go home when a baritone rumble emerged from the woods.

I held my breath. Gus sat up, his cheeks fat with acorns, his ears cupped and pointed in the direction of the sound.

It took all of my courage, but I spoke nonetheless. "Hello?"

Another rumble, then a wet wheeze.

Gus bolted away from me, away from the sound, and disappeared into the woods on the other end of the cemetery.

I wanted to stand. In my head, I shouted at my legs, commanding them to move, but they would not. My knees stayed pinned to my chest, my shoulders hunched, my courage small.

The rumble came closer and opened into a throaty growl that moved through the night, crescendoing into a moan. It came at me, then it was high above me, roaring down. I squeezed my eyes closed and covered my ears, but I could feel its hot breath on the top of my head.

I can't do this.

Mom, help me.

I opened my eyes a slit to seek an escape route into the woods, and a spiderweb of drool dangled in front of my face, sparkling and swaying. My eyes followed that tendril of drool up to a chin, to a jaw, to a mouth with lips rotted clear off, exposing a mouth void of teeth but full of green and black sludge that whorled with the growls coming from the thing's throat. His eyes, those empty sockets, caverns inside his massive head, stared down at me, hungry and angry and laughing.

I screamed.

I could feel it clenching my diaphragm, blasting out of my throat, the air moving across my tongue, but I couldn't hear my noise. I was so scared all I could hear was the ringing of panic in my ears, and all I could see were spots of impending blackout pirouetting across my vision as Old Man Merle reached for me with his skeletal hands coated in pus and ooze and gore.

Another hand reached out across my vision, brushing away the drool and lacing its fingers through Merle's. Merle stopped making noise. His chin tilted up, away from me, as he looked at the owner of the hand.

With Merle distracted, I scrambled on hands and

knees until I was several meters away and could evaluate what was happening.

New Friend and Old Man Merle were holding hands. The sounds coming from him weren't rough, or growling, or menacing, but had changed into a series of lilting coos as he examined New Friend from neck to toe. She curtsied, and he bowed, which was awful because his clothes were all eaten away, leaving gangrenous flesh and yellowed bone exposed, and his mini Merle swinging between his legs. His bones shifted and rotated as he bent at the waist, and remnants of sinew and muscle stretched and compressed as he righted himself to standing again.

New Friend let go of Merle's hand and came to me. She reached out and helped me to my feet. I wanted to hug her, wanted her to protect me, but more than that, I wanted to be her. I wanted to be brave, to be confident, to be special, to be impossible. But I was none of those things. I wasn't even a witch, so far as I knew. New Friend had to place her palm in the middle of my back and push me towards Merle. But still I hesitated as I looked up, up, up at Merle as we stood toe to toe, him looking down at me, quiet and curious. It wasn't until New Friend went into my backpack and put the mason jar in my hands that I remembered my mission, and I mustered up enough courage to carry it out.

"Hi, um, Merle. I'm Anna, and I thought, I, well, I'm pretty alone here, and—"

New Friend elbowed me in the ribs.

"Okay, yeah, well, I'm new here, and I'm a bit different, and I don't get along with normal people, usually, but I do get along with people like …"

Like what?

Like you, I was going to say, but it wasn't dead people. Not necessarily. But not normal, living people.

"Here," I said, and I thrust the mason jar at him. "I got you this. That is, I made it for you. Not the jar, but the water, well I didn't *make* the water—"

New Friend elbowed me again.

"It's saltwater," I said. "I dissolved sea salt in it so it's saltwater. I know it's not actually from the ocean, but it's close, and I heard you were a fisherman, and I thought that having some saltwater might make you happy."

I bit my lip and stepped away from Merle. I didn't know what else to say. Didn't know what I was really doing. I was lonely, and I was weird, and people like Merle weren't scared of me, so maybe Merle wouldn't be scared of me and we could hang out. New Friend had no head, Gus was a squirrel, so if I added Merle to the group, I could almost have one complete friend.

Merle studied the jar, moving it from hand to hand, bringing it to his face to sniff and lick it. Then his mouth contorted and stretched, revealing his back molars, which were caked with meat and decay.

He was smiling.

"You like it?" I asked.

Merle looked at me, and his smile grew wider, splitting his face from ear to ear. I jumped when he lurched toward me, reaching me in one loping stride and bending down to hug me. I felt his bones, his gooey, oozing organs soaking into my hoodie, and I gasped and jumped back, trying to avoid feeling his rot and nakedness. Merle stepped back too and hugged his jar.

"I'm glad you like it," I said.

"Gahhhh," he said.

I was still nervous, but I was warming up to the big galoot.

Merle sat on the top of the crooked headstone, admiring his jar of saltwater while New Friend explored the graves. Gus came scampering out of the woods to sniff Merle and his single rubber boot that survived on his left foot. I was walking over to sit closer to Merle, maybe strike up a conversation, but something snapped in the woods. We all looked towards the sound, which was coming from beyond the lych-gate. It was a snicker that swelled into high-pitched, manic laughter that screeched through the woods like a banshee.

Old Man Merle howled and loped off into the woods, clutching his jar of saltwater against his chest. Gus scrambled into the trees, and New Friend stood her ground beside me.

The voice coming at me from the lych-gate was awful, a blade on glass, shrill and piercing. The owner of the voice walked out, his movements broken and jarring, his bones clicking and clacking with each ragged step.

"Helllllooowww, little girrrelll."

I didn't answer. I couldn't. My voice was hiding with Gus in the trees. The thing walked to me, glitching and contorting. Its skin was black and shiny, pulled taut over jagged bones that were too thick and too long. It was quite tall, featureless, with a smooth, solid face and no hair. No eyes with which to see, no mouth to speak, and yet it could. It heard everything, saw everything, and spoke.

The Blankness, I called it.

Between its legs, both a penis and tail swung to and fro, each tipped by jagged arrowheads.

"Something is very wrong heeerrre, dontcha think so, girrlliiee?"

I looked around the cemetery.

Two great wings unfolded on either side of his broken body, and he flew through the air, landing right in front of me with a whoosh that almost blew me off my feet.

"Not in this cemetery, you fool! Heeeerrreee. In Eden's Edge."

When we'd arrived, I noticed a heaviness here. A murky aura.

"Ohhhhh," he said. "You don't knoowww." And he

laughed a horrible, braying chortle that sprayed hot spittle over my face. "You are still so busy trusting Mama, still longing for the feeling of her erect nipple pressed against your tongue that you could never imagine what is waiting for you to find. For you to be."

I shook my head. I didn't know what I was disagreeing with, but my head shook, and my tears flowed.

"What are you, lovely Anna? What is there for you here, in Eden's Edge? Why did your mommy pick this place, oh so far away?"

"B-because it's safe, and Allison—"

"Safe?" It laughed again, and my stomach roiled at the sound. "My dear. You were safe before."

"No," I said. "My dad—"

"And how is Daddy Dearest, eh? His ticker still ticking? Or did you open up the valve and let his life spray out everywhere, over everyone, drown the beast?"

My body jerked as New Friend yanked my arm and pulled me into the woods. We ran through the trees, branches whipping through the air where her head should have been and slicing my face. It felt good to bleed. To feel something tangible. Fear trickled down my face in that blood, away from my heart and my brain. Behind me, The Blankness heckled and jested, his voice was many, all around me like the darkness of night:

> *"Fog and steam,*
> *gossamer and pitch,*
> *halfbreed tainted, rotten bitch!"*

\#

My skin prickled with heat by the time I got home. Part of it was from keeping pace with New Friend, part of it was from anger. Mom was hiding something from me. And now we were here, and I was starting over, and I had no friends, and my old room and all my stuff was far, far away. I wanted to run away, to start my own life, with my own stuff, somewhere I could hide and be myself so nobody would know.

And The Blankness, this monster in the woods who lived beyond the lych-gate, was going to kill me. Whatever it was, it was here for me. And Mom had brought me here, served me up on a platter.

I slammed into the house and locked the door behind me, being sure to be as noisy as I could. Mom didn't prefer a racket, so surely, she would come out and address it if she was home. I got a glass from the cupboard, slamming the door shut when I was done, and downed a full glass of water as I listened for movement within the house. But there was nothing. No way Mom was home and didn't come out to see what all my fuss was about.

The water cooled my rage, leaving me with only sadness. Mom wasn't there, and somewhere along the way, New Friend had left too. I was all alone with the thoughts and voices in my head. The voice of The Blankness.

You were safe before
Something is very wrong here
Drown the beast

I chugged another glass of water and retreated to my bedroom. I wanted to sleep it all away. I wanted dreams to save me like they do in books, but my dreams were darkness and silence. Nothing ever came to me in my sleep. All my dreams and nightmares stretched and flexed during my waking hours, where they didn't belong.

Things would be so much easier if I were normal.

I took the jar with Dad's heart off the windowsill and sat on the edge of my bed, hugging it.

Did he hate me?
Did he really want me dead?

Dad would always be a part of me. There were bad things, but there were good things too. If I lost Dad, I'd lose half of myself.

I unscrewed the lid, grabbed the heart out of the gin, and held it in front of my face. It didn't smell like Dad. It smelled like alcohol and death. I pressed it to my lips, opened my mouth, fondled it with my tongue. I took a huge bite, wincing from the shock of the booze. I cradled the mouthful of Dad's meat on my tongue as saliva pooled beneath, and the sting of the alcohol made my eyes water. I thought of Dad's eyes watering too. Tears pouring out of his eyes and filling my mouth. I swallowed my spit, the gin, and Dad's tears and blood, and it all burned its way to my belly. I cried, and Dad cried too, filling my mouth faster than I could swallow. I chewed, and Dad's heart squelched between my teeth, and I let all of that slide down my throat in mushy clumps.

I felt every millimeter of his meat's journey as it gurgled its way down my esophagus, into my stomach, and started churning, burning in acid and bile. And for a brief moment, one that felt like forever and the length of my blink, I saw.

I saw Dad holding me. His baby girl, swaddled in a yellow blanket with embroidered strawberries around the border. I saw me holding his fingers as we walked across the lawn, felt the cool blue grass tickling my pudgy pink feet. I smelled his pipe, sweet vanilla, as smoke coiled from his mouth when he whooped and hollered as the Oilers shot the puck into the net.

Acid rose up my gullet, trying to push out the rancid meat in my belly, and the sugar-sweet memories turned sour. Dad's pipe smoke turned to burning hair in my nostrils, and his teeth grew sharp and eyes red. Now Mom was there, fingers, her hair, and torso too long and too white. She was floating above him, wailing. Dad was below her, dragging her down as she pulled him up, both screaming in pain and moaning in pleasure. I tried to turn my head, to look away, but as I sat on my new bed in my new house, my eyes were already closed. What I was seeing was behind my eyes and also somewhere else. Someplace I'd never known, never been.

I couldn't look away, even as shame and embarrassment tingled on my insides at the sight of Dad's penis swelling, stretching long and hard until it went inside Mom, and they were moving, and screaming, and laughing, and crying, and then suddenly, his penis was so engorged, and splitting like an overcooked hotdog, and it was too long and thick and was tearing Mom in half …

And then everything tore and exploded, and I was there, alone, standing by those grain elevators, covered in blood and wearing a yellow dress with strawberries embroidered along the hem.

Anna.

My eyes opened. I was in my new room, sitting on the edge of my new bed with the empty mason jar in my hands. I hiccupped, and the taste of gin filled my mouth.

Anna.

It was dark. Really dark. Must have been the middle of the night, but I wasn't sure. I'd left for the woods real late, and I had no idea how long I'd been out there, or how long it took me to get to the cemetery and back, or how long I'd been sitting on my bed with my eyes closed, dreaming.

Except … I never dreamed.

Anna.

I woke a bit more and became aware of my surroundings. The voice. It wasn't in the room with me, but it was close. The tempo of my heart increased, spreading from my chest to my ears as my eyes flickered to the window, my closet door, the door to my bedroom, which was open a crack. I could see through none of them. It was dark outside, so nothing to see outside that dirty glass even if I was closer to the window. The closet door was closed, and the bedroom door was almost closed, and there were no lights on anywhere for me to see anything at all.

I set the jar down on the floor and dove beneath the covers on my bed, pulling them up over my head and cocooning inside. I took small, slow breaths, trying to be quiet, trying to not exist at all. The house was conversing with the woods outside; the walls settled, and the floorboards creaked in response to the rustle of leaves and knock of branches from the forest. My breathing was heavy panting to my ears, so I put my hand over my mouth, trying to stifle the sound. Inhale, a pull, exhale, a puff. Something was just above the blanket, breathing out of rhythm with my own breaths. I tried not to shake, tried not to squeak, but my whole body trembled and my teeth clicked together, no matter how hard I tried to hold my jaw shut.

Anna.

The voice was close. Muffled through the blanket but still whispering in my ear. The fabric compressed around my face like a hand pressing over my mouth and nose. I wriggled away, noise belting from my lungs as I slithered out of bed, scrambled to my feet, yanked the door open, and ran shouting down the hall.

"MOM!"

I didn't look back at what was on my bed, breathing my name, my blanket grasped in its hands. I ran by Mom's bedroom, and I did not stop to look. If she was there, she would have heard me and come to my rescue. I continued on, past the kitchen, and the gleam of the knives hanging from the magnetic strip above the stove caught my eye.

I'm going to need something way bigger. Sharper.

I reached the front door, intent on screaming down the road until Mom heard me or a neighbour came to help

but nobody ever comes to help

but I didn't get a single step outside the door. When I yanked it open, I was greeted by my mom's confused face and Allison's furled unibrow and scowl.

"Anna, what's wrong?" Mom asked.

"I ..."

I don't know what was more terrifying: the sour, judging expression on Allison's face, or the scratch of a single fingernail up my backbone, twirling underneath my hair, and finally coming to rest, full palm wrapped around my shoulder, claws sunk into my flesh.

"May we come in?" Allison said, and another voice echoed in my ear, mimicking Allison and her impatient words.

May we come in, it said in a voice that was hollow, baritone, bitonal.

I shook my head.

Mom took me by the shoulders and pulled me in for a hug. We breathed together, her chest against mine, my rhythm matching hers. Over her shoulder, I spied New Friend in the front yard, her arms out to the side, balancing a bowl in each hand.

Blood and tears.

She was so strong to be able to hold the bowls like that. So brave to be able to stand there while the thing at my back slithered by me, its arms like snakes, its fingertips like tongues brushing my breasts as it detached from me and went towards her. But she did not run or stand down. In fact, she stepped forward, brandishing the bowls like weapons.

Allison crossed her arms. "What is going on?"

Mom released me, then turned, blocking me from Allison completely.

"Goodnight, Allison," Mom said.

Mom backed up, forcing me inside. Before she could shut the door, I saw a swath of a paintbrush through the sky. A streak of red colliding with the crystal sheen of tears as New Friend tossed the bowls at the creature, dousing it. It recoiled and screeched like Elphaba before lunging at New Friend. New Friend was quick enough to dodge its attack, and then she ran, and that thing did too, and Mom shut the door.

"Anna."

I went to the bay window, parted the curtains, and pressed my nose against the glass. I looked this way, then that, and back again, but there was no trace of New Friend or the creature that had been at my back. Just Allison, her frown, and her clenched fists and jaw.

Mom closed the curtains.

"Listen," Mom said, "Are you hurt?"

"No."

"Are you sick? Did something happen?"

Of course it did. But I didn't know what to tell her. That I was seeing things?

"Do you see things too?" I asked.

Mom was taken aback. She bit her lip and looked everywhere but in my eyes. I sat on the couch and looked at my feet so she could have a minute to compose herself. She went to the kitchen, and the tap turned out, then the click of the kettle. After a few minutes, Mom appeared, carrying two mugs with tendrils of steam lapping at the ceiling. She sat beside me, but not up against me, and turned her knees to face me.

"I don't see things," she said. "Do you?"

I nodded. If I gave her something, maybe she'd give me something in return.

"I see a little girl," I said. "She has no head."

Mom was sitting very still. I wondered if she was trying not to react.

"Is she dead?" Mom asked.

"I don't think so," I said. "I mean, she's got no head, but she walks around and plays and stuff."

"When did you first see her?"

"At the diner. The night we left home."

Mom nodded.

"I'm not crazy, I don't think," I said.

"You're not." Mom's voice was very small and guarded.

"Do you see her too?"

Mom shook her head.

"What am I? What's wrong with me?"

Mom set her tea down on the coffee table really hard. So hard that I wondered if she broke it.

"I told you," she said. "There's nothing wrong with you. You're just different."

"Bullshit!" My words were harder and sharper than I intended, but I'm glad they were. "You are hiding something from me, aren't you?"

"What would I be hiding from you?"

I felt the rant oncoming. Long overdue.

"Oh, I don't know, Mom, that you're a witch? Or that you're not, or that I'm not. That I'm just sick, and we're awful, and we've nowhere to go, and I'm destined to be alone."

"Anna—"

With all the force in all my blood and bones and muscles, I screamed.

"Tell me the truth!"

And Mom did. Quiet, matter-of-fact. And her words struck me like knuckles.

"I am a witch," Mom said. "You are not."

My body shivered. Gooseflesh swelled on my skin. My hair ached, and the taste of metal bloomed in my saliva.

"You are something else."

#

Mom told me her tale as our tea grew cold in our cups, never touching our lips.

"I was born of a witch, who was born of a witch, and back as long as there was time."

"Can you do magic?"

"I am magic."

"What does that mean?"

"I feel things. I am strong, I am power, I am capable of all the things. And people fear a strong woman, a woman who has no limits, no constraints. My flesh would be charred to a crisp if it weren't for the time I was placed in."

I scrunched my brow. "I've never seen you do magic stuff."

"Power is everywhere. It needn't be flashy."

"Can you tell the future?"

"Not exactly. I know when the events of the present are cogs in a bigger machine."

"Can you fly?"

She laughed. "No. Only on an airplane, and I quite dislike that, truth be told. I like my feet on the earth, my skin enveloped by natural air. I feel, I absorb, I use all that nature gives me."

"I like to garden," I said. Perhaps I could relate to her. Perhaps I could be her.

"Yes," she said. "You have that connection too. And I see you also have a familiar."

My eyes and hers found the window and the chittering ball of fur balanced on the maple branch outside.

"Gus?" I asked.

"You named him Gus?"

"It's his name."

"Ah."

She did not look surprised.

"Do you have a familiar?" I asked.

She nodded and smiled. Her lips were red, her eyes black. Both lips and eyes spread across her face, her lips splitting, slicing to feathers, her eyes shifting on her face to the sides, black orbs reflecting our new living room in our new house.

"The cardinal," I said.

The ruby bird was outside the window, heckling Gus as passionately as he was goading her.

"Yes," she said. "She's both my eyes and my comfort. Her name is Erinyes. I don't know if that was her name, but it's the one I gave her."

"Why?"

"Like you love studying witches, I liked Greek Mythology. I was obsessed, so when I first met Erinyes, I knew what she reminded me of. Blood falling through the night sky, soaking into the earth and water. See, when the Titan Chronus castrated Uranus and tossed his testicles and penis into the sea, the blood of his genitals fell like rain. The Erinyes were birthed from those droplets that landed on Gaia, a symbol of destructive vengeance, and the unity of blood, sky, and night."

The bird had such pretty feathers. Such a sweet song.

"She doesn't seem angry," I said.

"She's not," Mom answered, looking lovingly out the window at her familiar. "But she is power, strength, and growth. Rebirth and possibility."

I had so many questions. I had doubt. After all these years studying witches and being around one, I felt even a pinch wouldn't wake me from this dream telling me it was all real. I was excited, knowing witch blood was in me. But …

"You said I'm not a witch."

She clenched her teeth. Did I need to ask the right questions before she told me?

I continued to prod. "Was Grandpa a witch? Your dad?"

"No. Just a man who owned a Ford dealership."

"So, both parents don't need to be witches."

She hesitated, then shook her head. She knew where I was going with this.

"Anyone can be a witch," she explained, "But not

everyone is. There's no rhyme or reason. Sometimes, the line just fizzles."

Disappointment surged in my belly. "And it did with me."

Mom shrugged.

"You said I was something else."

A nod.

"A half-witch?"

half-breed tainted, rotten bitch

She looked unsure.

Light flickered on her face, which startled me, but she didn't seem to notice. I looked out the window at Gus and Erinyes, but they were only bones now. The tree where they'd been bickering was on fire, the flames roaring against the house. Wallpaper glue melted from the heat, and strips of wallpaper curled, peeling like flesh. The wood crackled and glowed, and embers floated up to the ceiling. The room was dark, spotted with angry red and orange stars floating, threatening destruction.

But Mom didn't notice.

Something else.

"There is something bad here," I said.

Her expression was taut and tired, strong but unsure. She nodded.

"Is that why we came?"

Despite the embers raining down on her hair like glitter, burning holes in her jumper, searing my skin, she remained calm. And for the first time since our conversation had started, she took a sip of her now-tepid tea.

"We came because it was a way out. And we were in a pinch."

A pinch. Running from the law, but they weren't really looking, were they? Dad was little more than ash in the trees.

"But you don't like the church," I said.

Church was somewhere we never went. Mom didn't talk about it much, only to say that Christians were hateful, judgmental, unhealthy, and dangerous.

"I didn't realize," Mom said, "That this was a faith-based arrangement. Allison did not sell it as such."

Of course she didn't.

"We're not stuck here, are we?"

"No," Mom said. "We're not. I just like that it's secluded and away from everything. There are other small communities. Maybe, one day, we'll even find a farm out in the middle of nowhere. Or a cabin in the mountains."

"But … you're a criminal."

She winced. It was slight, but I caught it. The tiniest creasing at the corners of her eyes.

"It was protection. Defense," she said.

"But … have you hurt people? As a witch, I mean."

"I concoct poultices for healing, for lifting negativity, for fertility. I can make well what's sick, heal what's broken."

She didn't answer about the people.

"You can hurt people with spells."

"I'm not destruction, Anna. I'm life and protection."

"Okay, but … can you heal this place? Make it a nice place to stay?"

Everything shifted. My body was slick, crackling with heat. I was both scared and thrilled. My skin ached from the fire rippling through the burning room, but the destruction was exhilarating. I thought of my garden, of the forest, of how if it burned to ash, new growth would emerge, twice as strong, clean, and lush.

"Anna."

There was fear in Mom's voice.

"Anna, what do you see?"

Fire and life.

"What do you feel?"

Power. Strength. Courage.

Mom slammed her cup down on the table. The fire extinguished, and like the forest had inhaled a sharp, deep breath, the smoke, ash, and lingering embers sucked out the window and dissipated into the night sky, leaving everything as it truly was—undamaged, unmolested by flame.

"That is quite enough for one night," Mom said.

"But—"

"Enough."

Mom punctuated the statement by standing and leaving. No goodnight, no hug. She just set her cup in the sink and disappeared into her bedroom, closing the door behind her.

And locking it.

Chapter Fourteen

In the morning, it was like nothing had happened at all the night before. Mom was soft, kind, and warm. Nothing was on fire. And I knew one new thing. I knew Erinyes, who trilled a morning ballad from her perch outside the window.

It was Sunday, and Sundays were for church, according to lots of people, including Allison. Mom had told her that was fine, but not for us. Church was for people who believed, and Mom supported that. Church was for people who needed community, who needed coping strategies, who needed. We did not need. Not church anyways.

Allison had reminded Mom several times since we'd arrived. Sunday. Ten in the morning. Not too early, not too late. Mom had declined—at first politely, then not so—but Allison wouldn't have it.

"Community," she'd said.

"Fitting in," she'd insisted.

And the not-so-subtle-or-kind: "The church's money is what enables us to provide the services we do."

And that was true. Allison's church and all its tax

breaks and donations had provided us a place after the Incident. But Mom had sought them out, had she not? Would The Incident have happened if Mom wasn't confident we had somewhere to go?

Regardless of what the church had or had not provided, ten o'clock came and left, and we did not go. We were in our jammies, Mom drinking coffee and me, tea while we cozied on the couch reading books. Outside the window, Erinyes ruffled her feathers against the fall chill, and Gus chittered, his cheeks crammed full of nuts and berries to stash somewhere in a hidey-hole.

Lunch had come and gone, the only hint the mildest of grumbles in my belly telling me to at least start preparing food to eat. Good books will do that. Stop clocks and speed them all at once, pages turning without notice, worries absorbed by the paper, replaced by stories.

We never got to finish our books. Our meditative read-a-thon was interrupted by a bang at the door. Loud, aggressive.

Allison.

Erinyes and Gus grew fangs, their eyes stretching to slits as they growled like feral goblins baring their teeth at the front door from their perch on the tree. Mom noticed this too. She cooed something to Erinyes, who flew off to another tree. For a bird so small and delicate, the sound of her wings was thunder in a canyon. I figured that was her rage making an appearance.

Gus didn't leave, though. He balanced on his haunches on the branch, watching as Mom rose and went to the door.

Mom did not seem anxious. She was calm, her movements unhurried, her gait casual.

When the door opened, Allison shoved her way in. She was anything but calm.

"I hope you two ladies had a lovely morning,"

Allison said through a tight jaw.

"We did," Mom said. "Good books, good drinks, good company."

Allison glared at me, then at the book in my hand and the one spread open on the couch beside me.

"There's only one book that should concern you today," Allison said.

The gleam of gilded pages reflecting the light sliced across my vision. I hadn't noticed the bible tucked beneath Allison's arm, but the light alerted me to its presence as she shifted to tap her fingernails against it in judgmental staccato.

"No," Mom said. It was an answer to every question, suggestion, or demand Allison might have had on the tip of her tongue.

Allison picked Mom's book off the couch and tucked it under her arm.

New Friend appeared from the kitchen, her hands balled into fists, her shoulders squared like she was about to punch.

"You lost Mom's place!" I yelled.

"Watch your mouth, child!" Allison yelled, and lifted her hand, aiming the back of it as if she meant to strike me, but Mom loped over in a too-long stride and grabbed Allison by the wrist.

Allison squealed and pulled her wrist away. I could see the smoke rise, smell the sizzle of skin, see the sweat of grease from the cooked meat in the shape of Mom's hand on Allison's forearm. Allison saw all that too, judging by the look of horror and disbelief splattered on her wicked face. She shook her head, drew a breath, and looked again.

She calmed. Her skin had changed, as if the initial injury hadn't been there at all; her skin was unmarred, save a slight redness from Mom's brief grasp.

But I could still smell the singe of hair and sour cook

of flesh. And the tiniest of upturns at the corners of Mom's mouth told me all I needed to know about what she'd done.

"You owe me," Allison said.

"How much?" Mom asked.

"Appreciation," Allison said.

"For what?" Mom asked.

"For bringing you here. For *saving* you. For giving you shelter and food and health during your time of need."

"And we do appreciate that. But we will not be abused and bullied."

Allison held up her arm, shaking it at Mom. "You are the abuser!"

Mom stepped forward. Allison did not step back.

"Make no mistake," Mom said, her consonants swords slicing the air, "You will never lay a hand on my daughter."

Allison's lips moved. She was jumbling words in her head, trying to put them in a clever order to spit at my mom. But, of course, nothing clever could be constructed in so little time from someone so mentally stunted.

"Be that as it may," Allison said, "It is expected that you come to church. We are a community, and there are certain rules. I need absolute order if this is to work."

Mom stood firm. "We signed nothing."

"Nor did we." Now Allison was the one smirking. "This is my house, on the church's land. If you aren't able to be a part of the community, this house might be more fit for someone more … willing."

Mom hesitated. I knew Allison had her. We all knew it.

"We have an understanding then." Allison did not form that as a question, nor did Mom acknowledge it as a statement.

Allison turned to leave, meant to leave, but something out the window caught her attention. I wondered if it was Gus, or Erinyes, or both. It very well could have been, judging by the look of abject horror that contorted her face into something even uglier than her own.

"What did you do?" she spat.

Allison didn't wait for an answer. She charged past us, shouldering Mom on her way by, and burst out the patio door to the backyard.

Mom rubbed her arm where Allison's shoulder had stuck her. Although Allison had bumped her enough to knock her back a step, I don't think she hurt Mom. I think Mom was rubbing her arm to soothe her rage. To pet it, keep it docile so it didn't get us evicted. Mom took off after Allison, and I took off after Mom, and we all ended up in the backyard.

"What is this?" Allison screeched.

"What is what?" Mom replied. She seemed genuinely oblivious to the target of Allison's ire.

I was not, though.

"My garden," I said.

Allison's head snapped in my direction, her eyes narrowed, and her fingers curled into clenched fists.

"Your … garden?"

I answered slowly, articulating each and every consonant and vowel so she might be able to better understand the obvious. "Yes. G-a-r-d-e-n."

The entire yard had been tilled and formed beneath my touch, loosened and changed into a world teeming with new life. Sprouts were already popping up here and there, and the bigger flora that I had transported had already taken root and were solid and steady in their new home. Just like I longed to be.

"I didn't approve this," Allison said with arms akimbo.

Mom and I looked at her, confused.

"It's a garden," Mom said. "In our backyard."

"I would never have approved this," Allison said. "This is vandalism."

Mom laughed. "Ridiculous."

Allison did not find it funny. The scowl on her face suggested she found it quite the opposite of funny. Her voice filled my ears; it was high-pitched and whiny, but the noise did not form words in my brain. There was something distorting her irritating tones, something emanating from the house. I wandered into the yard, taking care not to step on any life, old or new, and looked back at the house.

New Friend was in my bedroom window facing us. Blood was spurting from her neck, up into the air like a fountain. She raised a hand and pointed out to the yard.

Mom's voice joined Allison's. It, too, was a mishmash of hostile sounds, angry sentiments tacked together by force. The two sparred as I approached the window and New Friend. I studied the reflection—Mom, my garden, Allison. And clearer than all of those things was the sharp, long, violent shape that was perched on Allison's shoulders. The same shape that had ridden me to the door not long ago. I gasped and turned, but the reflection did not match reality. There was nothing on Allison, or hovering over her, or wrapped around her. I looked back at the window, where the reflection was alive with a shuddering creature. It was lanky, with snakes for arms and tentacles for hair. It was covered in black shining scales, its body muscular and sleek. In the reflection, it roared, cracking open a bloody mouth sharp with many rows of teeth, but no sound came out. It was a roar, though. Deep, angry, and loud. I could feel it in the air like a release of thunder.

"Anna."

Mom spoke my name, and I understood her voice clear as English in my ears. I went to her, to Allison, to the thing that sat upon Allison's shoulders. I stared at the nothing that was there and tried to decipher even the slightest distortion of light as evidence of its existence.

"This is not okay," Allison said.

"I can understand you not wanting us to alter the front of the house, but this is the back," Mom argued. "But if you wish, when we find new accommodations, we will sod this all over."

What?!

"My garden?" I shrieked.

Mom put a hand on my shoulder. New Friend appeared beside me and put her hand on my other shoulder.

"Not *your* garden," Allison said. "*My* yard!"

Allison was sputtering, and her face was red. She took one step towards my garden, and I took one step towards her.

"No."

I spoke the word, but it was not mine. The voice was filled with ash and gravel, a coughing growl of a syllable. It was a man's voice mixed with that of a girl's, but whatever it was, there was no fear in it. No hesitation. It reminded me of New Friend and her bravery, and I wondered if she had spoken it, but surely she couldn't have because she had no mouth. Besides, I had felt it come from my body like a rough and powerful belch.

Mom and Allison stared at me. Allison looked afraid—the angry-red of her cheeks fading to pale, her eyes widening, exposing the whites of fear. Mom was afraid too, but it was different. It was fear without shock.

"Anna," Mom said as she rested her hand on my shoulder. "Anna, be calm."

"This isn't the end of this," Allison declared as she backed up the steps to the patio door.

"We'll start looking for somewhere to go," Mom said. The waver in her voice broke my heart.

Allison still stared at me like I might spew rabies at any moment, but when she looked at Mom, her tight lips wrinkled into a smirk.

"It's okay," Allison said, her tone suddenly saccharine. "I understand it's been a difficult time. We'll work something out."

And then back at me with a glare before turning tail and charging through the house, leaving Mom and me alone in a weird silence, which I quickly broke.

"Mom, I'm sorry." And I was, even though Mom knew about the garden. She saw it, allowed it, even helped me with it. But I was sorry. Like I was always sorry when we were in a rough spot, a spot that I put us in. Me. The troublemaker. The one that wasn't quite right.

Why couldn't I just be a witch and not a weirdo?

Mom didn't look at me. She didn't say anything.

"Mom?"

She went inside the house. It was as if there was a string on her silence that was attached to my heart, dragging it behind her as she left without acknowledging me or comforting me. She dragged me and my heart over gravel, wood, inside across the linoleum, banging it against baseboards and door jambs as she turned into the hallway. The muscle of my heart was pulverized to gruel by the time she was out of sight, leaving me all alone in the Garden of Destruction.

She's had enough.

She hates me.

Like everyone hates me.

She'll leave me.

I'll be all alone.

I am always alone.

And then, a comforting thought.

I'll die.

Chapter Fifteen

I never did go back inside. I stood there, watching the path Mom had dragged my heart, hoping she'd use the streak of blood to find her way back to me. But she never came. So I left.

I hopped the back fence and walked into the woods. I didn't know where I was going, so I just moved forward with my head down, watching my feet shuffle through leaves and branches, crunching them like small, brittle bones. Every so often, when I was tired and fed up, New Friend's black patent shoes would show up beside my own grubby Converse and we would walk together. I never looked up to see her, but I watched her feet march forward, and mine followed.

We ended up at the cemetery. Of course we did; I didn't know anywhere else to go, to be. I didn't belong anywhere.

It was midday, and the sun leaked through the canopy, spilling over my skin, touching me when I didn't want to be touched. Because the sun would leave too, and my skin would be cold in her absence.

I sat crisscross applesauce in the center of the cemetery, thinking. Dwelling.

Mom was a witch, and I wasn't.

I turned my face from the sun, curled into a ball, remembering all the paths that brought me here.

Mom growing plants, flowers, fruit. A mortar and pestle to mash up concoctions as she hummed melodic poetry in her chest. The way she moved was ethereal, fluid, like silk in water.

I had come home with a scraped knee. There was blood, but it wasn't so bad. What was bad was all the kids who had seen me fall. All the fingers pointing, all the mouths laughing. Mom made a poultice but put it on my face instead. My knee still stung, but my inside hurt was quelled. That fluttery feeling in my belly when I thought about all the kids laughing, pointing, had dissolved into the cool slather she smeared on my cheeks. Her magic lotion and strange language softened the harsh laughter in my mind until it was silent, and the pointing fingers faded, changed, contorting into friendly branches and vines and growth in my memories.

I thought of our old place. Of the tree out front with the crook in its trunk where Dad had hung my swing. The dandelions that we would pick for tea for me and wine for mom. That had been my home of firsts. First day of school, first time riding a bike. And also the home of my joys. My hiding spot beneath the porch where I used to build small fires to provide light for my notebook so I could write my poems. The home where all my things were, trinkets and treasures hidden in every nook and cranny. I knew the feel of the floorboards, the smell hanging from the curtains. It was familiar, and quiet, and safe. And mine.

Why did she kill him?

Why are we running?

Mom was running. But she had nowhere to go,

nowhere to hide, because what she was running from was with her wherever she went.

She was running from me.

Dad was going to kill me. Mom killed him to protect me, and now we were here, in this awful place, controlled by that awful woman, and all I wanted to do was go home.

To have a home.

Did I ever really have a home?

Mom and Dad fought. Always about me. There was always a heavy uncertainty, a hesitation, a conflict.

... what's best for her ...

... what she needs ...

... what's safe ...

Was I unsafe? Had my home, my place of comfort, really been unsafe? I hadn't thought so, but then I was a child. Mom and Dad were not children, and adults know more about ugliness than children do.

I was crying. I didn't know when I started, but I allowed the tears to flow. I hoped they would wash me away to the coast, into the ocean, where I would sink and my hair would float above me like a veil, so pretty and glimmering in the deep blue cold.

"Gahhhh."

I screamed at the voice that blared in my right ear and looked up into a pair of milky eyes leaking green pus.

"Oh," I breathed. "Merle. You startled me."

"Gahhhh?"

I wasn't sure what he was asking me. His head was tilted, and he was leaned down so far I thought he might crack in two.

"You need something?" I asked as I wiped my nose on my sleeve.

Merle twirled his fingers, then reached a skeletal arm my way. I cringed, imagining bones wrapped around my neck, choking the air out of me, but he put his hand on my back. And although he thumped me several times, quite hard, I recognized it for what it was. A pat.

"Thanks, Merle."

I patted the ground beside me. Merle circled like a dog, trying to figure out how to get all the way down to the ground. In the end, he just crumpled like a suit to the floor, then balanced himself on his hip bones beside me.

"There's something wrong with me, Merle."

"Gahhhh." He shook his head.

"Thanks. That's kind. But I'm not right. I don't belong, and what I see and feel doesn't make sense."

"Gahhhh." Merle motioned to himself.

"Exactly," I said. "I see *you*."

"Gaaaaahhhhhh." Merle patted his ribcage over the spot where his heart had once been. Now, there was just a tangle of decay and kelp there, knotted between his bones like tangled yarn.

My attention wandered to the lych-gate. "I see other things too. Impossible, horrible things."

All the children eating New Friend.

New Friend herself.

As if entering on cue, New Friend joined us in the clearing and sat down facing Merle and I. Our own little weirdo circle.

"What are you?" I asked.

Neither answered. Neither could. One had no head; the other had no tongue.

"How are you possible? Are you really here?"

I was talking to myself. I decided not to interrupt. I talked and talked, telling New Friend and Old Man Merle all about how weird I was—about Gus, about Mom, about Dad's heart, about the thing riding Allison. I told them all the painful stuff, like The Incident and about coming here, and how I had nothing and no one. They listened intently, occasionally reaching out to touch my arm, or my leg, or my face. They listened until I was too tired to speak, then they lay down beside me when I laid down to gaze up at the stars, trying to forget even what planet I was on.

I started drifting. So did they. I could tell New Friend was by the rise and fall of her chest. I could tell Old Man Merle was by the rasping, drowning breaths coming from his throat. I held her hand on one side and his on the other, not wanting to ever let go, get up, leave. Maybe we all three could grow, sink like roots into the ground, be here forever as part of the forest.

As my eyes fluttered, slower and slower, and Merle's breathing faded into the distance, I heard another sound. The soft chittering of Gus, the delicate chirp of Erinyes, and singing. An awful voice.

Fog and steam
Gossamer and Pitch

I jumped up and ran. I didn't look anywhere near the lych-gate, didn't stop to see if Merle or New Friend had heard it as well. I was on my feet and running before the voice ever reached the third line of the horrible song. It followed me, though. Single words snapping at me from all corners of the forest.

HALFBREEEEEED

I screamed as the voice came out of nowhere, beside my left ear, lunging at me from an owl's hole in a tree.

TAINNNNNTED

This time from the ground as roots heaved up, grabbing at my feet. It was like running through molasses, and my muscles screamed along with my voice as I fought my way through the woods.

ROTTTENNNNNN

I must have left the path. The forest was thick, too thick. I put my head down and kept moving, but the branches were slicing my flesh, biting me like teeth. My clothes were bloodied, everything hurt, but still I kept going.

BIITTTCCCCCHHH

Erinyes came diving down from the trees, screeching and cawing like a bird ten times her size. Gus scrambled through the treetops, frantic, chattering and screaming vile threats.

Then a louder sound came, drowning all the other sounds out. But it wasn't an unpleasant sound. It was low, melodic, and haunting. A choir.

I turned, and the music went silent. The whole forest went silent. Not even the trees dared rustle. New Friend was standing in the path from where I had just run. She was not scared or frantic or running. She was still, calm, strong.

She came and took my hand. I walked at her pace, my back straight like hers, my confidence and courage matching hers too. We walked all the way home, where she took me into the house, got me a glass of water, and tucked me into bed. I felt her arms around me as I went to sleep, and in my dream, all I saw was her face. It was blank, smooth, but oh so familiar.

Chapter Sixteen

School was awful.

I couldn't keep my head in my work, but I didn't want my head to be anywhere else. I didn't want to think about the chant in the woods, about the other kids making fun of me, and I certainly didn't want to think about Mom or Dad or home. Either home.

Mr. Charles droned on for what seemed like hours. I didn't dislike him, but he irritated me. The whole place bothered me, and I didn't see the point.

Classes changed, and everything was so loud. Voices—both the other kids and something else—rattled around in my head as I walked across the hall. I heard giggling, talks of crushes

tainted

and the other voice was there too. The voice from the woods, beneath every other noise, jabbing at me like a splinter beneath my fingernail.

I closed my eyes.

BITCH

But that made it worse. So I opened them, looked

around, covered my ears. All the kids were looking at me. They were pointing and laughing, and New Friend's body parts were hanging from the ceiling, blood dripping from meat, urine and feces oozing from her insides, splashing on the floor and dirtying my pants…

"Anna?"

Miss Mojo took me by the arm and guided me away from the classrooms to an office down the hall.

"Here, honey, come into my office."

Everything went away. The sounds, the smells, the fear. Her office was an oasis. A hiding spot tucked at the tip of a tentacle.

"This is amazing," I said, breathless.

The walls were painted sage green and covered with old black-and-white photos. There were shelves fully stocked with plants, jars, and ornaments. The ceiling was covered with hanging plants, dreamcatchers, and what looked like taxidermied animal tails of many varieties.

"My tails," she confirmed. "That there is a red fox; that one is a marmot. And that wee little thing is an old rat that met its end out in the cat's barn."

There was an entire garden of plants on her shelves, contained in pots, jars, Tupperware. I knew most of them.

"You like to garden too?" she asked. I figured she already knew.

"Are you a witch?" I asked.

Her eyes twinkled, mouth curved into a plump smile.

"Why do you think your momma and I have been spending so much time together?" she whispered.

I gasped.

"How did you know about Mom?"

"I know," she said. "We knew about each other."

Mom had been away a lot. I wondered what she and Miss Mojo had been up to. More secrets.

She patted the loveseat beneath her window. I sat.

She sat beside me and took my hand.

"Am I a witch?" I asked.

She didn't answer.

"There are many witches, child. Most don't know it. It's just something that grows in your bones. You can keep it there, tucked away, or you can coax it out. Nurture it and bring it to life."

"Like a plant."

Another huge smile. "Yes! Like a plant."

"But how do I know …"

I focused on my body, trying to feel the insides of my bones and if there was anything there, lying in wait.

"How do you know if there's a seed in there?" she asked. "If there's a possibility?"

I nodded. "But Mom said I'm not a witch."

"Moms protect," Miss Mojo said. "I think your momma is just trying to figure it all out too."

It was exhausting. All this secrecy and not knowing. I had no control and no knowledge. I trembled, and tears shook loose. Then, like a dam had burst, the feeling of moisture on my cheeks summoned a sob from my throat. I cried out loud, and Miss Mojo jumped.

"Oh goodness," she said as she wrapped her arm around me and pulled me into her breast. "It's a lot, child, I know. And there aren't easy answers. Yours are more complicated than most."

I sniffled and sat back. "What does that mean?"

"I can't see you," she said. "Your momma, now, I could see her. We've been spending time together, your momma and I. I've been driving her to do the shopping, showing her around. Can't get much out of her, especially about you, but I certainly tried. I'm damn curious about you, child."

I didn't like that they had been talking about me behind my back.

"Why are you curious?"

"Because your momma's a witch. Clean and clear. But you …"

But me.

Rotten

"Did she tell you why we're here?" I asked.

Miss Mojo shook her head. "I wondered. I didn't ask, though. There's a lot of pain there. And fear."

I so badly wanted to let go, to tell Miss Mojo everything that had happened, that Dad was dead and Mom killed him and now we were running with nowhere to go. But then Miss Mojo might turn us in. Or hate us.

"You say you see Mom."

"Yes. I see smoke, I see droplets of water. I see the dirt of the earth in her veins."

"But you can't see me?"

A twitch of Miss Mojo's right eye.

"I only see … someone else."

A fly on the window buzzed. I looked at it and saw a thousand of its eyes staring back at me. Its buzzing swelled in my head until my vision was vibrating.

New Friend was on the couch beside me. I wasn't sure how she had gotten there, but she was sitting forward, hands on her knees, paying close attention to Miss Mojo.

Miss Mojo looked right at New Friend.

"You can see her," I said, turning my attention away from the fly. "You saw her at my house that day too. You opened the door and let her in."

Miss Mojo's eyes were glued to New Friend. New Friend reached out her hands, palms up, and Miss Mojo placed her hands there. Her eyes fluttered closed, her hands clenched hard to New Friend's, and they breathed together, deep and exaggerated, moving in rhythm as Miss Mojo's voice filled the room.

"Zirdo ol. Zirdo ge."

The room filled with bugs. The ceiling was blue and shimmering with them, and the floor beneath my feet heaved with mounds of fire ants.

"Miss Mojo?"

She was naked now. Her eyes were black, the lids burnt to a crisp. Blood seeped from the torn corners of her mouth, and black pitch oozed from her nipples and her vagina, pouring down her golden skin.

"Stop," I said.

New Friend and Miss Mojo swayed, hands locked, Miss Mojo's chanting rising in pitch and volume.

"Zirdo ol. Zirdo ge. Gohulim ge ipamis!"

"Please!" I pleaded, but to no avail. It got worse. So much worse.

New Friend's hands crawled up Miss Mojo's arms. They were violent, sharp spiders that clawed and tore away Miss Mojo's skin, revealing layers of compacted, writhing millepedes instead of blood and black shards instead of bones.

"ZIRDO OL! ZIRDO GE! GOHULIM GE IPAMIS!"

As she screamed, her words carved into the walls, over every centimeter of wallpaper, paint, wood. And those words bled, leaking trails of blood that pooled on the floor, filling the room faster and faster as she hollered.

"ZIRDO OL! ZIRDO GE! GOHULIM GE IPAMIS! ZIRDO OL! ZIRDO GE! GOHULIM GE IPAMIS! ZIRDO OL! ZIRDO GE! GOHULIM GE IPAMIS! ZIRDO OL! ZIRDO GE! GOHULIM GE—"

New Friend released Miss Mojo. Miss Mojo sucked in air, put her hand to her chest, and sat back on the couch. Sweat glistened on her upper lip and along her hairline, and her eyes belonged to a terrified rabbit—wide and white and frantic.

"Oh," was all she said as she looked around the room.

It was fading, all the evidence. The bugs shriveled to dust, clothes wrapped over her body, the bleeding words etched into every surface healed, and the blood evaporated. But I could still taste it in the air.

"Oh," she repeated as she looked around. Then at me. New Friend was no longer beside me. She was standing by the door, hand rested on the knob.

"I see you now, child."

I waited. I was too terrified to ask. Did I want to know what she knew? Did I want to be shown what she saw?

New Friend turned the door knob with a creak. Miss Mojo and I both jumped and looked at the door. New Friend dipped her legs into a curtsy and opened the door.

Laz came running in.

"Miss Mojo, I need your help."

Miss Mojo beckoned Laz over with a wave of her hand. She was still breathless and shook.

"It's Mary."

Miss Mojo snapped to attention.

"Mary? What's happened?" she asked, now fully focused on Laz.

"She's … I can't find her."

"Can't find her?"

"She didn't show up for school today. I went to her house, and her mom wasn't there, and Mary wasn't in her bed or anywhere—"

"Shhhh." Miss Mojo gathered Laz up in a hug, then looked over at me. "I haven't heard anything of this. Did you report her missing?"

Laz pulled back and shook his head. "I searched everywhere. The woods, the library house, all the places Mary like to go or hide or play. Nothing."

Miss Mojo's face was the darkest I had ever seen it. All crinkled lines, nothing smooth.

"Well, this won't do at all," Miss Mojo said. "I'll

take this now, Laz. You stay here and rest while I contact those who need to be contacted, and we'll all go out and search, okay?"

Laz nodded. His face was very stiff. I could see he was trying not to cry.

Miss Mojo hesitated. Looked at me. Then she stood, went to her desk, and scrawled something on a piece of notepaper, her lips moving as she wrote. When she was done, she folded the paper once, twice, three times.

"Okay. Laz, you stay here and take a break. Anna, will you stay with him until I get back? Might be a spell."

Of course I would. My heart was racing as I thought of Mary, lost out in those woods with The Blankness. And why did she wander away? Why wasn't she in her bed or safe in her home?

Before she left, Miss Mojo hugged us both and pressed the piece of paper into my palm. New Friend put her hand over mine and curled it closed, trapping the paper and its secret message inside.

"I'll be back, kids. Hang tight."

I slipped the paper into my pocket as Miss Mojo left, then sat on the couch with Laz.

"What could have happened to her?" I asked.

Laz shrugged. "Dunno. She was fine yesterday. We played, then I walked her home, and she was laughing when she went inside."

"Would she have run away?"

"No way," Laz said. "Her mom is here, and they get along just fine. And nothing was bothering her."

Not that you could see.

"I can't lose her, Anna," Laz said.

He started to cry, and New Friend put an arm around his shoulders. I wondered if he could feel it.

"She'll be okay," I said. Why did I say that? Nothing was ever okay. "Let's wait. Like Miss Mojo said. She'll

help."
Laz rested his head on my shoulder.
The paper crinkled in my pocket, jabbing into my leg.

Chapter Seventeen

Not quite an hour had passed before Miss Mojo organized a search party. Only the adults, though. She said she didn't want to worry the children or put any other kids at risk, in case there was something weird going on.

"I can't just sit here," Laz argued.

He was pacing. And so was my mind. I wanted to go out there and join the search party. I had an awful feeling.

And Laz knew it.

"You wanna go look too."

Miss Mojo told us to stay. And she was good, and she was going to help.

But she also didn't know me. She didn't know everything.

"Yeah," I said. "Let's do it."

Laz and I didn't have to sneak. Mister Charles was in charge of all the kids in one classroom, so he had his eyes and ears full, and every other adult was out scouring Eden's Edge and the surrounding woods. All Laz and I had to do was stay low to the ground and watch out for anyone who might see us.

"You think we should try the cemetery?" he asked.

NO!

"Of course," I said, despite my terror. I knew full well that Mary liked the place, and the other kids weren't actually scared of it like me.

So that's where we went. We crept out of the anus of The Beast, checked for people, then darted into the woods. I was nervous, both of being caught and of what we might find at the cemetery, but New Friend led the way, charging soundlessly through the brush in front of me while Laz brought up the rear.

The forest was alive with all the sounds—the shuddering of leaves in the trees, the groan of heavy branches, the chirp and whistle of insects and birds. It was unpleasant. Unsettled. There was a buzz beneath everything, a quiet and persistent baseline vibrating. It threatened to drive me mad.

We reached the cemetery in no time. It looked the same; I noted that none of the gravestones had been cleaned off. Most of the slabs were covered in deadfall and dirt.

"Mary's not been here," I said.

"How can you be sure?" Laz asked.

He didn't wait for an answer. He scoured the graves and just inside the perimeter of the trees, examining every stone, every fallen branch. What did he hope to find? Mary herself? Or pieces of Mary, hidden beneath things that were too small to conceal the whole of her?

Old Man Merle stood at the edge of the trees looking puzzled. He watched Laz scampering around, searching frantically until he, too, started searching. He lifted sticks, then put them back down, moved pebbles, scratched holes in the grass.

I walked up behind Merle and touched him on the shoulder. I had to be quiet. I didn't want Laz to see me doing something I didn't want to explain.

"Merle," I whispered. "Do you know what you're looking for?"

Merle pointed a crooked finger at Laz.

"Gahhhh?"

"Yes, he's searching. And thank you for helping, but you don't know what you're looking for."

With a look of defeat on his face, Merle dropped the stone in his hand, and it landed in the dirt with a small thud. Laz looked over, and I shoved the stone with my foot, hoping he'd think I dropped it. When he looked away again, I turned to Merle.

"Mary is missing."

A puzzled look, then, "Gahhhh?"

"Mary. The little girl with the red hair that's usually with Laz and Liza."

"Gahhhh."

Merle put a hand at his brow and gazed into the woods, searching like it was the high seas.

"Have you seen her lately? Like, at all today?"

Merle shook his head. "Gahhhh."

"Yesterday?"

Another shake. "Gahhhh."

He sounded upset and disappointed. I made sure Laz wasn't watching, then I gave Merle a hug to make him feel better.

"It's okay, Merle. It's not your fault. We didn't really know where to look, so we're just checking places we know she likes to hang out. This was number one."

Merle leaned into my hug, and if he had lips, I knew they would be smiling.

"Have you seen anyone out here today?"

Merle pulled away. He didn't have a smile on his face as his neck creaked and his head turned toward the lych-gate.

The Blankness was there, atop the lych-gate, balanced on his haunches. He was watching us without a sound, with no movement at all. I hadn't noticed him sitting there because his contorted, mangled limbs looked like tree branches silhouetted by the sun. I had never seen The Blankness in the light of day before. He was all black and dull, with striations all over his charcoal body. His face was a shiny, blank piece of glass with no openings. And one more thing was shining—a rectangular patch over his breast. Black but glowing somehow.

I looked away. Merle did not. He glared at The Blankness and balled his skeletal hands into fists.

"What is it?" I whispered.

Merle answered with enthusiasm. "Gahhhh! Gahhhh Gahhhh, Blarga Gahhhhg Blargh."

"Oh," I said, not wanting to embarrass him about his speech. "Okay. Thanks."

I imagined how hard it would be to speak with just a nub of a tongue.

"I can't find anything," Laz said.

He came stomping over to me, his face an angry red. "I don't think she was here. And I guess she wouldn't come out here alone. She never has, being a bit afraid of ghosts and all."

Merle's feelings were hurt, so I gave his arm a squeeze.

"So, what do you think we should do?"

I spoke to Laz, focused on the redness of his face and the desperation in his eyes, trying not to watch The Blankness as he shimmied down the lych-gate, onto the ground, and slowly chittered and jerked his way towards us.

"I say we search the woods," Laz said. "Go in one direction, then come back here. Then straight out in another direction and back. Do it again and again until we've covered every bit of forest between here and Eden's Edge."

The Blankness had reached us. He coiled around my legs, his forked tongue licking up the inside of my pants. His long arms stretched up to the back of my neck, and his talon scratched a straight line down my backbone, piercing me at my tailbone.

I tried not to yelp. I tried to hold a determined expression rather than terrified.

"You okay?" Laz asked?

"Just upset about Mary," I said. "And I think we shouldn't be going through the woods alone."

"But we have to find her!" Laz said.

"And we don't know she's there. Besides, if she was in the woods and got herself in some trouble, we could find that same trouble, right? Then that's three people missing, and Liza would come, and then we'd all be missing."

Laz thought on it, then hung his head.

"I say we go back to Miss Mojo's office," I said. "They can't keep us after school, so maybe we can join the search party then. I'm sure my mom will let us help."

Laz looked angry but agreed.

This time, Laz took the lead out of the forest. New Friend was nowhere in sight. Once Laz was a few meters deep into the trees, I turned and waved at Old Man Merle, but he didn't see. He was still turning over rocks and roots, searching for Mary.

The Blankness stayed with us, though. I refused to look at him, but I could hear him as he slithered behind us, pulling himself along like a lizard. Every so often, I would steal a glance, until he went biped and walked beside me in that creepy, jerky gait.

"You seek answers from witches, bitch?"

The wet words he whispered in my ears were from many voices, high and low, male and female. And in those voices was screaming, wailing, crying.

"Go away," I whispered.

He dragged his rough tongue up my cheek, and I swatted it away.

Laz stopped. "You okay?"

"Yeah, I … just a bug."

"Huh." Laz studied my face for a moment, then kept on going.

My feet started again, and so did The Blankness's. That's when I noticed his feet. They were huge and black and like human feet, but the toes were fused together into hoof-like things.

"I know who has answers, and it ain't no cunting witchessssss."

Though he still walked beside me, I could feel his tongue in my mouth, thick and dry and meaty, pressing on my tongue and the insides of my teeth, licking the back of my throat.

I gagged.

"What's wrong?!" Laz said.

This time, Laz came back to me and put his hands on my shoulders as The Blankness giggled into my throat, low and hard.

"It's nothing," I said. "I'm just freaked out."

Laz knew I was lying. I could tell by the look on his face. But he wasn't mad. He hugged me.

"What's that for?" I asked.

"You're a weirdo," he said. "But I like you. Don't be embarrassed to be yourself. You're interesting. And more importantly, you're kind. You're out here, in these woods, searching for someone you barely know because you care about her, and about me."

He was bright red, but it was no longer anger. The heat on my face told me I was bright red too.

"But whatever, let's keep going," he said as he turned and kept walking.

We got back to The Beast just before the end bell

rang at three o'clock, and we were back in Miss Mojo's office right before Mister Charles dismissed the class.

Liza was in the hall waiting for us.

"Playing hookey, are we?" she asked. Her smile faded almost immediately. "What's wrong?"

"Mary," Laz said. "She's missing. And we went to look for her at the cemetery, but she wasn't there."

"What?" Liza said. "Oh, my fuck! Did you go to her house?"

Laz was about to explain everything again when Mister Charles started leading us to the Belly.

"What are we doing?" I asked.

"Well," Mister Charles explained as the kids lined up in the hall, "Allison wants to update everyone. We're having a brief community meeting to put everyone's minds at ease."

At ease?

They found her?

Or Allison knew where she was all along.

Chapter Eighteen

Miss Allison was the ugliest, snarkiest preacher I'd ever seen. And a preacher she sure was. That or a politician, the way she blasted the audience with the off-white of her crooked teeth speckled in cheap red lipstick, and the way her voice sounded like she was wooing a small puppy. She was full of pomp and bullshit.

"Thank you, everyone, for coming," she said. "And thank you to Miss Mojo, who organized a search party without my knowledge."

Miss Allison glared at Miss Mojo, and Miss Mojo returned that glare tenfold with extra daggers attached.

"I will meet with Miss Mojo to discuss protocols, but in the future, things like these will need to be cleared with me so we don't have a misunderstanding like we did today."

"A misunderstanding?" Laz whispered.

Mom didn't look at me. She was staring at Miss Allison, occasionally slipping a glance over at Miss Mojo, whose eyes were firmly trained on the brat at the pulpit. Everyone in the pews, adults and children alike, looked confused and worried.

"Mary is not missing," Miss Allison said. "There were some … custody issues. Mary has been taken elsewhere, I'm afraid. I do apologize that her friends did not have a chance to tell her goodbye."

"What?" Laz said as he jumped to his feet. "That's bullshit!"

"Control yourself, young man," Allison scolded.

New Friend, who was seated beside me, took Laz's hand and guided him back into his seat.

I leaned over New Friend and whispered to Laz, "Is Mary's mom here?"

Laz did a quick scan of the crowd. Then a slower one, just to be sure.

"No," he said. "She isn't."

Laz was on his feet again. "Where's Mary's mom?"

Allison bared her teeth and banged her fist on the pulpit. "I told you to control yourself, young man."

Mom stood, taking the attention off Laz.

"I think the kids are just worried. I think offering them a little kindness and information might go a long way."

Allison did not thaw. Anger remained in her posture and her voice.

"We need to remain respectful and orderly," Allison spat.

"Yes," Mom confirmed. "All of us."

They stared at each other, and all the air sucked out of the room. I wasn't sure who was going to look away first, but I kinda hoped I might get to witness Mom's powers. Maybe Allison would explode into green smoke, would melt into a puddle upon that altar. Whatever it took to get rid of her.

"The young man has a very good point," Miss Mojo said, breaking the tension as she walked up to Allison. "We are a small community. Mary and her mom are … were part of this community. It's like losing family. It would be helpful to know what happened."

Allison held Mom's stare for a beat, then addressed Miss Mojo.

"I do not disagree, but no matter what, there needs to be order, and there needs to be process, and there needs to be respect."

"Then respect us and don't keep us in the dark," Mom said. "And while you're at it, try being civil to your neighbours. And a good role model for the kids."

I could hear the pressure and cracking of Allison's teeth grinding together as she glared at Mom. Everyone was silent, watching the exchange, gawking back and forth between the women.

"What has become of Mary and her mother is none of your business," Allison snapped. "There will be no more discussion of it here or anywhere. They have chosen to leave, and they are gone. That's the end of it."

No one made a peep. Mom sat down, and Laz fumed quietly in his seat.

Allison put her head down, and I studied the top of it—her dark, mousy roots, her scalp through her thinning hair—until she raised her head and flashed a smile so fake and big I thought I might puke.

"All right then," Allison said, her voice sing-songy. "Moving on. I think we may need to have a meeting after our next church service to brush up on some of our community rules and expectations. I think some of us may be forgetting or neglecting these things," she looked at Laz, "and some of us," looking at Mom, "are new and need to understand the importance of conducting themselves as part of the group. You are all lucky to be here, at Eden's Edge, and we will provide, as the Lord provided. But many folks would love to take your spot if you cannot abide by our system."

I was in a convection oven. Mom's rage steamed from my left side and Laz's from my right. I was sweating so bad from their heat that my butt was sticking to the pew and getting itchy.

Allison snuck some scripture in before dismissing everyone. Miss Mojo came over to us as people filtered down the center aisle and out the mouth of The Beast.

"Oh, kids," she said. "This isn't the outcome you wanted, but it could be worse."

"It is worse," Laz said. "Because what Allison said is bullshit."

Miss Mojo clucked her tongue. "Son, be that as it may, we need to watch our language and our manners. Your beef is not with me."

"Do you think this is for real?" Mom asked.

Miss Mojo shrugged and looked back. Allison had already ducked out the side door, probably so no one could get to her to argue or ask questions.

"I just don't know," Miss Mojo said. "People have just left here before. In the middle of the night, without a word. But remember, this is a place for people who are lost, or running, or have trauma attached to them. Disappearing is not an unusual ending."

"But …" Mom hesitated. She and Miss Mojo locked eyes. "What do you feel?"

Miss Mojo seemed to look very hard and deep into Mom's eyes. She didn't say anything, but she shook her head.

"Okay," Mom said. "Let's all get on home for now."

"But what about Mary?" Laz said.

"I won't let that get buried in the dirt, young man," Miss Mojo whispered. "Have no worries. We just gotta be quiet 'bout it."

"And smart," Mom added.

Laz silently agreed, then went off with the foster mother while Mom and I bid Miss Mojo adieu and headed towards home. New Friend walked beside us. She was acting odd and nervous, shoulders twisting this way and that as if she were looking around. Watching for someone. Or something.

"You think something happened to Mary?" I asked.

"Yes. Something happened to Mary," Mom confirmed. "But whether it's legitimate or is something more nefarious is yet to be seen."

We didn't have enough details. And we didn't have Mary. We might never have Mary again.

New Friend stepped in front of me on the dirt road and stopped. When I tried to keep walking so Mom wouldn't realize there was something wrong, New Friend blocked my path. Mom took two strides before realizing I had stopped.

"Anna, what is it?"

"It's nothing I—"

New Friend pointed back behind me. I didn't turn to look. When I tried to take another step, New Friend planted her palms on my chest and pushed me backwards. Mom watched, brows furrowed, studying the empty space around me.

"It's nothing," I said.

Mom's face told me she knew it was absolutely something.

I stepped around New Friend, and she grabbed my hand, trying to pull me back.

"Stop it," I whispered. "I just want to go home."

New Friend did not listen. But I was stronger than her. I kept walking forward, swatting her away while Mom shot me glances that were both curious and fearful. As we approached our house, New Friend gave up. She gave me a long, hard hug, then her shoulders slumped, and she walked away. Defeated.

What don't you want me to see? I wondered.

Dirt. I only noticed it once New Friend was gone. It was dark, and it blended in fairly well with the gravel driveway, but I noticed it. It was a trail of dirt leading from our driveway, up the side of the house to our gate, and into our backyard.

No. That's not quite right. *Out* of our backyard.

"Mom?"

But Mom had already noticed. She was examining her shoe. Her heel had stuck in a patch of dirt in our driveway. Her brow was furrowed as she took her shoe off and examined the dirt, then did the same with the other shoe, which looked relatively clean. Her eyes left her shoes and found more patches of dirt and the trail I'd discovered.

"Anna." It was a statement. I didn't quite know what it meant.

Mom's shoes slipped from her fingers, and she ran to the gate and into the backyard. I wanted to follow, but I was afraid. I looked over my shoulder, hoping New Friend would be there to hold my hand and walk with me or to put her hands on my shoulder blades and push me forward, but she was long gone.

"Fuck!"

Mom's scream pierced me. I doubled over, sick with panic and horror.

What was there? Was it Mary's body? Was it the police, come to arrest Mom and take her away and leave me all alone in Allison's custody?

My body shuddered with sobs, and my feet refused to go. Gus was up on the eaves, screaming at the stars, and Erinyes was flapping around in a panic, cawing like she was the size of a vengeful raven.

"Unfuckingbelievable!" Mom yelled.

I had to do it. I had to go see what Mom was seeing. I couldn't just stand there like a fool, like a weak little sapling taking root in the front yard. But I didn't follow the dirt path to the back gate. I fished my key out of my pocket and went in through the front door, then grabbed a throw off the couch and shrouded myself in it for protection. Discovery and truth can be cold and suffocating, and I wanted to cocoon myself away and have something to cover my face with.

I went out onto the patio. Mom was raging around the backyard, pacing trenches in the ground, muttering words I didn't understand.

It wasn't Mary. But it was awful.

My garden was no more. Someone had destroyed it. With intent and vigor. Everything green had been yanked from the ground, every bit of bark chopped to bits, every colourful flower stomped to mush. And all of it, the bones and organs and soul of my garden, had been put into a ring of stones and lit aflame. It was smoldering, with only hints of the life that once was glowing in the ash and embers.

"Mom?"

Mom did not stop her pacing or her chanting. She was scouring every square centimeter of the property, speaking words in a language that sounded distant, guttural, enchanting. I didn't know what she was doing, but I let her finish. She was a witch, and she was on my side.

Finally, after the moon ascended the stars like stairs to the pinnacle of the sky, Mom came over to the porch steps where I was sitting wrapped in my blanket.

"This was done with intent," Mom said. "Every little sprig, root, berry, flower. All gone."

I knew that. I could see that for myself, but tears welled in my eyes, nonetheless.

"Why?" I asked.

"Hate," Mom said. "And it took a lot of energy and time to do this."

"While we were looking for Mary," I said.

"Yeah," Mom said. "But Allison didn't know we were looking for Mary. We didn't tell her."

I knew I wasn't allowed to swear. But language was

the least of our concerns.

"The fuck she didn't," I spat.

Mom startled, taken aback, and then her upper lip pulled back, revealing her teeth. She was canine, she was bitch, and she was angry.

"Enough," Mom said. She pulled me up off the porch and hugged me. I breathed in her lotion, the lavender in her hair. I felt her muscles bulge as she hugged, felt the blood coursing through her veins.

"I love you, Anna. Please go inside. This will all be okay."

I believed her. I kissed her on the cheek. She tasted of tears, oranges, and ash.

I didn't stop to get a drink of water; I didn't stop to pee. I didn't care if I wet the bed because that wasn't hurting anything. Wasn't killing anything. I didn't want to think anymore. I just wanted to sleep.

As I crawled under the covers fully clothed, New Friend's weight on the bed caused me to roll to the side, into her, and she covered me with the blanket. A haunting ballad came from her belly as she hummed, trying to mask the sounds of Mom's increasingly rage-fueled chanting and heavy breathing outside my window.

Chapter Nineteen

It was dawn when I woke. I peeked over my blanket, and the sliver of sky I could see over the top of my plastic blinds was watercolour strokes of blush and orange and fading lavender. The burst of morning colour did not alleviate the sense of doom resting on my chest as I thought about my garden that no longer was and my Mom who had been sent into a whirlwind of rage.

I sat up, got up, went to my window. Mom was still outside, though she had shed all her clothes. She was caked in dirt and filth from head to toe, and trails of sweat had spread across her skin, turning her into a cracked windshield. Her lips were moving, and her stomach heaving, both from exertion and whatever she was chanting.

There were two wheelbarrows in the yard. I wasn't sure where she had gotten them, but they were full of all sorts of things—white dust, red dust, stones, feathers, and jars of liquids. Mom was intensely focused on the task at hand. She'd spread out patterns of powder here, then lit a candle there. Then she'd spritzed all of it with the bottles of liquid, her voice rising in tempo enough that I could hear her. I still didn't understand what she was saying.

I went to the kitchen because that's what we do in the mornings, but I wasn't hungry. I wasn't sure what to do. I didn't want to interrupt Mom. I was a bit scared of what she was doing. I wondered if I should go to school, act like everything was normal when everything was, in fact, not normal. Not that it ever was.

I peed, then scrubbed myself off in the shower. Gus watched me, a nut in his hands, nibbling away. When I was all done and dressed, Gus hopped on my shoulder and we went outside.

"Should I go to school?" I asked from the porch.

Mom didn't hear me. She was putting the finishing touches on a ring she'd built around the yard in orangish chalk and red feathers.

"Where did you get so many feathers?" I asked.

Mom's fingers were bloody. Her hands were bloody, and her arms, and her breasts. I kept Mom in the corner of my eye as I went to the ring around the perimeter. It wasn't just feathers. It was birds—cardinals, with half a dozen ravens throughout. They were all arranged on their backs, wings spread, necks snapped back so they were touching beak to foot, all around the circle.

"Mom."

She came to me. I could smell the musk of her body. There were smears on the insides of her thighs where she'd obviously relieved herself more than once through the night. No time to stop, I supposed.

"I can't explain this in full," Mom said, motioning to her work. "But it's protection."

"But the yard's already destroyed."

Mom shook her head and smiled. "Not destroyed. Changed. No one can destroy something completely. It takes a great deal of power to destroy life like you created here. Its heartbeat is still here, in the earth. And no one will touch it again."

I thought on it.

"But what if someone did have power? And really bad power?"

Mom hesitated. Suddenly, she seemed very aware of her nudity. She put an arm across her chest and a hand over her lady bits. I held out my blanket, and she took it and wrapped it around herself.

"There is something bad here, Anna. But I don't think it's power. If it is …"

Mom looked afraid again. And smaller, like she'd sunk into the ground.

"Can't you fight it?" I asked. "If there is a bad power? Can't you cleanse it?"

Mom shook her head. "If it was a witch doing bad things, yes. Or a good person doing bad things. But if it's something more … a witch can only match powers and intentions."

I didn't quite know what that meant, but Mom looked really bothered, so I didn't push her.

"Should I go to school today?" I asked.

"School." The thought obviously hadn't occurred to her. "I suppose. Yes. This," she said, motioning to the yard, "Is awful, but not worth us being stranded. Not yet."

I couldn't even look out at what used to be my garden. All my work, my love, my energy. Destroyed for no good reason. I couldn't even have that in this place that wasn't even my home.

"I guess," I said.

Mom put her arm around me and guided me inside.

"I know it's hard," she said. "But one moment at a time. Only focus on what's in front of you. You risk getting lost in a spiral of Mary, of the Garden, of Allison … of Dad …"

Mom trailed off. All these things were her whirlpool

too, threatening to drown us both.

"Give me five minutes," Mom said. "I'm going to have a quick shower, get dressed, then I'll walk you to school."

"It's okay," I said. "I can get there on my own."

Mom hesitated. I could tell she was exhausted, and I knew that exhaustion would win.

"You sure?" she asked.

"Positive," I said. "I'll go straight there," I lied.

"Okay. Well. Try not to get lost in your own head, okay? And if anything goes sideways, or you feel uncomfortable, or if Allison gets on with her bullshit, just run home."

What home?

"I will, Mom."

Mom planted a soft, warm kiss on my forehead.

"I love you," she said.

"I love you," I said back.

Mom was the only one I loved. Ever.

When I heard the shower turn on, I skipped out the front door and around the circle to New Friend's house. She was sitting on her front stoop as if she'd been awaiting my arrival. When I approached, she hopped up and joined me on my journey to The Beast. We were just about there when, from behind one of the houses, a hissing noise caught my attention. Must have caught New Friend's attention before mine because, unbeknownst to me, she'd stopped walking before the sound had occurred.

"Pssttt."

I looked over at the house and saw Laz and Liza peeking from around the corner, furiously waving me over. I took a precautionary scan of the lane, The Beast, and the other houses before New Friend and I ran over to where Laz and Liza were hunched down beside a wood pile at the back of a small bungalow.

"What are you guys doing?" I whispered, because it felt like we were sneaking.

"It's Mary," Laz blurted. His hands were shaking and his eyes wild.

"Shhh," Liza said. "Not here. Come inside."

"This is your place?" I asked.

Liza nodded and took us up the back steps, into a kitchen not that dissimilar to my own. The ten houses on this property were cookie-cutter floor plans of each other. Probably cheaper for Allison to have everything built the same.

"We aren't gonna let this go," Laz growled as Liza poured us some coffee.

"Coffee?" I said. "But we're kids."

I cupped my hands around the hot mug. The smell attached to its tendrils of steam was bitter.

"Best grow up real fast, Little Goat," Liza said.

"But … a little goat is a kid."

Both Laz and Liza looked at me. Liza laughed. Laz did not.

"I'm glad you two can joke around," he muttered.

"Lighten up," Liza said. "Now tell Anna what you told me."

Laz took two hard swallows of his coffee. "I found Mary's bloodstone. It was on the floor of her room, and it was cracked."

"You were in her room?" I asked.

He continued as if he hadn't heard me. "Mary never goes anywhere without that stupid crystal. And her chair was tipped, and her bed all rumpled. Mary'd never leave a rumpled bed. She's all prim and proper and pretty."

Laz blushed and his eyes moistened.

He loves her.

"Was her mom there?" I asked.

He shook his head. "Nope. But her mom's purse was.

Who goes somewhere without their purse?"

"Was their car there?"

"They don't have a car," Liza said. "No one does, except for Miss Mojo, Mister Charles, and Miss Allison."

Curious.

"No cars?" I said. "Why?"

"Most people come here running," Liza said. "Mary's mom did have a car, but Miss Allison made her get rid of it. Said it was too easy for people to find her with a car."

"Besides," Laz said, his voice high and mocking, "Everything we need is here, Allison says."

"So … what now?" I asked.

Laz took another gulp of coffee and started pacing.

"There's obviously something not right here," Liza said. "Have we seen any of the three cars come and go, Laz?"

"Nope," he said. "And I've been watching the road in."

"But if she's missing, she'd have been taken, or just gone, before we knew, yes?" I said.

Laz glared at me. He didn't want the impossible. He wanted a solution. A win.

"Be that as it may," Liza said, "Let's go easy on ourselves and assume they are still in Eden's Edge. And there's only so many places Mary and her mom could be tucked away."

I thought of the buildings I'd seen in Eden's Edge. All small bungalows, including Library House. Then there was The Beast, which was open to everyone, and Allison's house.

"Allison's house," I said.

"Stop," Liza said at Laz as he opened his mouth. "Be smart here. It's one thing to break into Mary's place while everyone's attention is on her. But Allison's? She'd skin you at the pulpit and serve you for dinner."

Sweat beaded on my upper lip. I thought of New Friend, hacked up and served on silver platters beneath those spastic fluorescent lights.

"Not actually," Liza said, obviously noticing my stomach sink into my bowels, "But a pissed off Allison is not something I'm interested in summoning."

"But what if that's where they are?" Laz said. "I ain't doing nothing."

"What if we just watch Allison's place?" I offered. "From, like, the woods or something."

Liza pressed her tongue to the roof of her mouth, posturing to say no, but closed her mouth instead.

"We dress dark, cover ourselves in moss and stuff," I said. "No lights. I think we could do it."

And I would ensure we had someone to watch our backs.

"Okay," Lisa conceded.

Laz pumped his fist. "Good! Let's get her!"

"Hold on, cowboy," Liza said. "At night. Meaning we all need to go grab naps if we're gonna be in any shape to stay up on patrol all night."

"I can't go back to the Foster House. Martha will drag me straight to school. Allison has been up her ass lately. Super strict."

"No," Liza said softly. "Martha's as worried as we are. And she has about as much love for Allison as we do. She'll understand. Maybe you're sick or something."

"What about your dad?" Laz asked. "Will he let you stay home and nap?"

"Dad's out today," Liza said. "He's cutting some wood for Allison. Some ridiculous project, I'm sure."

"Probably a big ole pedestal for a golden statue of herself."

"Well," I said. "I can tell my mom precisely what we're doing and she'd be completely on board. In fact, I bet she'd let you two bunk up and nap."

My stomach clenched. Did I just invite other kids into my house? Around my things? What if they saw my jars or my notebooks? What if they see who I am

what you are

and they realize how weird I am and never want to see me again?

But what did I care? I never had friends. Why start now?

"You mom sounds cool," Laz said.

My heart was a butterfly, all warm wing flaps when I thought of Mom's face, her touch, the song of her voice.

"She is," I said. "The coolest."

Laz and Liza, in unison, cooed, "AWWWWWWWW!"

Heat pounded in my head, and I looked at my shoes. New Friend's shoes were there, beside mine, shining both her reflection and mine. Neither of us had heads.

"Okay, let's do it," Liza said. "Let's go get some rest and meet behind the school at, say … eight o'clock?"

"Good plan," Laz said.

"And hey, go for a jog," Liza said as she poked Laz in the ribs. "Burn off some of that caffeine or you'll be up for two weeks."

"That's what we want!" Laz argued.

Liza shoved Laz out the door but stopped me when I tried to leave.

"Hey," she said. "Witch. You doing okay?"

Was I? Absolutely not. For a great many reasons.

"It's okay," Liza said. "We're a team. I appreciate you diving in with us, and we've got your six."

Liza didn't let me respond. She hugged me, and it was good, like a Mom hug. I never wanted her to let go. But she had to, and she did, and I left without saying a word, which was weird, but I didn't want to breathe and have the feeling of the words on my tongue erase the feeling of Liza's pressure on my body.

I walked. But I did not walk home. I walked to Library House, then behind, and into the woods, the whole way feeling Liza's embrace on my body.

Chapter Twenty

Merle listened intently while I explained the plan.

"We're just gonna watch," I said, "And see if we can, I don't know, see anything through the windows. See if Mary's in there, or her mom, or if anyone is acting sketchy."

Pretty sure Merle had no idea what I was talking about, but he listened just the same. He did, however, perk up at the mention of watching our backs.

"If you keep an eye behind, like in the woods, that would be a huge help."

Merle nodded, and a tendril of drool swung from his lip. But then he shrugged.

"Gahhhh?"

"Keep an eye out for what?"

"Gahhhh."

"Well …"

My eyes found the lych-gate and the gangly blank creature perched atop like a grotesque.

"Keep an eye behind us. In case there's anything … anyone there."

Merle nodded and cracked his knuckles. Though he seemed ready for a fight, he was a softy through and through. Whatever he did to Old Bobby Pickton, I doubted he'd ever hurt another fly.

"I gotta try to nap," I said. "But I don't want to go home."

Mom was there, and she'd gone mad. The corpse of my garden was there. My home that was supposed to be my new home but wasn't really a home at all was there.

"Is it okay if I crash here?"

Merle nodded and got to his feet. I was going to curl up right there on the ground, but Merle loped into the trees, appearing moments later with an armful of moss and leaves. He proceeded to make me a little bed complete with a pillow, which looked like a full piece of sod he'd uprooted from somewhere.

"Thank you, Merle. You're a good guy."

Grey as he was, I believe Merle blushed. I laid down and closed my eyes, and Merle sat beside me. I was about to suggest Merle get some rest too because it was going to be a long night, but I supposed people like Merle didn't need rest. They were already at rest, all the time. Or permanent unrest. That was their state. He seemed content to just sit with me, and I was glad for that. I felt safer with his eyes open.

My thoughts grew as heavy as my eyes, and soon, my body pressed into the earth and the dirt swallowed me whole. My land of dreams was on the underside, all grave dirt and barren landscape. There were fires on the horizon; reds, oranges, and whites flickered and rippled, the heat distorting the dead trees peppering the landscape. There were creatures around, livestock and birds, but they were all broken and wrong. Necks twisted backwards, limbs snapped in half, eyes hanging out of sockets. And they just existed that way, roaming the land, chewing on sand and rock while they mewled tunes of suffering.

The soles of my feet were on fire. I looked down. I was barefoot, and my skin had bubbled and blistered from the heat of the burning sand. I looked behind and saw an endless trail of my footsteps.

"Where ..."

But my feet did not stop. We kept walking, my feet and I, across the hellscape teeming with death. Corpses, wilted flora, the smell of shit and piss and rotting meat. Insects landed on my skin, tearing away chunks and leaving bloody pocks. A wasp landed on my eye, and all I could do was watch its stinger pierce my cornea and blink as blood pooled in my eye and dribbled down my cheek like a tear. But I could do nothing to stop it. I couldn't swat at my face, I couldn't hold my eye, I couldn't scream. All I could do was walk.

Something squiggled in my vagina. It was long and sharp, with a thousand teeth and twice as many tongues. I looked down at the landscape I traversed and found it was not sand but a heaving floor of fat millipedes, one of which had crawled up my leg and inside of me. Then another, and another, until I was heavy and bloated and sinking in the squiggling ground.

The whine of mosquitos lit my brain aflame, and they got louder, closer, and they thrust their proboscises into my inner ears, causing an itch so great I would have stabbed knives in my head to dig it out, brain be damned.

And they were buzzing. So loud, monotone, driving me mad. But not buzzing. Speaking. Teasing.

"Fog and steam ..."

"No!" I screamed, and my feet ran in response. The ground was no longer millepedes but shards of shattered crystal all pointed upwards, into me. They sliced open the flesh on the arches of my feet, then the muscle, then carved the bone until I was running on stumps.

"Gossamer and pitch ..."

"Stop!"

And I did stop. Or at least slowed down. I was walking now, not running, and the ground was stone. Not just stone but some sort of black gem, pure and gleaming beneath my feet. And through the dark stone, crimson veined through like spiderwebs of rubies.

HALFBREED, TAINTED, ROTTEN BITCH!

I was standing in front of a throne made of human bones. Hundreds of them, maybe thousands. At the base of the throne was a four-headed dog and eight-headed snake, each guarding their half of the throne with vigorous growls and hisses, all teeth and spittle and hunger for pain.

I was surprised to see what sat upon the throne.

It was a man. Or perhaps a woman, but it was square like a man, and it had no hair. It was smooth, faceless, featureless. No clothes, no colour, no muscles. No nipples or genitalia, though I still felt a great deal of shame, seeing them exposed there like they were.

There was something, though. A rise in the flesh where their left nipple should have been. A scar, or a deformity, something I couldn't quite make out.

Come, it said.

And I came.

I ascended the steps, and the higher I got, the smaller I became, until, when I arrived at the base of the throne, I was barely the size of the thing's cloven hoof. It bent down to speak to me, though it had no mouth, and I could smell its meals—freshly bathed babies, kittens covered in birth, rotting moose meat.

I'll show you.

"What?" I stammered. "What will you show me?"

Who you are.

"I'm Anna."

No.

What you are.

And with that, the four-headed dog grabbed one of my legs in one of its jaws, and one of the snake-heads grabbed my other leg. They pulled, and I split down the middle, half of me going with one creature, the other half with the other.

I couldn't breathe. I made my way down each digestive tract of each creature, getting squeezed, compressed, and sloshed around, gas popping in my ears, pushing around one curve, then another, burning with acid and bile until my body was coated in the warm sludge of feces and I was expelled into the fresh air of the forest.

I gulped air. Sat up, touched myself. I was covered in shit, blood, and mucus, but I wasn't hurt. Not really. Just shaken up a bit and nauseated. I puked, and the vomit rinsed some of the filth from my mouth.

"Gahhhh! Gahhhh!"

Merle was sobbing. He was standing over me with tears pouring from his eye sockets and snot from his nose.

"It's … it's okay, Merle. I'm okay."

Merle was unconvinced. He hugged me, then hugged me again before disappearing into the woods.

I took in my surroundings. I was underneath the lych-gate, facing the cemetery. Meaning I had come from beyond the lych-gate. I rolled over onto my belly and crawled a few centimeters back to the bowels from where I'd come when Merle came hollering through the cemetery with his jar of saltwater under his arm.

"GAHHHH!"

New Friend was there too, and she wanted what Merle did. And that was to have me away from the opposite side of the lych-gate. She grabbed me by the ankles and hauled me out into the center of the cemetery, then she and Merle propped me up against one of the graves.

"Hey, guys, I'm okay."

But they fussed over me. New Friend shimmied me

out of my clothes while Merle poured his saltwater in my hair and over my skin. New Friend tenderly rubbed away the grime while Merle fetched her flowers from the forest to use as both soap and scent.

In the end, I came out pretty clean, though my hair needed a good shampooing.

"Thanks," I said.

They hugged me, one at a time, and then stood facing me in expectation.

"What was that?"

Silence. And Merle wouldn't look at me.

"Okay."

It wasn't their place to tell me. If they even knew. As if they could even say.

But I felt awful. I felt like crying, and the soles of my feet still hurt, and I felt shame in my privates and in my butt where the bugs had violated me. I grabbed a pinecone and scrubbed my skin violently, drawing blood. Merle and New Friend tried to stop me, but I screamed, and I vomited again, and they left me alone. But they couldn't watch. They stepped into the woods while I tried to scour myself clean using bark, rocks, branches. I scraped every inch of myself, inside and out, but it felt no better, so I crumpled to the ground and cried. I cried every bit of soul I had out into that dirt, and with my pain soaking into the earth, I slept.

Chapter Twenty-One

There were no fewer hours in the day, but nightfall was upon me before I was ready. I awoke to find New Friend and Merle standing guard, both wringing their hands in worry as they watched both me and the surrounding woods. I activated my muscles and sat up, feeling every bit of the pain I had caused myself with the abrasive forest debris.

New Friend helped me to my feet and back into my clothes. I was half-focused on the task at hand but also on the lych-gate. I'd been dreaming. Hallucinating. Something.

I am insane, I thought as I noted all the bloody abrasions over my body. Self-inflicted horrors.

But there was no time for any of that now. Now was about my, *dare I say,* friends. Mary, Laz. Liza. My insanity would be waiting for me once we were done solving the mystery of Mary.

New Friend led the way, like she always did, and Merle brought up the rear. I felt safe sandwiched between them as we walked through the darkening woods. Even so, my eyes betrayed me, sneaking peeks over my shoulder, through the trees, and up in the air. Where was the Blankness? I kept expecting a bony hand to seize my shoulder or a dry tongue to force itself into my ear. But nothing happened. When we finally broke through the trees into Eden's Edge, I wondered if I was still dreaming and in fact still back laying naked in that cemetery with bugs and bones and tongues all over me.

We crept around the back of Library House, keeping low to the ground. Merle had trouble with this. He was so tall and rigid. I tried to help him, but he would not bow or bend.

"Maybe we should stick to the trees," I suggested.

He shrugged, and New Friend also lifted her shoulders.

Oh. Right. He didn't need to hide. Nor did she. The only one that could be seen was me.

"Gahhhh," he agreed anyways. For me, I think.

For my benefit and peace of mind, the three of us retreated back into the cover of the forest and crept the entire perimeter of Eden's Edge until Allison's two-story monstrosity came into view. New Friend found us a cozy little nook behind a fallen oak, and we hunkered down there to wait.

That's when I spotted The Blankness. The reason he hadn't been stalking me in the forest, haunting me from behind, was that he must have been ahead of me the whole time. He was perched at the peak of Allison's house, a hungry buzzard sniffing for blood.

"Anna!"

A whisper in the dark, coming from the woods.

"Laz," I said.

New Friend and Merle retreated as Laz and Liza approached. Liza passed through Merle, and she gave a violent shiver.

"You okay?" I asked.

"Chilled, I guess," she said.

"Wimp," Laz said. "It's not that cold."

She shrugged. But I knew. It was that cold inside Merle.

"See anything?" Laz asked me.

My eyes went to the peak of the house and the jagged figure looming there. "Not really sure what I'm looking for," I said.

"Any people?" Liza said. "Cars, movement from within the house."

"Just got here," I said. "But nothing yet."

All five of us stayed still and quiet, each examining the house. The inside was bright, but the curtains were drawn. I could make out the vague shapes of furniture, perhaps the glow of a television in an upper bedroom, but no movement or silhouettes of people.

"What about the basement?" I asked. "If I was gonna keep someone, that's where I would keep them. Hidden and soundproofed by the dirt."

Laz and Liza both gave me a look, and New Friend placed a hand on my shoulder to silence that particular train of thought.

"Those little windows?" Laz said. "Dark. I bet there's nothing down there. Just an unfinished basement. All the other places are just on concrete slabs."

or shoes and feet

"Because that was the cheapest way to go. Miss Mojo told me."

"Even her house?" I said, pointing to Miss Allison's extravagant shanty.

Liza furrowed her brow and looked at Laz, who shrugged.

Miss Allison would have a finished basement. She would have a good and proper house, with a sturdy foundation and a dark and dank basement to hold people prisoner and feed them rat meat for breakfast, lunch, and supper.

We waited a good while, watching the windows, the drive, the sneaky lane behind the house, but there was a whole bunch of nothing. Merle grew restless behind us, shuffling soundlessly through leaves while New Friend played an odd game of hopscotch across uneven rocks scattered on the forest floor. Even The Blankness sprawled out, his tail hanging loose and swinging from the peak like a pendulum as he lay on his back, blank face aimed at the now full-bright stars.

Liza finally removed her attention from the house, shed the backpack she'd been wearing, and dumped its contents on the ground.

"Energy," she said. "Come on, guys. Snack up."

Chocolate bars, chips, candies, sandwiches in baggies. Liza had an entire pantry with her.

"Awesome!" Laz said as he stuffed half a chocolate bar into his mouth at once.

"Go easy," Liza said. "It isn't coffee, but it'll spike you. And I ain't wrangling you all night, hauling you down from the trees."

I chose a sandwich. My tummy was unsettled, and all I really wanted was some soda crackers and Canada Dry, but I figured some food might help. And eating would pass the time.

"You make this?" I asked as I bit into the delicious Havarti and turkey sandwich with extra mustard. I loved mustard.

Liza nodded. "I always make sandwiches for Dad when he goes to work. These are his favorites. He hates working for Allison, so I figured I could at least do this to make him feel better."

My dad would never feel better again. He'd never feel again.

As I chewed, I questioned, again, why Mom had to do what she did. Did she have to do what she did? Was Dad so bad that he would come after us if she took me somewhere? Was he dangerous?

I did not like my dad. But he had moments where he tried. Teaching me the piano, my tiny fingers atop his rough, thick ones as we plinked and plunked our way through "Für Elise." The way he held the back of my banana seat as I wobbled my way up and down the road, over and over again. He taught me to build fires

"stack the wood like a teepee, Anna, and make sure there's room for air to get in. Fuel, fire, oxygen, remember that"

and how to whittle wood into things I needed, like poker sticks to roast hotdogs and dowels for birdhouses. He even let me drive his truck once or twice when Mom was out, even though I could barely reach the pedals. And much to my joy, he even snuck me snippets of brandy at Christmas, after we'd lit the fruitcake in a blast of blue and orange flame, the three of us cheering around the table.

But there was also the yelling. The slamming of doors, the scorch of his words, and the slice of his tongue. That dark look in his eyes when he crawled in late, all smiles and sharp words, smelling of violence and energy. And the way Mom cried. She cried so much.

And I was crying too. The bread of my delicious sandwich was wet. Liza noticed, and she put her hand on my shoulder at the same time New Friend put hers on my other shoulder.

"Anna?" Liza said, her words warm caramel, just like her touch.

But I couldn't focus on that for long. Nor did I answer her. My head snapped in the direction of movement on the house. The Blankness stirred, then got up his haunches and peered into the darkness down the back lane. I looked there too but saw and heard nothing.

"You okay?" Anna asked.

The Blankness stood up straight—a tall, slick pole, dancing from foot to foot in anticipation of whatever was headed its way. Its member was standing at attention too, long and thick and engorged, pointing from its crotch out into the night.

"Something's coming," I said.

Before Liza and Laz could ask any follow-up questions, headlights appeared through the trees, bouncing moons getting bigger and brighter as the quiet rumble of an engine crescendoed.

"It's Allison," Liza said.

The nose of Allison's bland little SUV appeared around the last corner of the lane leading to her house. Her garage door rolled open as she approached. We all squinted and strained to see her, and I spied more than just Allison in that vehicle. It was full. She backed into the garage, got out of the driver's seat, and her dark creature slipped out of the backseat behind her before taking its place on her shoulders. Her passenger door opened, and a scraggly bearded man stepped out. But not just him. He had a thing riding his shoulders too. Both Allison and The Beard seemed oblivious to their riders, though. He walked around the car, and they embraced, and the creatures skittered off like roaches, ducking out of the garage as Beard's hands groped all of Allison. Beard backed Allison up the three steps in the garage, his hands on her boobs and in her pants, and she smashed her hand on the garage door button. The garage door closed as they fumbled into the house, and their riders skittered up the siding to the roof. They were braying and yelping like hyenas, jiggling and nipping at each other until they spotted The Blankness. This shut them up really quick. Tails between their legs, they found a spot together above one of the second-story windows, with The Blankness looming on the peak above them.

"Ew," Laz said.

"Yeah," Liza said. "Didn't know she had a boyfriend. I wonder what Jesus thinks of that."

The light in the window below the riders came on, and we watched, mouths agape, at the silhouettes that peeled off each other's clothing and wrestled around the room, banging into things, each other, with a violent, heaving rhythm.

"Oh my God," Liza said as she covered Laz's eyes.

The riders were doing the same. On the roof, one had its talons pierced into the other's hips, pumping away, his penis thrusting through her entire body and bursting out from her mouth with gushes of dark fluid. They howled and cried as liquid rained down from where they were connected, and from their mouths, until it was a torrential downpour coating the house in a thick, murky sheen.

"Ugh," Laz said. "I didn't wanna come here just to see that old bitch doing it!"

"Don't watch then," Liza said. "We just gotta wait."

Liza turned her back and tore open a bag of ketchup chips. Laz turned too, but frequently stole glances over his shoulder at the porn show upstairs. The Blankness sat very still, focused on the shenanigans of the riders.

It went on for a while, then there was nothing for a spell. When the lights upstairs extinguished, Laz stomped his foot in the dirt.

"Shit," he said. "Did they go to sleep?"

"Maybe," Liza said, carefully watching the window.

Five minutes went by. Then ten. Merle was wavering on his feet, and New Friend was twiddling a blade of grass between her rotting fingers, terribly bored. I was about to suggest calling it a bust when the garage door rolled open.

That's when Hell was revealed.

The Blankness jumped down to the ground, looked

at me, and pointed at the open garage door. Allison came out by herself but did not turn on the light. She walked outside, and the light of a cigarette cherry breathed to life as she glanced around, scouring along the forest and up and down the lanes. She tilted her head, listening.

Liza raised her finger to her lips and pushed her other palm to the ground, telling us to stay quiet and stay down. Allison surveyed the situation for many minutes before opening the hatch to her SUV.

Beard came out of the house with Mary in his arms.

Liza put her hand over Laz's mouth, and I put my arms around him to keep him from jumping up.

Mary was conscious. Kinda. Her limbs were swinging limp, but her mouth was moving, and her eyes were blinking slowly. Beard did not put her in the hatch where we couldn't see her but in the backseat, where he buckled her in, said something to her, and kissed her on the mouth.

Laz struggled beneath our grasp.

Mary's hand came up, pushing Beard away, but she was weak, and her arm fell into her lap.

Beard put his hand up Mary's shirt and groped around, and his other hand found its way up her skirt. She shied away, tried to move across the seat, but eventually gave up and went limp.

Tears were streaming down Laz's face and over Liza's hand. Mary cried too. The wet on her cheeks was gleaming in the moonlight that snuck into the garage.

Beard stayed at it for several minutes, then kissed her again and shut the door. Allison got in the driver's seat as Beard went into the house. Several moments later, Beard came out with someone else, this person stiff and lifeless. An adult woman, naked, with her abdomen sliced open from neck to pubic hair, her entrails trailing behind her. Judging by the reaction from both Liza and Laz, this was Mary's mom.

There was a roll of black plastic laid out on the floor of the garage. Beard set Mary's mom on the plastic, rolled her up a couple of times, then applied duct tape around her. Then, simple as that, he put her in the hatch, got in the passenger seat, and Allison pulled out of the garage. The riders jumped down from the roof and entered the SUV, sitting together in the back seat beside Mary and slapping at each other like siblings.

For a brief moment, as Allison was pulling away, I caught Mary's eyes, and she caught mine. She was dopey, cloudy, and in absolute anguish.

We all watched until the tail lights disappeared. Then Liza held Laz for a few minutes longer. When she finally released him, he exploded to his feet, screaming, punching the trees, kicking rocks. Whatever he was saying was unintelligible, but we got his meaning, and his emotion.

Liza was so pale. I didn't know brown skin could turn so pale.

"Oh my fuck," she said. "Holy shit."

New Friend took me by the hand and nudged me forward.

"What?" I screamed. "What do you want me to do?"

Laz stopped thrashing around, and Liza looked up into my face.

"I am useless!" I screamed.

New Friend nudged me again.

"I have no power! I am nothing!"

Another nudge.

"I can't do anything, I have nothing, and I can't do this anymore!"

Nudge, nudge, nudge.

She wasn't going to give up. I breathed in, tasted the forest, exhaled, tasted my sour breath on my tongue. I envisioned my mother, her light, her heat. She was the sun.

"My mom," I said, quieter. "We need to tell my mom. She'll help. She'll know what to do."

They didn't need convincing. Laz and Liza were on their feet, ignoring the need for stealth as they bounded right out of the trees and into Eden's Edge. I followed, then looked back to see if New Friend was coming. She wasn't. She wasn't even there anymore. Merle was, and he looked as horrified as we all felt about what we had just witnessed.

"Go home," I said gently. "And thank you for your help. I'll let you know how it goes."

I turned back to Liza and Laz. They had heard me, and I didn't care. They didn't seem to care either. Liza grabbed my hand, and Laz grabbed hers, and we ran for my house and my mom.

Chapter Twenty-Two

I was breathless after explaining everything to Mom. Once the whole story had come out—from Laz's discovery in Mary's house to the scene we'd witnessed with Beard, Allison, Mary, and her mom's body—I was exhausted. Had it taken hours to tell that whole story? It felt like it. And it was a relief to have all that knowledge transferred from my brain to Mom's. The burden no longer weighed me down, and I felt I could float like dandelion fluff into slumber.

The memory of The Blankness and the riders brought me back to my feet like anchors, though. Those were details I had omitted from my story, of course. They weren't helpful.

"Okay."

That's what Mom said any time she was processing anything.

"It's all true," Liza said.

"Oh," Mom said to her. "I know. I believe Anna. I always do. I'm just putting it all together in my head. Give me a moment."

Mom stood from her chair and went to the kitchen. I was already standing; when I had big pieces of information to tell, I liked to be standing and pacing, my body moving the entire time to keep my anxiety tamped down. Laz and Liza were sitting together on the couch, hip to hip, both staring at my mom. I wondered why they were so fixated on her.

"What?" I said to them, defensive and self-conscious.

"Um," Laz said as he pointed at Mom, who was now preparing tea.

I didn't understand. I cocked my head. Liza patted her shoulder, then also pointed to Mom.

"Oh," I said. "That's Erinyes."

Mom was hiding nothing. This was new to me. Mom always tiptoed around the fact that she was a witch, hiding her rituals, keeping her friends away. Now here she was, confident and positively beaming, with Erinyes on her shoulder, herbs in her belt, and crystals and plants around her neck.

"Your mom has a pet cardinal?" Laz asked.

"Well … kind of," I said. I still wasn't confident like Mom. Mostly because I didn't understand fully what she was, what she could do

and what I am

what am I

and how to explain it to people who maybe didn't believe in witches and all that.

Mom came back into the living room carrying a tray of cups and a pot of tea.

"I don't know who drinks tea and who doesn't, but please, help yourselves."

I poured myself a cup, then Liza poured one too. When Laz didn't make a move, Liza poured one for him.

"There could be caffeine in it," she whispered to him.

He didn't smile, but he did take a sip. I wondered if he would ever smile again.

"I'm going to talk to Allison," Mom said.

"What?" we all said in unison.

"Mom, is that a good idea?" I asked.

"It's simple," Mom said. "She's committed a crime, or so it appears. She needs to be held responsible for her actions and for the actions of her bearded friend."

"But, aren't you scared?" Laz asked. "I mean, Mary's mom …"

Mom took a sip of her tea, then her smile extended beyond the width of her cup.

"No," she said after she'd swallowed. "I'm not scared. I've done nothing wrong."

Except kill my dad.

"But what if she kicks you two outta here?" Liza asked.

A flutter of heat touched my cheeks. Liza looked genuinely worried. Even upset.

"I don't want … it would suck if you left," Liza said.

She likes me?

A real friend?

"I think getting kicked out might not be a bad thing," Mom said. "This place is wrong. If what appears to have happened has really happened, then Allison has some explaining to do. I think I won't get kicked. I think nobody will, except for perhaps her."

"But she owns everything here," Liza said.

Mom's smile faded. She took another, slower sip of her tea, then offered a drink to Erinyes.

"Yes. I should have questioned that more," Mom said. "But we were in a pinch, and needed a place fast, and this was hidden …"

Mom was upset. The others probably couldn't see, but I could. And I could smell the guilt steaming from her pores.

"It's okay, Mom."

I went over and hugged her. She hugged me back, and Erinyes playfully tugged at a strand of my hair. I lingered a moment to let Mom swipe away a tear, so the others didn't see.

"I will go get Miss Mojo," she said. "She has a vehicle. And perhaps she has a phone, since none of us seem to."

"Miss Allison said she was trying to get the fibre optics guys to come out," Liza said, "but—"

"Yes, but but but," Mom snarked. "There's a damn good reason none of us have phones. She didn't want us to have them. And nobody questioned it because this place is small, and we have everything we need, and most of us are hiding anyways …"

Laz and Liza looked at me. I know they wondered what we were hiding from. I did too.

"I will go to Miss Mojo," Mom said, "Ensure we have a vehicle, then we will alert the authorities. You kids need to stay safe until this is resolved."

"Should we go to school?" I asked. "So everything seems normal?"

"Uh, no," Liza said. "Not on a Saturday."

I had lost all track of time. Between my encounters through the lych-gate, my travels through the forest, and the trauma at Miss Allison's, I wasn't sure I even knew what year it was.

"Just act normal," Mom said. "Go home, do the things you do, try not to arouse suspicion. Quiet and under the radar, please."

"Yes, ma'am," Liza and Laz said.

Everyone quietly sipped their tea before moving to the door.

"Would you like us to walk you home?" Mom asked

them.

"That's kinda suspicious, isn't it?" Liza said. "Us all scrunched together?"

"Maybe so," Mom said. "Allison's gone anyways. For now. Hurry home and stay inside, okay?"

"Okay," Liza said. "And thank you. Both of you."

Mom and I smiled, mirror images.

We watched them out the window as they went down the lane for as long as we could still see them. Then Mom took my hand and squeezed.

"Friends," she said.

"I dunno," I said, shrugging.

"Seems like it. And they seem like good people."

"They are," I said. And I believed that.

Was there a way I could stay with the other kids? Maybe they could come with us. Maybe Liza's dad could marry Mom. Maybe we could adopt Laz ...

"I want you to get your stuff ready, Anna. Things you want to take with you."

"Are we really leaving?"

"We sure as hell aren't staying," Mom said. "Let's get ready to go, please. On the fly. Moment's notice."

I didn't want to be ready to go. I didn't want to run, to have to grab only what I could carry and leave the rest behind. Because I would be leaving little bits of myself behind as well. Again.

"Will Gus and Erinyes come too?"

Erinyes warbled a lovely solo on Mom's shoulder, answering the question.

"She came here, didn't she?" Mom answered.

"What about Gus?"

Mom looked out the window. Gus wasn't in the tree, but I could hear him chittering and complaining nearby.

"I don't know," Mom said. "I suppose that's up to him."

Mom hugged me. I breathed in her scents of lavender musk and L'Air Du Temps. I could also smell blood, but she looked clean, so I wondered if what I was smelling was actually flowing through her veins.

I'm a vampire?

Erinyes chirped out what sounded like a laugh.

Maybe not.

Mom started gathering up her things—her knitting, her book, a jumper. I wandered out into the backyard. All the stuff in my bedroom was basically already together. But out in the backyard, I wondered if there was anything I could take. Any of the life or death back there remaining for me to salvage. I went back there to see and found Gus digging holes all over the dirt.

"Hey, buddy," I said.

Gus jumped at the sound of my voice, then scampered over to me and leapt up on my shoulder.

"Are you gonna come with me?"

Gus nestled into my neck, his little hot breath warming my skin. I got down on my knees and plunged my fingers into one of the holes he'd been digging and fished out a nut.

"Planting trees, are you?"

Gus screamed at me, jumped down, ripped the nut from my fingers, and reburied it in its hole.

"Hey, I'm sorry. Continue, little guy. Bring this place back to life."

It made me a bit sad. Gus was rebuilding what had been destroyed, which meant he had no intention of leaving. I refused to think about it, though, because then I'd think about Old Man Merle, and Liza, and Laz, and the things I would be leaving here. Things that wouldn't fit into my box.

I stood and brushed the dirt from my pants, and I felt something in my pocket.

The paper from Miss Mojo. With all the panic and

business and plans, I had completely forgotten about it. I took it out, smudging it with dirt as I carefully unfolded it.

The words written on the paper were the ones Miss Mojo was chanting in her office.

Zirdo ol. Zirdo ge! Gohulim ge ipamis.

I folded the paper back up and went inside the house. Mom had her coat on.

"I'm going to—"

"Miss Mojo's," I finished.

"Yes," Mom said. "You're gonna be okay?"

"You don't usually form that as a question," I said.

Mom smiled. She hugged me, long and hard. When she pulled back, her eyes were wet.

"You are going to be okay," Mom said. "We both are. We are strong and we are smart. We will *be* strong and smart."

"Yes," I said. "I love you, Mom."

"I love you, Anna."

Mom left. I watched her go, just like we'd watched Laz and Liza go. Once she was out of sight, and a few minutes after that, I threw on a hoodie, went out the back door, over the fence, and ran to Library House.

\#

I swore in my head. The library was locked. It hadn't been locked before when I only wanted inside, but now that I *needed* in, I couldn't get in. I thought about breaking a window, but I was supposed to lie low and not draw attention before Mom and Miss Mojo could deal with the Allison mess. Someone might hear breaking glass, or Allison could even pass by. That could be a whole lot of trouble. I sure didn't want to end up like Mary or, worse, Mom end up like Mary's mom.

So, I sat on the back step and bit my nails. I didn't know what else to do. I looked at the note Miss Mojo had given me and read it over and over again. No matter how much I said it out loud or read it silently, the words made no sense. And they weren't even a little bit familiar. I balled the paper up in my fist, threw in on the ground, and buried my face in my hands.

A tingling sensation started at the base of my spine. I scratched my skin, examined my limbs and butt for ants, but found nothing unusual, so I put my head back in my hands and concentrated on my breath to keep myself calm.

Another tingle, then a poke. I stopped my breath, my movement, my sound, and focused on my back. Fingertips crawled their way up my backbone, using my spine like a ladder. I made sure to arch my back, allowing whatever it was to have solid footing to get where it was going, even though I was so scared I was shaking.

The fingers reached the base of my skull, then slithered down my neck to my collarbone and over to my shoulder.

Tap tap tap.

I did nothing. Said nothing.

TAP. TAP. TAP. Harder. More pronounced.

I looked up into the face of The Blankness. He was standing right above me, his wheezing wet breath misting on my face, his smooth body twitching and crackling as he lifted his arm. Long, black fingers uncurled into a flat palm, and in that palm, a key.

"What?" I asked.

A clicking sound came from his throat, then a soft flapping. It sounded like … the turning of paper.

"Books."

He thrust the key at me. I reached out and took it, and when his skin touched mine, it burned and blistered, and I nearly dropped the key. I screamed, and the blister swelled and burst, releasing a flood of ichor over the ground. It was so painful and smelled so bad, but I had nothing to wash with. A hardy laugh came from within The Blankness as I flailed around, shaking off my own infected pus.

But I had a key.

I focused on the key and only the key, trying to ignore the carnage of my hand. I jammed the key in the door of Library House and turned it, and the click of the lock jarred some sense into my mind. My hand was clean and unmarred, and the pain was gone.

The smell, however, remained. Because The Blankness didn't go anywhere. He was still standing there, lurking and stinking.

"Why did you let me in?" I asked.

The Blankness growled. I opened the door, and The Blankness clucked and chittered. He was holding out my crumpled piece of paper. I was in disbelief. First the key, now he was handing me this? This horrible monster, who was awful, and felt awful, and smelled awful. Was he helping me? Or would this, too, result in my pain?

I snatched the paper from him and went inside.

I clicked on the green lamps on some of the tables but not the overhead lights. I figured it was light enough outside that people wouldn't see the dim glow of the table lamps, but the big light might be pushing it.

I wondered where to start. There weren't any nonfiction books in here, Miss Mojo had said.

Of course not. Miss Allison is trying to brainwash us all.

But maybe there was something. I ran my hands along the books, trying to feel something. Anything. If there was a witch in me, I needed her to come out and help.

My fingertips sizzled.

There's something!

I closed my eyes as my body took over. I let my limbs move on their own, my hands pushing against the wall. Someone pushed me, and I fell to my knees. I clawed at the floor with my fingers, my fingernails, my bones. Then someone handed the strings to me. I was back in control of my own body.

I stood and opened my eyes. Scrawled on the floor in gouges filled with blood was a word I didn't recognize.

ENOCHIAN

Okay. It was something.

I looked up the E's, first the authors, then the book titles. Nothing but romance—Eternal, Everlasting, all that junk—and authors I hadn't heard of.

"Enochian …"

Sounded like a race of people. If there was an encyclopedia, a map, something that was real in here …

BANG.

The sound blasted from the other room. Something heavy had hit the floor. I hadn't heard the door, and there were no windows that opened up. I hadn't thought to check if there was anyone else in there with me, but who would be in here?

"Liza? Laz?"

If I was going to get in trouble, or if it was Liz or Laz, they would have said something.

I crept around the corner, waiting for something to grab me, to sink its teeth into me and pull away a chunk of my meat. But nothing lunged at me. The Blankness was there, completely still like a pillar, standing beside a bookshelf. And there was a leather-bound book splayed face-down on the floor in front of him. I looked over at the shelves, at the blank slot where the book had been …

waiting for me.

I walked over to the tome on the floor. I stood staring at the nothing that was The Blankness's face, looking for any hint that there might be eyes staring at me, or teeth waiting to rip the flesh from my bones. But there was nothing. Not even a ripple. It was black glass, smooth and flawless. But still, I did not want to bend down right in front of him. Maybe that face would come to life, open up to devour me, or there'd be eyes that would bewitch me and drive me to madness. Perhaps he would grab me with those too-long arms and violate me with those too-long talons like Beard did to Mary. Or perhaps, while I was bent over to pick up the book, he would stomp my head like a watermelon with his huge cloven hoof.

These were all the things I was imagining as I bent down and picked up the book. None of them happened. I stood up quickly, looked into that glass face, and backed away. He didn't move. Not a single muscle twitched. I went to the table farthest from The Blankness and sat in a chair with its back again a bookshelf and pulled the table to me.

I looked at the book.

The title was *Tongues of the Devil*.

I opened the cover. There was no year and no author.

I flipped through the first few pages. They weren't in English. It looked like French, or maybe Latin, but I didn't know much of either, just a word here or there. A little way in, there were drawings, and they were awful. Demons violating humans, animals eating other animals, pain and suffering and torture. There were different hellscapes, creatures I had never ever seen, and people with all sorts of deformities. All the demons were gleeful, and all the people's faces were twisted into hellish anguish.

Enough.

I quickly turned past the pictures and found a section written in English. It was a collection of languages: Latin, German, Italian, Aramaic. And each section had a translation. I flipped to the E's.

ENOCHIAN TO ENGLISH TRANSLATION

I uncrumpled the paper Miss Mojo had given me.

Zirdo ol. Zirdo ge. Gohulim ge ipamis.

My fingers pressed against words, riffled pages, searched like it was braille. As I read, I wrote, my finger writing the words in blood on the table beside the book. Behind me, chanting a soundtrack, was The Blankness. And with each word I deciphered, his words became clear. Actual words. Enochian.

"Zirdo ol. Zirdo ge. Gohulim ge ipamas," he chanted, over and over, crescendoing with each word I translated.

Finally, it was complete. I looked at the words I had scrawled on the table. My words were rough and ugly, not like Miss Mojo's pretty curly ones.

Zirdo ol. *I am me.*

Zirdo ge. *I am we.*

Gohulim ge ipamas. *It is said we cannot be.*

I am me. I am we. It is said we cannot be.

It made no sense. That was what Miss Mojo said, what Miss Mojo had written in this weird language, and what The Blankness was singing behind me now.

I flipped through the book, trying to put together the meaning of those words and why Miss Mojo would say them. From what I gathered, Enochian was a language from the 1500s made up by two radical religious fools, John Lee and Edward Kelly. They claimed it was the language of angels, but linguists tore it apart and diagnosed it as nothing more than nonsense. Still, there were hidden factions of occultists who believed that Lee and Kelly were not grifters, or insane, or making everything up. That they were, in fact, angels—not heavenly ones but those with black eyes and stone hearts, walking as if they were men, introducing the language of hell to the earth.

I slammed the book closed.

The language of hell?

Witches were ostracized and murdered for canoodling with Satan. Miss Mojo was a witch, and she knew this language. I thought it was bullshit, the whole heaven and Earth thing, Devil and the Lord. But then why would she write this? Are witches bad? Are they aligned with the devil?

I'm not bad.

A tap at the window drew me from my thoughts. It was The Blankness, but he was on the outside of the window, tap tap tapping with his long, sharp nail. When I looked, he flipped his hand and curled his talon, beckoning me outside. He was still the same awfulness, all long and lanky and gyrating muscles, but I wasn't as afraid. I was, however, curious, so I crumpled the paper into my pocket and went outside. He waited until I was a meter away, then dropped to all fours and crawled down the lane. I followed, and with each step, my heart pounded harder and harder. I looked back to see if there was anything behind me, even though The Blankness was in front, leading the way. I wanted New Friend there. I wanted her to hold my hand, give me a push on the small of my back, to hug me and to encourage me to keep going. But it was only The Blankness and I, and no one to protect me if he decided to turn and tear me to strips.

We ended up in front of Allison's house. And it was the beginning of chaos.

The Blankness skittered up the side of the house, roosted on the peak, and watched. I saw his stomach heaving with laughter, and it made me sick with fear.

Miss Mojo and my mom pulled up to the house in Miss Mojo's wood-paneled station wagon just as The Blankness and I arrived.

"What are you doing here?" Mom asked as she was jumping out of the car.

I looked up at the peak of the house.

Allison's front door opened with a groan, and she came charging out. Her rider was coiled around her neck like a boa, its limbs and tongue hanging limp down her body.

"What are you all doing here?" Allison asked.

Mom was still looking at me. Wondering why I was there. The Blankness tilted his head, and so did I, as

Allison's rider slithered off of her and started nipping at Miss Mojo's legs.

"We have a problem," Mom said.

"Is that so," Allison said. She stepped to Mom, and Mom pulled me behind her. Miss Mojo joined Mom at her side.

"Best not come close," Miss Mojo barked at Allison. "I've had plenty of you for one lifetime, and I could snap that little turkey neck of yours with a twist!"

Allison looked startled. She took a step back, but her face flamed with anger.

"You best not talk to me that way," Allison said.

"Or what?" Miss Mojo said. Her large hands were balled into tight fists, and I wished upon every star that she would smash not one but both of those fists into Allison's mouth, smearing that too-red lipstick and shattering her gross, stained, too-large teeth.

"What happened to Mary?" Mom asked. "And her mother?"

Allison stuttered a bit, then, "Like I said, they left."

"Left?" Mom said.

"I won't be repeating myself," Allison said.

"No need to repeat the lie," Mom said.

Allison's hand flew to her chest in a gesture of shock. "I am not lying! How dare you even suggest that?"

Mom was to the point, unemotional, matter-of-fact. "You were seen with Mary. You brought a bearded man home with you, and you two left with Mary after he assaulted her. And he brought Mary's mom out and put her in the hatch. I'm not going to assume more than was actually witnessed, but there is a suggestion that Mary appeared to be drugged and that Mary's mom was deceased."

Venomous was the only word I could think of to describe the look on Allison's face. She had no words, but she moved her body around as if trying to shit them out.

"Nonsense," she finally said. "Absurd. I think maybe you are under the influence. Both of you."

Mom shrugged. "Well, we'll sort it out either way. We went into Faulten and spoke with the police. They should be out shortly."

Allison's face was a cooked lobster. She was red, sweating, her eyes watery and bulging from her head.

"You cannot …"

"Uh huh," Miss Mojo said, "We sure did. And that's good, yes? The police will help. If you're not guilty, you're not guilty. If Mary and her mom were dealing with some legal business, the cops will know, and this will all be fine. Better safe than sorry, though."

I worried about the police. Of course, I was concerned about Mary and her mom and what was going on here, but Mom and I were running. Mom spoke to the police? She didn't seem rattled, but what if …

"Anna." Mom had her hands on my shoulders. "It's okay, Anna. Go home. I'll be there soon. And we are leaving Eden's Edge."

Allison laughed. "No, you are not."

Mom ignored her.

"No rush," Mom said. "We are going to be fine. Let's take our things, and Miss Mojo will give us a lift into Faulten."

"You owe me," Allison said. "You stayed here for free."

"And I'll pay, if that's what you'd like," Mom said.

I had no idea how we were gonna pay. Mom had left everything behind with Dad.

In the distance, I heard the wail of sirens. I clutched onto Mom with every inch of strength I had.

"Mom, I'm scared."

"I know, Anna," Mom spoke into my hair. "But we're strong, and we're smart, and we are going to be just fine."

"I love you, Mom."

"I love you too."

When Mom pulled away, New Friend took her place, tenderly grasping my shoulders and turning me towards my house. Her hands slid to the small of my back and gave me the push I needed to get moving. As we walked, the trees surrounding Eden's Edge lit with dancing reds and blues, ominous and threatening in the night. I closed my eyes, pressing tears out that poured down my cheeks as New Friend covered my face and took me home.

Chapter Twenty-Three

I was quite certain that my skin was going to split open and my blood, muscles, and bones were going to fall out onto the floor, making a huge mess in the living room for Mom to clean up. My fear, my anxiety, my hopelessness would certainly tear me apart if I had to wait another moment to find out what was going on. I wanted Mom home with me. I didn't want her to be there at Allison's with the police. How long would it take? Would she be there all night? Tomorrow? How long was I going to be alone in this house?

New Friend took my hand and led me to the couch. I would have rather stayed pacing in front of the window, even though I had the blinds closed so no one could see in and spy on me. Moving felt good, and just being near the window felt like watching because I could hear the sounds from outside—the crunching of gravel as a few police cruisers rolled through Eden's Edge, the drone of raised voices. What I didn't hear was nature. I needed to hear the birds, the leaves caressing each other in the trees, the silence of the stars.

"I'd feel better outside," I told New Friend.

She tightened her grip.

"Out back, though. Where no one's gonna see."

She hesitated but eventually conceded and let me go.

The cool air engulfed me as I opened the back door. It wrapped its arms around me, embracing me with my mom's breath. It smelled like her. I had forgotten about the destruction of my garden, but it was okay because Mom had applied magic to it. I wasn't sure what it was, but it was everywhere. Piles of ash and plants speckled over the lawn, red and white dust lines around the perimeter. And something I hadn't noticed before. Something startlingly scarlet on the inside of the dust lines. Glowing, flickering.

As I moved closer to the line, the definition became clear. Feathers, singed and curling, red and shining. Not just feathers but full birds. Cardinals.

I covered my mouth and pinched my nose to block the taste of cooking fowl. There was no smoke, but they were definitely burning. They were writhing and gasping, beaks wide and gulping for air as their flesh crackled like burning embers. They were all connected like melted wax, but they were not dying. They were living as some sort of mass, feathers gorgeous and full, eyes pouring down their faces.

"Oh," was all I could think of to say.

It was awful, but also magic. Mom had done this. Erinyes flew down from the eavestrough and landed beside the row of bird fire. She pecked at their faces, preened their feathers, warbled them songs of peace and harmony.

What does it do, I wondered, *this barrier of bird*?

Mom would have to tell me when she got home.

If *she comes home.*

"No!" I shouted at the voice inside my head.

"Come home," The Blankness said.

He was standing just outside the yard, in front of the fence but just outside the line of scorching birds. He was a tall, imposing pole with no sense or purpose. And though he didn't look threatening in any way, more like the burned corpse of a tree, he filled me with horror. My feet wanted to run, my eyes wanted to cry, my throat wanted to scream.

"Come home." His words were air squeezing from a pin-punctured balloon, forced and tight.

"I am home," I said.

The Blankness laughed, and the line of simmering birds shuddered, igniting into a chorus of feeble chirps and caws.

"Home," he laughed.

Just as panic was about to overtake me, throw me down and violate me, New Friend stood beside me and held my hand.

He cannot cross the birds, I thought.

I am safe.

"You are never safe," he grumbled through wheezing laughter.

"What do you want from me?" I yelled.

He laughed, but this time, there was more menace there. It was slow, drawn out, pure wickedness.

"What do *you* want from you?" The Blankness asked.

His laughter ceased. And with it, the forest fell silent as well. No wind, no whispers. Even the perimeter of burning birds had ceased their song and woes to listen for what might come next. First there was a crack. Then a creak. Then The Blankness turned on his hooves and walked slowly into the woods. His head turned to look back, and his talon came up, beckoning me. Then he went on his way without turning back again.

I did not go. I wasn't curious, not any more. He only ever took me to show me bad things, and I was full up on all the bad things I ever wanted to see.

I went inside the house. I was both so tired and buzzing awake, the dichotomy threatening to break both my body and my mind. I was determined to wait for Mom. I wanted her home, on the couch, drinking tea with me and reading. I went to her book, which was splayed out on the coffee table, and touched its pages. I could feel her. I smelled its pages where her lotion permeated the story.

Clutching the book to my chest, I went to her bedroom. Everything was in boxes. We really were leaving. I had no reason to be happy about it, but also no reason to be sad. Yet I *was* sad. Why, though? There was nothing here but awful Allison, and the vision of Mary's violation, and that awful Beast waiting to gobble me up.

But there was also Merle and his droopy eyes and pronounced gimp. And the feeling of Gus's puffy tail against my cheek. Laz and his razzing, and Liza. Liza and her kind heart, perfect skin, dark eyes, hair of black glass.

I crawled up on Mom's bed and curled under her covers, making a cozy cocoon that smelled like Mom and felt like Mom. But it still wasn't Mom. She was out there, fighting with Allison, talking with the cops.

Is she in the back of a police car?

Mom's voice was screaming in my head. I had never heard my mom scream. It was terrifying, and I screamed too. Along with me, I heard all the voices screaming in agony: Mary, Liza, Laz, Merle's garbled *"Gahhhh."* Even Gus and Erinyes were screaming, and everything was burning, and I woke up in a pile of sweat with Mom's comforter tangled in my limbs and my sweaty hair glued over my face. I flailed, fell off the bed with a hard thud, threw the blanket to the side.

Sunlight. It was daytime. I was in Mom's room, but she wasn't there. There was screaming. Anxious and shrill. But it was only one voice, and it wasn't Mom. Or human.

"Erinyes?"

SLAM

The bedroom window shuddered under the impact.

SLAM

I was sure the glass was going to break.

SLAM

I opened the blinds and was greeted by tiny streaks of blood and globs of feathers. Erinyes was flying into the window, over and over again, screaming and bashing in her tiny skull.

"No!"

I ran out of the bedroom, down the hall, and to the front door. I had to stop Erinyes. Mom would be devastated if she died. Could she die? I didn't know, and I wasn't about to find out.

I flung open the door and was greeted by the sun. It warmed my face, tingled my skin. It was Mom. And she was smiling.

"Oh, Mom!"

I threw my arms around her and squeezed her tight. She placed her hand on my back and pulled me in tighter than she ever had. Her lips kissed the top of my head, and her breathing matched my own. For only a moment, before it became ragged. Gasping.

"Mom?"

The front of her jumper was soaked with my happy tears. But it was too wet. There were too many tears. I pulled away. My face was wet, just like the jumper, but it was both tears and blood, like both of New Friend's bowls had been poured over Mom.

But it's okay.

She's smiling.

SLAM.

Erinyes continued to smash into the window.

"Mom, what happened?"

Mom didn't speak. She just kept smiling.

Behind me bloomed another sound. A horrible, mournful wail. It was The Blankness. He was on his knees, his mangled, taloned hands over the nothingness of his face.

Black tears of sludge rained down on the ground at his knees as he mewled and sobbed.

Mom?

Her smile was so beautiful. So plump, so wide, so red. It dribbled down, coating her shirt, but it was too low and too wide, and went from one ear across her slender, perfect throat to the other ear like a necklace of rubies. Her other mouth was moving as she tried to speak words, but only dark blood poured out, pooling with the blood gushing from her throat.

MOM!

I screamed, but I don't know if it was out loud. The Blankness screamed with me, in my voice, and New Friend did too.

Mom crumpled to the ground. I went with her, holding my too-small hands over the wound on her throat.

"Mom, what do I do?" I screamed. "Who do I call, where do I go, do you need water? A bandage? What do I do?"

WHY CAN'T I KNOW THE MAGIC TO FIX THIS!?

9-1-1. But there were no phones, and Mom needed an ambulance, and she needed it right away, and I had to get help.

Mom lifted her hand. It was cold as she put it on my cheek, but her touch was the sun and soft rose petals.

You are strong, she mouthed. *You are smart.*

"No!" I screamed, and the line of burning birds screamed with me.

Mom's eyes lost their diamonds, fading to rheumy with her last breathed words.

"I love you."

Erinyes screamed and flew at the window one last time, snapping her neck so hard her head fell from her body.

I hugged my mom, who went limp in my arms. I screamed, wanting her to scream back, but our breaths were no longer in sync. I laid beside her with my head on her chest, hearing only the pounding of one heart, my heart, and I screamed and cried hard so maybe mine could beat enough for us both.

New Friend and Merle stood by and watched.

"Go get help!" I screamed.

Neither moved. Merle was crying, and great yellow gobs drooled out of his eyes, nose, and jawless maw.

"Do something!"

They did nothing. But something needed to be done. It was morning, and it was Sunday, and I knew just where to go for help.

Chapter Twenty-Four

The Beast had its jaw closed as I ran up the front stairs. I didn't feel like it wanted to eat me anymore. I feared that I would yank on the door, and it wouldn't give, and I'd be left out on the steps with no one and nothing while it became too late to help Mom.

But the door opened when I pulled on it.

"Help!" I screamed.

The Beast received my noise and blasted it back at me, amplified by the cathedral ceiling of its belly. The chapel was empty, save one bottle-bleached harpy standing at the pulpit and the rider perched upon her shoulders, giving her the appearance of widespread, leathery wings.

"Well, look at who's finally decided to join us for service," Allison said.

"My mom," I sputtered as I staggered up the aisle.

"Is she here with you?" Allison asked.

I hated Allison. Everything about her, but especially the smirk she had tugging at the corners of her mouth.

"What did you do?" I screamed. "What did you do to my mom?"

It didn't matter what she did, though. It was done. I looked around the chapel, searching for someone. Anyone.

"Help," I pleaded. "Please. My mom needs help."

Laz wasn't there. Liza wasn't there. Miss Mojo wasn't there. None of the other people were there. It was Sunday, and everyone was supposed to be there.

"Mom!" I screamed. "You have to help!"

At the front of the room, Allison clucked her tongue.

"The voices heard in this chapel are for reading sermon or scripture, or offering prayer to the Lord. Those are the only things I should be hearing on this day, in this place. How dare you interrupt the Lord's message today?"

Allison tapped her magenta nails on the pulpit. I focused in on her hands. They were covered in blood. The front of her blouse was too. It had lines and splotches of browning crimson splattered across it like ugly art.

"What …" I looked around the empty room. "You can't!"

"Listen, Anna," Allison said. "Once in a while, we have a select few that can't play nice. That are ungrateful brats like you and your mother."

"You are a monster!" I cried.

"I saved you!" Allison yelled. "Without me, your mother would be in jail and you'd be lost in the foster system to be beaten and raped and tossed to the streets before your breasts even start to bud."

"You can't do this!" I screamed.

Allison's smile grew wide, and she put her hand to her chest in shock. "Do what?" she said, saccharine sweet. "Help the needy? Feed and house the poor? Shelter the abused?"

"Killer!" I said.

"Why I never!" Allison said, her smile stretching impossibly large. "How dare you, after all I did for you and your mother?"

"Mom is …" I couldn't say it. I couldn't admit it yet. "Mom needs help!"

"She sure does," Allison said. "And I'm happy to provide."

"You can't," I growled. "You won't get away with this."

Allison laughed, and the sound blared off the cavernous room like thunder. "Get away with what? The police were here, darling. Investigating you and your friends' bullshit claims. But there's no proof of anything, Anna."

"I'm leaving," I declared.

"Are you now?"

"I am!" I shouted. "I'm gonna tell everyone here! And I'm taking Laz and Liza, and Miss Mojo will take us, and we will turn you in."

"With what evidence, my dear?"

I intended to say no more. I charged past the pulpit, into the hallway, and down to Miss Mojo's office. She wasn't there, which didn't surprise me, but I tried not to think of where she might be. Where Laz might be, or Liza, because I couldn't lose them, could I? I could lose no more. Right?

"And what of your father?" Allison was standing in the hallway, filling it with her presence. "Where is he in all of this? Perhaps if your mother is … unwell, we should encourage the authorities to fetch your father."

No.

"Or would you rather be alone with some foster family? Seems you have some mental health issues that might make that tough."

"I'm not crazy," I said.

"I have a documented episode in our basement that shows otherwise."

"You ain't got nothin'."

Miss Mojo came through the back door by her office and pulled me behind her. Just like Mom would have done.

"Mind your own," Miss Allison hissed.

"This is my own," Miss Mojo said. "And Eden's Edge is my own."

"It isn't!" Miss Allison screeched. "I paid for this place, and I continue to pay for it."

"Get paid for it, you mean."

Miss Mojo took a step toward Allison, and the air buzzed.

"Quite the business model," Miss Mojo said. "Acting holy, hiding people to sell 'em off."

Allison crunched her teeth together and clenched her fists.

Miss Mojo turned to me. "Where's your momma, Little Goat?"

All I could do was sob. I fell into Miss Mojo's bosom and let everything pour out there.

"There there," she said. "We'll go find her. And look. You aren't ill. Or wrong. You are powerful and tough, just unsure of yourself. We'll get you someplace safe, okay?"

"You aren't going anywhere," Allison said. "No one is."

"Because we'll blow your cover?" Miss Mojo said.

"You're a lunatic," Allison said with a hesitant laugh.

"Maybe so," Miss Mojo said. "But I'm a literate one."

Allison's face twitched. Her smile got a touch smaller. "What?"

"I can read, you Whore Bag. And I know my way around a computer, thanks to my nephew."

The smile returned. "The one you took the rap for so you're hiding here with me? What if I told the police the truth? And your darling nephew gets tossed in jail for life?"

"Yep!" Miss Mojo declared without shame. "And

you shan't be lording that over me anymore, you wretched hag. I gotchu. You're done."

"I welcome the police," Allison said. Her voice was shaky. "Everyone here has a story. Everyone here has sinned."

"Uh huh," Miss Mojo said. "And we can all go down together, shall we? And Eden's Edge can be returned to the woods as it belongs."

"No," I stammered. "I … where will I go?"

Miss Mojo turned her back to Allison and spoke to me.

"Listen here, Little Goat. Allison is into some bad stuff, but you already knew that. Turns out it's real bad. Selling kids to that bearded goon. Sold a good handful of them already. I got proof, you see. Wiped computer files. Your Mom and I, we stopped into my nephew's, got him to dig around in some accounts. Dark web, shit I don't really understand. We got her. We'll end this."

"Help me," I cried.

"Absofuckinglutely," Miss Mojo said.

Glass smashed in the hall behind Miss Mojo. Over her shoulder, I could see Allison's bloody fist clenched around a fire axe. Her feet crunched through the smashed glass of the emergency box as she charged toward us.

Miss Mojo didn't even turn.

"Go," she said to me. "Get your friends. Meet me out front of the chapel once you have them and all the stuff you need. Imma stay and take care of this bitch."

I was going to argue, to grab a weapon, do something to help, but there was no need. Miss Mojo raised her arms, and her eyes rolled into the back of her head as sparks rained down from the lights above. The buzzing in the air amplified as the walls shifted and the lights flickered. Allison stopped to cover her head, and swarms of bats and bees emerged like billows of smoke from the vents, engulfing Allison and turning the halls black. Miss Mojo stood still, her entire body crawling with all the things, bees crawling in and out of her nose and eyes and ears.

I ran like she told me. I didn't understand the magic, but it was working. And it wasn't mine to understand.

Chapter Twenty-Five

Liza wasn't home. Laz wasn't at Foster House either, but his home wasn't empty. There were eight other kids living there besides Laz, but the house was quiet.

"Hello?" I called out.

They're gone.

They got away already.

Miss Mojo saved them.

The house was rank with a warm humidity and the stench of copper.

I found the first child at the table, his lips blue, face beside an overturned bowl of cereal.

I found two more children in the downstairs shower. There was so much blood I didn't know where one began and the other ended. And I didn't know where they'd been hurt. Didn't matter. It was done.

The rest I found in their beds, bloody and grey and stiff.

Miss Martha was in a rocking chair by the master bedroom window, unfinished knitting in her hand, a knitting needle stabbed into her eye.

She must have been the first to die. She was the only one that looked calm. Unaware.

I tried all the other houses. Found much of the same. Blood, lifeless eyes, clothes stained with the incontinence of death.

There was no one left.

Miss Mojo was with Allison. She would kill her.

I did not know where Laz and Liza were. I did not want to know. I couldn't find them like that.

I dragged my feet to the cemetery, all the strength and will leeched out of me. New Friend did not come. She did not help. I imagined her dead too, buried way beneath the earth, choking on mouthfuls of soil and maggots.

I had nothing.

I had no one.

I was no one.

Chapter Twenty-Six

Merle wasn't at the cemetery. But The Blankness was there, perched atop the lych-gate.

"You can't do anything to me," I said. "I don't care anymore."

The Blankness didn't move.

I scoured the cemetery, kicking over stones and ripping through bushes until I found an old beer bottle. It was full of mushrooms and mold, and the glass was murky and discolored.

I wasn't scared. I wasn't sad. I was nothing. I actually felt relieved. There was no more wondering, no more waiting for something better, no expectations or stress about what I was or what I wasn't. It was just me and this moment, and for once, I finally had an exact grasp about what was going to happen. I was in control. I was powerful.

I smashed the beer bottle against a headstone and sat on the ground. Without hesitation, and with more strength than I thought I had left, I poked the jagged neck into my wrist and carved a trench down my forearm.

My pain poured out into the dirt.

All my sadness, my ambivalence, my worries, cleansed out with my spurting blood.

In that river of blood, I saw all the faces of every kid who had ever made fun of me, any ugly versions of myself I got used to seeing in the mirror, all my fears of adulthood. All those things drowned in the blood and soaked into the dirt. They were no longer mine.

"Gahhhh."

The stars were swirling above me. Black spots joined them, a waltz of the dying, as I got woozy and so, so thirsty …

"Gahhhh."

My arm was very cold, tingling, wet. I looked down and saw my reflection shining at me. I had no head.

"Gahhhh."

The stars stopped swirling; the black lightened to navy, then to robin's egg blue as the midday sky came back into focus.

Old Man Merle was there, holding me up with one hand and pouring salt water from his mason jar onto my wound. And somehow, he washed away every bit of blood.

"How?" I said, but I didn't have the energy to know.

Merle helped me to my feet, and New Friend was on my other side to help me walk.

"Where are we going?"

Neither could say, of course, one without a lower jaw and the other without a head.

I just let them take me. Even as we approached the lych-gate and The Blankness pounced down from above, I did not struggle. The rectangular scar on his chest was glowing now, so bright I had to shield my eyes. I didn't put up a fight. I wanted him to take me away, end me, end my misery. They transferred me into his arms. He picked me up and carried me through the lych-gate.

Chapter Twenty-Seven

The Blankness set me down on the other side. My eyes were closed. I did not want to see. I put my arms out, felt for him, but he was gone. The air was different. It was colder and tasted of canola crops and grain dust.

I opened my eyes. I wasn't in the forest or the cemetery. I looked over my shoulder. The lych-gate was there, but it shouldn't have been. It was out of place, dropped into a world that didn't belong to it. On either side of it were the grain elevators. My old home.

"Anna, please," The Blankness said. "You don't understand."

I didn't understand. Not at all. I was barefoot in front of The Blankness. And we were standing in the spot of the Incident. It was exactly like the night of it, right before we ran, right before …

"Anna, trust me," he said.

"You aren't to be trusted," I said, but the voice was not mine. It was someone else's. *Something* else's. It was a low, guttural growl.

I looked down at myself. At the blood over the front

of my jumper. It was crusty and dried.

"It's not yours, Anna." Two voices, coming out of The Blankness. Both his and Dad's. "It's not there at all, Anna."

I touched my face. It was not there. I touched my throat, and my hand rested atop the stump where my head used to be.

"Your head is there, Anna. It's okay."

The Blankness was talking, but Dad's voice was superimposed over the horrible vocals of that wretched thing.

"What are you?" I asked. "What am I?"

The Blankness shuddered, the blurry patch of black skin on his breast becoming more defined, brightening.

"An abomination, Anna. A beautiful, glorious abomination."

It was focused now. A patch of rectangular olive green with orange lettering.

LOUIS.

"Dad?" I said.

The Blankness trembled, twitched, creaked, and contorted as Dad shed the slick black skin to don his own.

"Anna," Dad said. All trace of The Blankness was gone, leaving only Dad.

"It's always with me," Dad said. "In me. Just like she's always in you."

My neck poured blood onto the ground, mixed with my tears.

"She's you," Dad said.

"What is she?"

"The strong bits of you. The dark side of you. The power in you."

"Why? How can this be? This isn't real."

"We are demons, Anna. Devils."

It was very real. New Friend was always there when

I struggled, helping me along, lifting me up, encouraging me to do the things I could not do. When I suffered, she suffered. But she fought back.

"It is real," Dad confirmed.

"I'm a witch," I said.

We must be. This headless girl and me.

"A witch, yes. But also, a demon." Dad's voice was sure and strong, spoken in unison with The Blankness's predatory tones.

My stomach roiled, the eyeball within turning and seeing. A beast on a throne of bones. A beautiful enchantress copulating with a grotesque incubus who filled her and split her in two.

"I thought it could work, Anna. I thought I could shun that part of me. Be good for her. For you."

Mom loved him. And he loved her. But he was more beast than man, she more witch than woman.

"You are more powerful than a witch, Anna. You could have so much more. Be so much more."

Mom and Dad sang in my ear, a lilting lullaby, haunting, beautiful, and threatening.

"Fog and steam,
gossamer and pitch,
halfbreed tainted, rotten bitch."

"Witch and demon," Dad and The Blankness chimed. "Best of both, worst of all."

"I am not bad," I said.

"Nor are you good," Dad answered. "You are everything else."

"And capable of so much more than these two could ever dream," The Blankness shouted directly in my brain.

I screamed, and the glamour dropped me directly back into the moment of the Incident.

"Come with me, Anna," Dad was pleading. "Let me show you our power."

The Blankness was Dad. He was wearing his work overalls, his name patch crudely stitched on his breast.

"No!" I barked in a voice that was more animal than me.

"She doesn't want to," Mom cried. "She has a choice of what she wants to be!"

Mom was standing behind Dad. The spade in her hand was clean, shining silver in the moonlight, reflecting three images: a beautiful maiden, New Friend, and The Blankness. One happy family.

"She is what she is!" Dad roared in The Blankness's voice. "My wing! She will come under my wing!"

"There's no reason we can't keep going," Mom cried. "All of us together."

"She can be more," Dad bellowed. He turned to face Mom now, his teeth gnashing together as he shouted. "She can be power! We can have EVERYTHING!"

Wide, leathery wings shredded through Dad's clothes and skin, sending a spray of carnage into the air like campfire embers.

I had been wrong. I had remembered almost right, but not quite. Mom had a before-face and an after-face, but not before and after The Incident. It was before and after this moment. The moment she knew what I was destined to be.

"Anna," she said, her tone soft and sure. "Only you can choose."

Her hands were steady. Her eyes flaming with the red of Erinyes's feathers.

"He can kill me," she said, "And if that is your choice, then so be it. I love you just the same."

I pointed at the spade in her hand as talons burst from Dad's fingers, shredding his hands into strips.

"Stop him, Mom!"

She smiled, and her face lit like the sun.

"I cannot stop him. A demon is powerful, your dad

more than most. He is lost in there, I'm afraid, and he is nothing more than bone and blood and lust. Your Dad is gone. Only Khuya remains."

Mom wept tears of red feathers, but she was not sad. A transformation was taking place. She loved a demon, and he loved her. I could taste their passion in the air. But it was doomed. It was always going to end, and that impending resolution was a relief for her, both devastating and liberating.

The heat of white fire seared in my fists. My blood joined the mist of Dad's in the air as bone shot from my knuckles and a forked tongue slivered from the hole in my neck. He turned, The Blankness's face rippling into Dad's features only briefly before the Incident occurred.

I felt the shock like electricity through my marrow as my claws opened a chasm across Dad's throat, their tips scraping the base of his skull like a knife on stone. Dad's neck smiled just like Mom's as hell poured from him. Steaming blood like river rapids carrying chunks of bones splashed over my feet, over Mom, until everything was an ocean of thick, burning blood. We were swimming, drowning; I was gulping down Dad's insides until, like a draining bathtub, it whorled away, dried up in the heat of hell, and Mom and I were left standing with after-faces in an empty lot flanked by grain elevators.

The spade in Mom's hand was clean. It had always been clean. The blood I saw there was on my eyes.

"Anna," she said, soft and true. "We need to go now."

It was only a man lying dead on the ground. Dad. My dad. Killed by my hand, a hand unnatural and full of power I didn't know.

New Friend stepped out of me, away from me, took my hand and led me to Mom. Mom gently guided me away from the corpse on the ground, then stopped.

"One moment," she said, and she put my hand in New Friend's.

Mom knelt down next to Dad and wept. She put her head on his bloody chest, mixed her tears with his blood, then kissed his lips, long and hard.

"Khuya," she said. "I loved you."

With a sudden strike, Mom plunged her hands into Dad's guts and pulled his ribs open with a crack. With slender fingers, she pulled out his heart, kissed it, and held it to her chest.

"You will be with her," Mom said. "Always. And the great things she will be."

Mom gave Dad one last kiss, and then we whisked away to the house, to the car, and to a dingy diner in the middle of nowhere.

Chapter Twenty-Eight

I could taste blood. My stomach roiled, reminding me that the meat of Dad's heart was digesting within me. Inside of me. Always with me.

My eyes opened to a landscape of tree branches and starlight. I was on my back in the cemetery. Old Man Merle was by my side, rinsing me with his seemingly endless supply of faux seawater.

I cried, but I wasn't sad. I had no time for that.

I had been awakened.

Demon witch.

Miss Mojo had said something to me that day in her office. When I wondered if I was a witch.

"Most don't know it. It's just something that grows in your bones. You can keep it there, tucked away, or you can coax it out. Nurture it and bring it to life."

The truth had coaxed me to life.

I sprang to my feet, and Gus leaped from a nearby tree onto my shoulder. Merle loped along with me for a few steps before I held my hand out.

"No, Merle."

He looked hurt.

"Gahhhh."

"I'll be okay," I said. "You've done so much."

Merle started crying and leaned down for a hug. I embraced him. He was huge but frail, hard but delicate. And in that skeletal form, he had the hugest, warmest heart.

"I love you, Ole Man Merle."

"Gahhhh," he said as he kissed the top of my head, his tongue drooping into my hair.

As I walked through the forest, I was alone. The Blankness wasn't there, though I felt him watching me. Maybe he was up in the trees; maybe he was back at the lych-gate waiting for me to come home.

To hell.

New Friend was gone too. But I didn't feel her inside me. All I felt was sad, scared, powerless little ole me, plodding towards an unknown with no tools or weapons or sense.

Eden's Edge was eerie and quiet. Of course it was. Everyone was dead.

Almost everyone.

As I passed, I saw clear people, echoes of the folk who had once been there not that long ago. People who Allison had traded, sold, killed. They were battered and bloody, their wounds shattered glass and their pain a fog. I tried not to look at them, but I couldn't help myself. The children were lined up outside Foster House, hovering a meter above the ground by invisible nooses attached to another realm, their mouths wide in screams and cries, their eyes dripping death.

The adults, limbless and faceless and clear like tarnished glass, were shambling to The Beast, chanting songs of sorrow and loss.

Your God will not save you, I thought. *No one will.*

Allison's house stood panting in the corner,

salivating over me like I was carrion as I approached. The lights were on, and there was music playing inside. Allison's silhouette was in the window. She was holding a drink, her arms waving, body moving, head bobbing

dancing?

and it enraged me.

She should be suffering, not dancing.

I walked around the back of the house and tried the door. Locked, of course. A criminal has fear because they're intimate with the evils of the world. I slid off my jumper and found a big rock to wrap inside it. It was dark in the basement, and the music upstairs was loud, so I took the gamble that Allison would take no notice. I smashed out a basement window with the rock wrapped in my jumper. After cleaning the glass away from the window frame with my shoe I wriggled inside.

The basement stank of feces, urine, and blood. Maybe vomit too, but it was hard to tell. Everything was steaming and acrid. I wanted to find a light switch so I could better see the horrors that awaited. It was the unknown terrors that were the worst. Their teeth were always bigger, their claws always sharper.

My hands groped the walls but found only unfinished boards and insulation. Beneath my feet was cold, solid concrete. An unfinished basement.

I moved slower, wary of open wires or exposed nails, and thank goodness I did. A wet patch on the floor found my foot, and I slip-slided my way a meter before I found purchase on the wall and braced myself. Face planting on concrete would have been an awful start to this quest.

On the remainder of my journey around the large open basement, my feet found several wet spots, some slick, some deep enough to actually splash. I finally reached the stairs, having found nothing along the walls but wood and insulation. At the base of the stairs, though, my nose found the dangling chain belonging to an overhead light. I pulled it and focused my eyes on the naked bulb that sizzled to light above my head.

Something in the corner groaned. In another corner, a muffled sob.

I turned around. There was only one light for the whole big basement, but it was enough to see the things I knew I might find but absolutely did not want to.

Laz was in his underwear, stretched out, wrists and ankles chained to the wall, suspending him in place like a star. In the far corner was Liza, in a bloody undershirt and equally bloody panties, shackled by the wrists to a chain on the floor. And stacked in the opposite corner were a few lifeless bodies, stiff but still oozing. Mister Charles was on top, naked, his entire midsection and groin caked with dry blood. His severed penis was stuffed in his throat, and his eyes were red and bulging.

I would have been embarrassed and disgusted seeing Mister Charles in that state, but I was too worried about Laz and Liza. I ran to her first because her eyes were open, and she was older, and she would know what to do. I ripped the strip of t-shirt that was tied into a gag over her mouth, and she sucked in a few huge breaths before speaking.

"Go," she said. "Run. She's insane. She's gonna … we're all dead. You have to go."

And I wanted to. So bad. But if I ran, if I got out and got safe somewhere, what would I have? Thoughts of my dead friends who were not dead the last time I saw them, when death had yet to find them? And where would I go? Live in the woods like an animal?

I yanked at Liza's chains.

"No use," she said. "I tried and tried."

Her panties were soaked with blood. She had bruises shaped like fingertips on the insides of her thighs. I couldn't help but stare, and I felt bad, and sad, but mostly mad.

"That's your period, right?" I said, pointing at her panties.

Somewhere in the house, a toilet flushed. A man coughed. Allison laughed. Liza put her fist in her mouth and screamed. Laz groaned.

"Laz," I said.

I went to him. There were so many broken bones jutting out here and there. His jaw was purple, smashed, and crooked. His top teeth didn't line up with his bottom teeth. I wondered how a dentist might fix that. One eye had burst out of his head and was swinging by its tendons on his pallid cheek. He was cold and sweating, and his one good eye was rolled into the back of his head.

"It's okay," I lied. "I'm here, and we're strong, and everything is going to be okay."

I frantically scoured the basement. There wasn't much, but there were a few piles of soiled bedding. I found the least offensive blanket and tried to wrap it around Laz. He was in shock, and he needed to be warmed up, but I couldn't quite reach to where he was suspended on the wall. I tried to throw the blanket around him, but it kept sliding off, and it took every ounce of strength I possessed to not scream every expletive I knew at the fucking thing.

"It's okay, Laz. We're leaving soon, and we'll get Mary, and then we'll all go to the doctor, and then maybe we'll get to stay in a hotel somewhere before we find a new home."

Laz didn't respond. His head lolled side to side, and he made some baby noises, but not much else happened.

The doorknob at the top of the stairs jiggled, then turned. Liza let out a yelp, and urine flowed out of Laz, splashing on the floor beneath him. I looked away. Laz would be embarrassed, so I didn't look. He wouldn't know we saw.

A man's voice crept into the room as the door opened

a slice.

"Calm down, woman. I'm just gonna go another quick round with these kids. There will be plenty left for you."

"You gonna pay for that too?" Allison said from somewhere on the upper floors.

"The buyer's payin' me huge," he said. "I told him this is the last bit of stock for a while so I hadda charge extra."

The conversation continued, but my mind was too busy to hear. It was too hard to get Laz and Liza freed quick enough, so I had to hide until I could. The basement was so exposed, I was so exposed. The only place I could think of to hide was beneath the crusty, stale pile of blankets in the corner. So I burrowed in there and slowed my breath, making it shallow and light so he wouldn't see the blankets move.

I heard every single heavy step as Beard clopped down those stairs. And I could smell him—sweat, booze, and something feral. Salty and wrong.

"Ya ain't lookin so fine, little man," Beard said.

His footsteps clopped over to Laz, and he bellowed up the stairs.

"Hey, you dumb bitch, you ruined this one! They ain't paying for broken merch!"

Allison was squawking and muttering something, but I didn't hear. All I could hear was the rattle of chains as Laz thrashed and struggled. I dared to peek out from beneath my hidey-hole, and I wished I hadn't. Beard had one hand on Laz's face, the other on his own crotch.

"Ain't much to work with here, little buddy," Beard said.

It all happened so fast. Beard bit into Laz's cheek, hard. Laz squeaked but stopped fighting. Then Beard took his other hand, put it on Laz's other cheek, and, with a sharp, sudden twist, cracked Laz's neck.

The contents of my friend's bowels dropped to the floor. His head thudded against the wall, loose and lifeless.

Beard turned to Liza.

"Well, sweetheart, guess it's you again."

Liza started screaming and pushing back into a corner that wouldn't budge as Beard liberated his penis from his stiff, stained jeans. His rider, who was attached to the back of his belt, started masturbating, shooting black semen onto the floor in dark, oily puddles.

My heart slowed. My jaw ached from my teeth clenching. I thought I might clench so hard my teeth would smash and drive into my brain.

Beard was facing Liza, so he didn't see me stand. He didn't see the blankets slide off to the floor, and he didn't see New Friend walk up in front of me. She held my hands, pressed our chests together, breathed with my breath, and pushed inside of me. My skin grew hot, taut, then I was suddenly bigger, stronger, just like her. My hands were steady, my mind clear.

"You look pretty," Beard said as he grabbed Liza and pulled her to her feet.

Liza still had some fight in her. She thrust forward, smashing the crown of her head into Beard's nose, opening a geyser of blood down his face and twisting him clear around.

Now he was facing me.

"What the actual fuck—"

I felt New Friend in me, rumbling, conjuring rage like a spell. I felt her confidence and power swell.

She coaxed me out and joined us together, witch and demon.

It did not hurt when my skin split and talons of bone shot out in place of my tiny fingers. It didn't hurt as my jaw unhinged and I sprouted rows of sharp, black teeth. I felt so strong as I drove one hand into Beard's chubby gut and lifted him in the air above me. I used those rows of teeth to grab hold of his shriveled, yeasty penis. I shook my head back and forth, a dog with a bone, and liberated that gross sausage from its owner. After spitting little Beard on the floor, I lowered the man to my face and kissed him, making sure he got a mouthful of his own genital blood before I sliced through his neck, decapitating him. His head was still rolling on the floor when I dropped his body like a sack of shit.

Beard's rider screamed and shriveled like an icy cold cock until it was little more than a drop of rat feces on the concrete.

Liza was terrified. She wasn't looking at him. She was looking at me.

It didn't matter. She could hate me and fear me all she liked. She was safe now.

I grabbed her shackles and broke them with my bare hands. Then tore the cuffs off as well before New Friend withered inside me, leaving only gentle Anna to say goodbye.

"Run," I said to her.

She was frozen. A deer on a highway.

I took her by the shoulders and hugged her. Then I undressed myself and dressed her in my clothes before leading her to the broken basement window.

"Run," I said, and I lifted her up.

Finally, she launched into action. Screaming erupted from her throat as she scrambled out into the woods.

"Keep running," I whispered after her.

I hoped she did. I'd never know, but I had to believe I had saved her. That she would go on and live her life, forget all these horrors.

Upstairs, there was a scratch of vinyl, and a new record started playing. Leonard Cohen's *"The Future."*

Perfect, I thought as I ascended the stairs.

Chapter Twenty-Nine

Allison was waltzing around the room with a glass of chardonnay clutched in her greedy fingers. Judging by the way she stumbled around the coffee table, all clumsy and unsteady, she'd had a few. She was stained from head to toe with blood. The blood of the residents of Eden's Edge.

And she was laughing as she danced.

What a shock she got when I appeared through the basement door. She stopped dancing, stopped laughing, and stared.

"Something the matter?" I asked.

"You …" She pointed at me, at my exposed parts. I'd even given my panties to Liza to replace her torn, soiled ones, which were now clenched in my fist. They were wet with her urine and blood, but that's not all. I could feel the squirm of Beard's semen in my palm, wringing out of those panties.

"Yes," I said. "Me."

Her eyes went to the basement door.

"Laz is dead," I said, my lower lip trembling. "You

killed him."

She looked shocked. I was enraged by her feign of innocence.

"I did no such … he was still alive when—"

"Shut up, you lying cunt."

She dared to smile.

I put my head up, chin out. "Liza's gone."

She scoffed. "Like fuck she is. You didn't have the key."

This time, I smirked.

"Didn't need it," I said.

She was puzzled. I wasn't going to explain. She was too daft for that.

"Robert!" she called.

Merle's face flashed in my mind.

Oh, I thought. It made sense now why Merle was here.

I brought Liza's panties to my face. That semen stank, but not just of Robert. It stank of dead hooker, and of the coast, and of a dirty pig farm.

"Bobby Picton's dead too," I said.

Now she looked shocked. Her hand dropped, and her wine spilled on the floor as Cohen reached the chorus.

"You can't do this," she said. "You'd be fucked if it wasn't for me!"

I let her rant. She was terrified.

"You and your weak, pathetic mother. I should have told the cops all about her and your father. That she murdered him and stole you away. You aren't worth the price you'd fetch, you little bitch!"

A smile bloomed on her face again. She sauntered toward me and let out a burping laugh.

"But Momma has been taken care of," she said. "All gone. Now it's just you and me, baby."

"What was your plan?" I asked. I was genuinely

curious.

"Start fresh!" she said. "This place is perfect. Secluded, beautiful. I can do whatever I want. And I have all the money to do it. Brats sell like gold."

"How're you gonna explain all the dead people?"

She laughed out loud. "The ones who were hiding here? That nobody knew was here?"

"The cops were here," I said. "They'll come back."

"Let them come," Allison said. "They love me, a God-fearing Christian do-gooder. I talked my way out of it once, I can do it again. Besides," she said as she slithered right up to me, "They didn't know there was anyone else here. It's an empty campground on farmland nobody wanted. And they sure as hell ain't gonna find bodies. I'll take care of that."

"Your bearded friend is dead," I reminded her.

She shrugged. "There's more where he came from. Plenty."

And like moths to a flame, those wretched men would find Miss Allison.

"Little Goat."

Allison spun around as Miss Mojo came out of the kitchen wielding a fireplace poker. Allison's rider snarled and nipped at Miss Mojo, but Miss Mojo only smiled as the thing was engulfed in a swarm of hornets.

"You whore," Allison said to Miss Mojo. "Betrayer!"

Allison grabbed the wine bottle off the coffee table and the two women squared off.

"Listen to me," Miss Mojo said as she looked deep into Allison's eyes. "Each evil wears a demon. A rider, like you say. Only you can see them. I have the power to slow them, but only you have the strength to stop them."

"What?" Allison said.

But I understood. Miss Mojo wasn't talking to

Allison.

"All them crazy fucks have a rider, but once the steed is down, the rider falls too. But the rider makes the steed impossibly lucky. Almost impervious to death or consequence."

"You're crazy," Allison said, laughing as she smashed the bottle against the wall, leaving her holding the jagged neck.

"What do I do?" I asked.

I thought of Mom. She was the sun.

"Light cannot kill dark," Miss Mojo said, reading me. "It only creates shadows for the dark to hide in."

"Raving lunatics," Allison said. "The both of you."

"Only one thing is vile enough, low enough to extinguish the dark."

Allison lunged, and Miss Mojo did too. The bottle pierced Miss Mojo's side as she thrust the poker into Allison's chest. The two of them danced together, grasping weapons that were stuck in each other, twirling a macabre waltz to the climax of Cohen's song.

The music slowed; Khuya was dragging his talon on the vinyl as New Friend stepped in front of me.

I was stuck in a slow, morbid fairy tale as I crossed the room in floating steps. Blood splattered through the air in arcs as my talons found flesh, slicing gouges like art across both human canvasses. Miss Mojo yelped and backed away as Allison yanked the poker out from between her ribs and jabbed it in my direction.

I laughed. Pointed at Allison's ribs and bowed.

"Messiah," I said.

She opened her mouth, readying a dumbass retort, no doubt, but I was all finished talking. One leap and I was on her, both of us crashing to the floor.

"Feel her," I growled. My voice was low and loud and shook the room like an avalanche. With one swipe, I tore away Allison's clothes, and using a single talon, I jammed Liza's panties into Allison's vagina, forcing them through her body until they were peeking out of her throat.

"Taste her," I chuckled and cried at the same time, vengeful and devastated.

Allison choked and gasped as blood poured inside and outside her body. I took her throat in my unhinged jaw. I ate until there was no more meat or bone keeping her head on her body.

New Friend deflated within me, and Soft Anna scrambled to Miss Mojo's side.

"You did good," Miss Mojo said.

"It's okay," I said. "I … Liza will get help."

Miss Mojo smiled. "No, Little Goat. There is no help. And no more is needed."

There was too much blood. It was pooled beneath Miss Mojo like Liza's hair, like a black glossy lake, and it was still growing, flooding—

Allison's rider was on top of her, screaming, melting away as if it'd been doused in acid.

"Only dark can kill dark," Miss Mojo said.

"I can't!" I cried. "What do I do?"

The song on the turntable ended, and the needle lifted. Miss Mojo's breathing softened, her eyes glittered like virgin snow, and she touched my cheek.

"Gossamer and Pitch," she said, her voice a song.

My Mom.

My Dad.

"Zirdo ol," Miss Mojo said as she tapped my chest.

"I am me," I said.

Miss Mojo died in my arms.

The floor shook, a gentle quake, and thousands of ladybugs crawled from every crack and every floorboard, engulfing Miss Mojo with their ruby shells and black spots and quivering antennae. Miss Mojo was humming a tune in her throat, ethereal and beautiful, and they devoured her entirely, bones and all. Then they retreated, back through the cracks and crevices and into the dirt of the earth.

I sat and cried. Rolled on the floor, covered in all the blood—mine, Allison's, Laz's, and Liza's. Mom's was in there too, I was sure.

Where do I go?

What do I do?

I knew no bug magic like Miss Mojo, or earth magic like Mom.

And I was a good person. I wanted no demon power like my dad, Khuya.

Because I was something else.

I was me.

A ladybug landed on my finger. When she was angry, when she was taking care of business, Miss Mojo was all hornets and ants. But there were ladybugs there too …

Chapter Thirty

I wanted Mom's ghost to be waiting at the house for me, but it wasn't. She wasn't where I had left her either. When I had run for the church, she was still on the front step, but now all that remained on my front porch was a stain of blood.

She's alive!

But the stain was too big. And trailing away from it was a wide streak. Drag marks. A body through blood.

I followed it around the house, over the line of burning birds, and into the backyard.

Old Man Merle stood there with The Blankness. With my dad, Khuya. Mom's body was there, propped up on a seat made out of stones and branches and logs. Mounted atop this makeshift seat was the rack from the moose where I had discovered Gus.

"Did you do this?" I asked Merle.

He looked down at his feet and nodded.

Mom was carefully decorated with wild roses all over her body. Erinyes's body had been placed in her hands, and the bird's wings had been plucked, her red feathers used to adorn my mom's hair.

"It's beautiful," I said.

Khuya had his arm around my mom. I went to him, and the three of us embraced.

I wanted Mom to be a part of me too. Equal to my dad. The best of both.

Khuya opened Mom's body cavity with his tongue and slurped out Mom's heart. Her heart was cold and still when I bit into it. Her life squelched between my teeth as I chewed. I ate until the whole of her heart was inside me, beating with my own, beating with Dad's.

Once I was done, with my mother's blood smeared over my naked body, I rolled back in the dirt and watched the stars twinkle. Merle got to work, cleaning up Mom's chest and putting her back the way she was. He filled her body with plants, feathers, and weeds, and though she was quite dead, her peach lips curled into a smile.

She is earth now. One and the same.

Khuya stood beside her, a hand to the throne, watching me with curiosity.

What was I going to do?

Cleanse. Start anew.

Chapter Thirty-One

New Friend helped me. Not inside me but beside me, guiding me and lending a hand. It took so many hours that the sun joined us and left again. We collected deadfall, dried brush, papers. Everything we could find. The gas from the furnaces, from jerry cans, from Miss Mojo's car and Allison's car and Beard's truck. Hours of prep led to one glorious ceremony. The Razing of Eden. Burn the old to grow the new.

The forest sang a vigorous chorale as the flames licked the sky, devouring every last centimeter of that awful place.

And for the last time, as the world burned, I walked New Friend home.

Her house burned too. She and I stood side by side, hand in hand, as the contents of the bowls on her porch evaporated into the air, a swirling tornado of smoke, blood, and tears.

I did not need her anymore. I was her.

She hugged me for many moments. I drank in the feeling of her skin on mine, her strength, her support. As she ascended her stairs, I wondered, again, what was inside her house. All the shoes that supported it … were they mine? The many versions of me that were, that could have been, parts of me that had lived and died and withered away?

It wasn't for me to know. Not yet.

I caught one last glimpse of her pinafore as the door shut. The lock clicked, and a lump formed in my throat. She was gone.

Chapter Thirty-Two

I watched for days as Eden's Edge burned. I didn't sleep. Somehow, I didn't need to.

Emergency workers came. Firefighters put out the blaze. Police and investigators scoured the area, collecting evidence.

They didn't find much. Burned-out vehicles, the ash of building and meager possessions.

They could not see within the perimeter of birds. They could not see my house, or my garden, or Mom's rotting body upon her throne, growing mushrooms and flowers and an entire ecosystem of its own.

They couldn't find the bones of all the other bodies because I had brought them all into my perimeter and used them to fertilize my land.

Over the next few years, people came and went. Surveyors, real estate agents, lawyers. They had no use for Eden's Edge.

"Vandals."

"Unusable."

"More of a headache than anything."

"More money to fix it than it's worth."
"Best left alone."

I thought of Liza, of her black glass hair, of her smile and her kind words. I wanted to believe I would see her again, feel her arms around me, hear her laughter like birdsong.

Once the fires had burned and the land was cleansed, still I sat, watching as the ash and dirt gave way to green sprouts and the critters came back, making themselves new homes within the rebirth.

One thing remained unchanged. My home. The house my mom had protected with burning cardinals and dirt magic stood exactly where it was, a sanctuary in the woods. And in the backyard, a throne. A corpse made of flowers and feathers and sun. A majestic rack tipped with greenery and blooms, marking this spot as sacred. Old Man Merle tended to the throne and its flowers, holding his jar of salt water with the charred nugget of Picton's rider sealed inside. Gus was sitting on the arm, gnawing on a freshly fallen chestnut he clutched in his paws. I smiled, and they looked. Because I was beaming with happiness. I was the sun.

I sat in the grass, listening to voices. The voices of children just outside my perimeter. Coming from the place where Foster House used to stand. Coming from the entirety of Eden's Edge. Miss Mojo and her insects, singing and buzzing, tiny wings vibrating. And way off in the distance, I heard the horrors of hell waiting for me through the lych-gate.

And Khuya's voice, beckoning me home.

"Come."

"No," I said. "I am home. For now."

I played back in the grass, feeling three hearts beating within me, wondering how I was going to choose to live my life, with my power, and the possibilities of what I was capable of.

"Zirdo ol. Zirdo ge. Ol Trian."
I am me. I am we.
I shall be.

* * *

About the Author

Jae Mazer is a Canadian who was born in Victoria, British Columbia, and grew up in the prairies of Northern Alberta. After spending the majority of her life battling sasquatches in the Great White North, she migrated south to Texas to have a go at the armadillos. She is a connoisseur and creator of gothic horror, splatterfolk, splatter westerns, and folk horror. She's degreed, won awards, been in anthologies, has chameleon hair and lots of skin ink, and enjoys mustard and alcohol.

Awards:
- ATAI 2017, WINNER, Best Horror Novel for *Chrysalis and Clan*
- American Book Fest 2019, Best Horror Novel for *Crone: A Witch's Tale*

- Next Generation Indie Book Awards 2019 Runner-up/Finalist for *Crone: A Witch's Tale*
- Next Generation Indie Book Awards 2021 Runner-up/Finalist for *Blood Wail*.
- New York City Midnight Finalist for Short Screenplay for *Just Like Momma*

OTHER HELLBOUND BOOKS

Snow White in his Glass Coffin

This Southern gothic, psychosexual horror story follows siblings Chastity and Jonathan Caldwell throughout their terribly troubled lives…

From spending their grim childhood in a ramshackle trailer with an unstable, cruel mother who prostitutes Jonathan out to fund her meth addiction, through a brutal murder that permanently alters their relationship, and into their adulthood, where Chastity begins to take increasing sadistic joy in controlling and tormenting her poor brother.

Told from Chastity's unique perspective, Snow White in His Glass Coffin dares you to empathize with two deeply disturbed people who commit and attempt to rationalize their unspeakable, brutal crimes.

A gut-wrenching tale most definitely not for the faint of heart.

Cain Consequence

In "The Great Secession," reality has gone unbelievably haywire!

Stu's dog has changed, his favorite cookie brand vanishes, and TV shows become completely different overnight.

To crack the case, Stu teams up with a bitter, former child star, a witch whose spells misfire more often than not, and an entrepreneur cursed with epic lousy luck. Can they get along long enough to stop the madness?

Meanwhile, occultist Barclay Cain stirs up trouble with his own motley crew of weirdos.

Get ready for a wild ride through the Lands – filled with haunted toilets, crazed soccer moms, and magic brothels. It's a showdown of bullets vs. magic, where even winning might not fix the cracked reality.

Join Stu and his gang in a quest in which wicked hilarity meets mayhem, and normalcy takes a back seat to the absurd. Who knew saving the world could be so crazy?

To Hell and Back

Step into the abyss of horror and dark fiction with To Hell and Back…where each story is a gateway to the unimaginable.

To Hell and Back serves as a mosaic of contemporary fears and timeless terrors, curated and edited by the Bram Stoker Award-winning Joe Mynhardt. This collection of horror stories brings together a diverse array of tales from both beloved and emerging voices in the horror genre, each story a unique exploration of the dark corners of the human psyche.

Published in collaboration with Crystal Lake Entertainment, with an introduction by Lee Murray, this horror anthology includes disturbing tales by Jeff Strand, Gage Greenwood, Gregg Stewart, Jasper Bark, Kenneth W. Cain, James Aquilone, Taylor Grant, Colin J. Northwood, Chad Lutzke, Felix Blackwell, J.P. Behrens, Bridget Nelson, Jay Bechtol, Nick Roberts, Kyle Toucher, Diana Olney, Devin Cabrera, Naching T. Kassa, John Durgin, Francesca Maria, James H. Longmore, and Rowan Hill.

To Hell and Back invites readers on a journey through cityscapes and small towns, into office blocks and family homes, along lonely roads, and wooded trails. It confronts external threats like predators and cults as well as internal battles with ambition, mental illness, and moral weakness. Themes of road rage, childhood trauma, the horrors of war, and the supernatural intertwine, offering a chilling snapshot of contemporary societal fears. With stories that range from political and cultural tensions to tales of creeping unease, this anthology not only aims to terrify but also to offer a means of confronting and reflecting on our fears from a safe distance.

Uncover the shadows lurking within and beyond with To Hell and Back—dare to turn the page and confront your darkest fears.

The Wet

"Paul Kane is a first-rate storyteller, never failing to marry his insights into the world and its anguish with the pleasures of phrases eloquently turned." (**Clive Barker** – Bestselling author of *The Hellbound Heart, Mr B. Gone* and *The Scarlet Gospels*)

In the quiet seaside village of Sable, something is stirring. Reclusive artist Jason Harding has retreated there to recover from a past trauma.

Lifeboat man Rob Woodhead returned because Sable is his home.

Disgruntled weathergirl Vicky West is on her way to interview windsurfers for her satellite TV channel.

All three will be brought together by a freak storm, one that remains stationary over the ocean and seems almost alive. What happens next will rock the entire community to its core…

The Wet is the very first novel written by #1 bestselling, award-winning author Paul Kane (The RED Trilogy, Before, Sherlock Holmes and the Servants of Hell). Penned in his early 20s and recently uncovered, this terrifying curiosity, influenced by those genre-busting '70s and '80s pulp horror novels, will shock and surprise you to the very last page.

Published for the very first time, The Wet is certain to cause a splash!

Jae Mazer

The Horror Writer
"The most definitive guide into the trials and tribulations of being a horror writer since Stephen King's 'On Writing.'"

We have assembled some of the very best in the business from whom you can learn so much about the craft of horror writing: Bram Stoker Award© winners, bestselling authors, a President of the Horror Writers' Association, and myriad contemporary horror authors of distinction.

The Horror Writer covers how to connect with your market and carve out a sustainable niche in the independent horror genre, how to tackle the writer's ever-lurking nemesis of productivity, writing good horror stories with powerful, effective scenes, realistic, flowing dialogue and relatable characters without resorting to clichéd jump scares and well-worn gimmicks. Also covered is the delicate subject of handling rejection with good grace, and how to use those inevitable "not quite the right fit for us at this time" letters as an opportunity to hone your craft.

Plus... perceptive interviews to provide an intimate peek into the psyche of the horror author and the challenges they work through to bring their nefarious ideas to the page.

And, as if that – and so much more – was not enough, we have for your delectation Ramsey Campbell's beautifully insightful analysis of the tales of HP Lovecraft.

Featuring:

Ramsey Campbell, John Palisano, Chad Lutzke, Lisa Morton, Kenneth W. Cain, Kevin J. Kennedy, Monique Snyman, Scott Nicholson, Lucy A. Snyder, Richard Thomas, Gene O'Neill, Jess Landry, Luke Walker, Stephanie M. Wytovich, Marie O'Regan, Armand Rosamilia, Kevin Lucia, Ben Eads, Kelli Owen, Jasper Bark, and Bret McCormick.

And interviews with: Steve Rasnic Tem, Stephen Graham Jones, David Owain Hughes, Tim Waggoner, and Mort Castle.

**A HellBound Books LLC
Publication**

www.hellboundbooks.com

Printed in the United States of America